JENNIFER WILCK

The Perfect Match

THE PERFECT MATCH BOOK 1

To Lisa Kanner & Michelle Mana for entertaining/helping me with speed-dating stories. It was fun and informative, and I couldn't have written this book without your help.

And to all of my self-published author friends, who convinced me that I could make a better book.

Other Books by Jennifer Wilck

Scarred Hearts Series

A Restless Heart
Unlock My Heart
A Heart Restrained

Stand Alone Romance Novels

In The Moment
A Heart of Little Faith

**Harlequin Special Edition:
Holidays, Heart & Chutzpah**

Home for the Challah Days
Matzah Ball Blues
Deadlines, Donuts & Dreidels

**Harlequin The Fortunes of Texas:
Fortune's Secret Children Book 5**

Fortune's Holiday Surprise

CHAPTER ONE

After another crazy workday at her Manhattan PR firm, Aviva Shulman slipped the key into her Hoboken apartment door lock, praying for quiet. In slow motion, she turned it to the right. The tumbler clicked. She held her breath. When neither of her roommates called out or made a sound, she eased the door open and tiptoed inside. Shutting the door, she removed her shoes, and padded through the living room toward her bedroom, treasuring the alone time that waited for her only a few feet away.

"Aviva, you're home! I was waiting for you."

Erica's voice made her freeze. Her stomach rolled. After spending extra time in her office, taking a later PATH train than usual, and eating out at a bar down the street to avoid cooking at home, she'd come so close to sneaking into the apartment without Erica knowing. With a sigh, she faced her roommate. Maybe she'd luck out and Erica would want to discuss global warming or politics.

"Guess what I found!"

She edged forward. This might not be too bad. "What?"

"There's a speed dating event at Urban Bistro Friday night. Come with me."

No such luck. "What? Why?" The last thing she wanted to do was judge or be judged in five minutes or less.

"Because there will be a lot of guys in one room, obviously, and you didn't like the date I set you up with last week."

Aviva sighed. Was it only a week ago? "Erica, I really appreciate all your efforts, but I think I'd like to take a break for a little while." Like the next century.

"Avs, you're not in mourning. You didn't just break up with the love of your life. You're alone. There is no *take a break for a little while* when you're single. You need a man."

Aviva cleared her throat and looked around the small living room. What she needed was a new coffee table, a new window shade, and potentially a new roommate. "I don't *need a man*. I'm perfectly fine on my own."

Erica laughed. Aviva cringed until the raspy noise stopped.

"I meant for sex," Erica said.

Aviva spluttered.

"Please tell me you know what sex is," Erica said, a look of horror pinching her narrow face.

Her other roommate was out, if the darkened bedroom with a wide-open door was any indication, but still Aviva lowered her voice. "Of course, I know what sex is. I just don't see why you're concerned with whether or not I get it."

"The question isn't why I'm concerned," she said. "It's why you're not."

Aviva shrugged. She'd been single for a while, and while sex would be nice, it wasn't worth the trouble of finding the perfect guy. Especially if that perfect guy was hidden among the horrible ones Erica had introduced her to. She'd rather abstain.

"That's it, if a shrug is the best you can do, you're in dire need. Girl, you're coming with me and that's that." Erica grabbed Aviva's hand and dragged her to the gray sofa they'd found at Goodwill. She sank into it, barely missing scraping her leg against the beat-up, faux-wood coffee table. Right in the middle of it was the speed dating flyer. Erica shoved it at her. Aviva took it with the tips of her fingers, wishing she was anywhere but here.

Tahiti would be nice.

"It won't bite you, Avs. It's tomorrow at seven."

If only she could plead a work engagement. In Tahiti. "Uh, I have to work late."

"Of course, you don't. It's a summer Friday. You always get home early on summer Fridays."

"Oh, right." Damn, she'd noticed. "Well, it's Shabbat. I probably should go to services."

Erica reared back. "Since when have you become observant? Come on, it'll be fun. The targeted ages are twenties and thirties. This company works with young professionals. I've done it before. The guys are all lawyers and investment bankers who work on Wall Street. It'll be great."

Yuck. Guys like her dad, devoted to their careers, above all else.

Or like the disaster from last night. A work colleague had set her up. He didn't stop talking about himself the entire time. According to his credentials, which he'd presented in writing upon his arrival at the bar, he closed multimillion-dollar real-estate deals with the über-wealthy on a regular basis. That date wasn't even the worst. Last weekend Erica set up with Mr. Helmethead. She wasn't sure there was even hair under the gel. And the weekend before, Mr. Grabbyhands wouldn't let go of her boobs. He probably thought they were squeaky toys. She'd met so many horrible guys, she'd lost count. And she'd had enough.

"You don't look very excited," Erica said, after Aviva set the flyer back on the table.

"I'm not. I really appreciate your attempt to help me, but speed dating isn't my thing. Neither are the awful, full-of-themselves professionals I've met recently. What's the point of a relationship with someone who's more turned on by the money they make than by me? I'm starting to think artists or creative people are more my type. You know, like back in high school."

"Oh, come on. You can't possibly want a starving artist. The goal is to get out of Hoboken and move into an apartment on the Upper West Side, Avs, not the Village. The right guy is out there for you. You'll never meet him if you stay home. This is an easy way to meet a whole lot of men at one time. No excuses, Avs."

She wanted to say no, to refuse flat out to go. But she needed peaceful coexistence with her roommate. Otherwise, their parents would hear about it. While Aviva's mom was always understanding, her dad and Erica's parents were less so. So, Aviva usually tried to make as few waves as possible to keep the peace between the families. She sighed. "Okay. One last time. But after this, I'm done. Good night."

She closed the door to her bedroom and fell onto her bed. Since when was Erica in charge of her sex life? Since she'd become too much of a wimp to protest. Well, that was ending now. Two hours of pretending to like a whole bunch of professional, single, most likely egotistical men for roommate harmony. And then she was doing things her way.

Jacob Black yawned as he walked into the upstairs lounge of the Urban Bistro. Another late-night study session followed by a day of third-year law classes. All he wanted to do was get some sleep. But he'd agreed to come with his roommate, Adam, to this event. He wouldn't break his word. Even if he had no intention of taking anyone here seriously.

Dimly lit, the lounge's purple lighting glinted off grey walls and bathed the black marble tables in a purple glow. Silver patterned carpeting and upholstered chairs lent a disco vibe to the place. Or it should have.

Unfortunately, the shadowed ambiance made Jacob sleepy. If he sat in one of the comfortable chairs, he'd conk out in five minutes.

The hostess of the evening checked his name off the list. She directed him to the black marble bar to get a drink.

"Scotch and soda." A pat on the back made him turn. "Hey, Adam. What can I get you?"

"I'll have what he's having," Adam said to the bartender. He looked out over the slowly filling tables. "So, you ready to find the woman of your dreams?"

"Here? I doubt it."

"That's what I love about you, Jake. You're always the optimist."

Jacob took a long swallow of his drink. Some of the tension of the day disappeared. "I'm a realist. It's not possible to find the woman of my dreams in five minutes. Besides, with the bar exam looming and the long hours we'll have to put into a job at a law firm, no woman in her right mind will want to get involved with either of us."

"We don't need one in her right mind, Jake, just…" Adam molded his hands into an hourglass. Jacob elbowed him in the ribs. "Ow!"

"Grow up."

The hostess began her instructions, and the chatter died down. "Okay, ladies, you're going to stay seated while the men move from table to table at five-minute intervals. Make sure to write down the name of each person you meet. Circle the name of anyone you're interested in. At the end of the evening, turn your program in to me. I'll provide you with the contact info of anyone for whom there is a mutual interest. That's it. Have fun. If you have any questions, ask. Ready, set, date!"

The bell rang. Jacob sat across from a petite blonde.

"Hi, I'm Samantha."

"Hi, Samantha, I'm Jacob."

"Nice to meet you, Jacob. I'm a dietician. Do you know how much weight you can gain from alcohol?"

"Uh, no, hadn't thought about it." He pushed his glass to the side.

She sipped from her bottle of water. "Most people don't. That's why I only drink water. What do you do?"

"I'm a law student at Seton Hall."

"Oh, student diets are the worst. You should make sure to get lots of fiber and vitamin C in your diet. Potassium, like from bananas, is also important."

As she continued her list of essential ingredients, Jacob stared blindly into space. Just when he thought he couldn't stand any more of her advice, the bell rang.

"Well, it was nice to meet you, Jacob."

He moved to the next table where another blonde bounced in her seat. She rose and their heads banged together. Jacob rubbed his forehead as the first threads of a headache formed.

"Oh, I'm sorry. Are you okay? Do you need ice?" she asked.

"No, I'm fine. I'm Jacob, by the way."

"I'm Marcy. Do you like animals? I love animals."

"Yeah, I like them." Okay, maybe she was normal, if a little clumsy.

"If you could be any animal, what would it be?"

Or not. Was this woman serious? He coughed as he tried to think. Why was he bothering? But he didn't want to be rude, so he said the first animal to come to mind. "I guess I'd want to be an elephant."

"Really? That's cool. I'd want to be a gazelle. They're so graceful."

He clenched his jaw to keep from smiling at the irony.

It was the last time he wanted to smile. The next five speed dates consisted of a woman who spent the entire time listing every place she'd traveled, another who complained about New York City for the entire time, a third who talked about her medical conditions, and a fourth who discussed how soon she wanted to get pregnant. The icing on the cake was the drunken redhead who spilled her drink on him.

At the next bell, he sank into a seat, his only desire to make it through the rest of the evening with as little pain as possible so he could forget about this experience.

"You look about as happy to be here as I am," the petite woman across from him said, a merry sparkle in her green eyes. "I'm Aviva." She held out her hand and offered him her napkin at the same time.

"Thanks." He shook her hand and used the napkin to blot his shirt. "I'm Jacob. I didn't know my dislike was so obvious."

"Takes one to know one, I guess." She leaned forward with a conspiratorial wink. "So, who dragged you here?"

He laughed—the first real one all evening—balled up the napkin and placed it on the side of the table. With his arms folded on the table, he leaned forward. "My law school buddy. You?"

"Roommate." She pointed to a woman across the room whom he hadn't yet met. Her movement released a faint floral scent, not overpowering.

"You can't say no to a roommate without messing with the living arrangements," he said.

"Exactly! Plus, our families have a long history together, so it's even more complicated." She pushed a lock of hair behind her ear. Her brown hair was cut in a pixie style, but longer in front. If asked, he'd say he preferred long hair, but this style suited her. What was her name again? He studied his sheet. Right, Aviva. The lights glinted off her sparkling chai necklace, the Hebrew letter meaning "life," and drew his attention to her creamy neck.

"So, do you have a lot of experience with room-mates?" she asked.

He grinned. "I do. Adam," he searched until he spotted his friend and pointed so Aviva would see him, "is the one with the dirty blond hair. He's been mine throughout law school."

She scanned her pamphlet. "I haven't met him yet."

"He's a nice guy out for a good time." He winced. "Sorry, I didn't mean it that way. He's a nice guy."

"What about you?"

Jacob thrust his fingers through his hair. "I hope I'm a nice guy. As for a good time, I'd be more into it if I wasn't so tired."

She looked around the room with a furtive glance. "Want to escape?"

His favorite question of the night. "Yes."

At the bell, they strode to the door, ignoring the voice of the hostess behind them. The chilly night air was in stark contrast to the warmth of the crowded lounge, but Jacob didn't mind. Free from the mélange of perfume and vapid chatter, he took a deep breath for the first time all evening. He turned toward Aviva, then waited for her to finish texting. Her fingers were long and supple. She looked up from her phone. "Sorry, just letting my roommate know where I am, in case you turn out to be an axe murderer." Her careless shrug made Jacob smile.

He patted his pants pockets. "Drat, must have left my axe in my other pair of pants. Guess you're safe with me."

She laughed. They walked toward the corner together. The top of her head barely reached his shoulder in the flat shoes she wore. Once again, her floral perfume wafted toward his nose. Unlike the other perfumes he'd smelled earlier, this one was appealing.

"Can I get you a ride?" he asked as they approached Washington Street.

"No thanks. I can walk from here. It's only a few blocks."

"Are you sure? Why don't you let me walk you home?" He straightened as a sudden protective urge sliced through him.

"You don't need to walk me home. It's perfectly safe."

Jacob looked around at the people who milled about on the sidewalk, coming in and out of the local bars. He couldn't let a woman walk by herself in the dark. He'd never forgive himself if anything happened to her. "Look, call me crazy, but I'd feel better if I knew you got home safe. I promise I don't have any ulterior motive. Please?"

She nodded. "It's not necessary, but okay."

They stood together under the glow of the lamplight. Car headlights made patterns on the pavement. He stole a glance her way. She was staring at him with...interest? Maybe he should get to know her better. He was about to suggest they find a quiet place for coffee when the traffic lights changed. A cab approached. Aviva flagged it down, and it pulled to a stop. Jacob opened the door.

She started to climb in. "Thanks for escaping with me, Jacob."

"Escape artist at your service."

He closed the door and waved as the cab retreated into the distance. Her floral scent hung in the air around him. He inhaled and walked away. It was probably better this way. He didn't have time for a relationship. Right?

CHAPTER TWO

The next morning, as Aviva waited for her caffeine elixir to brew, Erica walked into the tiny kitchen. She wore earbuds and workout clothes. She looked more awake than Aviva could imagine at eight-thirty on a Saturday morning, especially after being out so late the night before. Aviva squinted at her. Erica turned off her music.

"Hey, I lost track of you last night. Why did you leave early?"

Aviva groaned. "Because it was awful." Thank goodness she was finished with Erica's set-ups.

"Really? I thought this one guy, Paul, was fabulous. All the women were hanging on his every word."

Of course, they were. They all fell for his "Look how important I am" flash. Until they try to spend time with him and switch the focus off him. She wished she could go back to bed. Erica's taste in men left a lot to be desired.

"I don't know. I didn't click with any of them." *Except maybe that one...* "But thanks for trying."

Erica patted her shoulder and squeezed past her to open the refrigerator. She grabbed a smoothie and took a few swallows. "Well, at least you got free drinks out of it. Let me give it some more thought. I'm sure I can find someone for you."

Aviva started to protest, to remind her that last night was the last time, but Erica replaced her earbuds and disappeared into the workout ether. With a sigh, Aviva stuck her mug under the coffee drip. She'd tell her, she just had to find the right time.

Their parents were best friends. Growing up in the suburbs, Aviva and Erica had been joined at the hip. But sometime during high school, the two diverged. Erica pursued any man with a hot body as well as a financial future like their dads. Aviva did all she could to avoid the same path, leaning toward musicians, Goths and artists. As roommates, though, they worked. Life wasn't perfect, but she couldn't afford an apartment on her own, and studios were too cramped. Relations with her roommates had been fine until Erica decided she was put on this earth to be a *shadchan* her own personal matchmaker. Aviva had no plans to get dating advice from a woman who changed men faster than most women changed their purse. But first, she had to drum up the nerve to tell her.

By the time Jacob finished reading and annotating fifty pages of Hart & Wechsler on Sunday night, it was two the next morning. He hadn't been able to concentrate because flashes of the woman he'd met on Friday night popped into his head. Pools of light splashed his desk, reminding him of the way the lights in the club caught her chai necklace. Voices outside made him look out the window, expecting to see her walk down the street. But it had only been a random twenty-something student walking with friends who gave him an odd look. Even staring at his book, he hadn't seen the text written on the page, but the way she swirled the A in her name when she'd written it in his pamphlet.

To make matters worse, Adam woke early on Monday. He made enough noise to serve as a human alarm clock. Three hours later, Jacob stumbled into federal courts class, large coffee in hand. He sank into a chair, yawned, and turned on his laptop to take notes. He leaned down, opened his backpack, and searched for his flash drive. Out of the corner of his eye, he saw female, jean-clad legs walk to the seat next to him. As he angled his head to say hello, he saw chestnut hair curled behind an ear, and froze. Adira...Alina...Aviva. Aviva? He whipped around and winced at the crick in his neck. It wasn't Aviva. It was Lori, the same woman who'd been in his class all semester. She'd also been in several of his classes each of the previous two years. And she looked nothing like the way he remembered Aviva.

He shook his head. He was losing it. This was why he wouldn't pursue a relationship. If he was this distracted by a random stranger, imagine how he'd be with a girlfriend.

"You okay there, Jacob?"

He gave her a grim smile and sat straight in his seat, overtaken by a sudden warmth. "Yeah, just tired." How in the world did he mistake Lori for Aviva? Sure, both had brown, short hair, but he couldn't pinpoint Aviva's features, not when Lori was next to him. Aviva was a mirage, a barely remembered memory from a few days ago. An incredible distraction he didn't have time for. Distraction didn't fit into his plan.

His professor's arrival forced him to pay attention to his class. No matter how tired he was, he needed to maintain excellent grades in order to get the prestigious law firm job he'd been offered after graduation. It had been his goal throughout law school: graduate with honors, get a high paying law firm job, pay off school loans, have a stellar career. He would finally be able to take care of his mother the way she'd taken care of him all these years. With his father gone, it was up to him. Nothing would distract him.

So, why couldn't he get Aviva out of his mind?

Hannah, another PR associate, and one of Aviva's closest friends, popped her auburn head into Aviva's office, messenger bag on her shoulder. "You ready to go?"

"Give me a sec." Aviva rummaged through her bag and pulled out lip-gloss. "Okay, I'm ready."

"You need lip-gloss for class?" Hannah said.

Aviva shot her a look. "I always need lip-gloss. Now come on, I don't want to be late."

"You're the one who put on the lip-gloss."

"How was your weekend in Boston?" Aviva asked, trying to change the subject. They made their way to the PATH station to catch the train to their writing class at Rutgers in Newark.

"Cold. I had fun with my nieces and nephews, though. Didn't study enough. You?"

"Erica dragged me to a speed dating thing, and spent the rest of the weekend—"

"Wait, tell me about the speed dating!"

"It was just as I expected. The guys were all full of themselves, except for one. He and I snuck out early."

Hannah stopped dead right before paying for the train. She spun around. A pedestrian behind them banged into Aviva. Two others muttered curses as they stomped around them. "You left early with someone? Who?"

"Han, we're going to be late. The train is coming."

"I don't care. I want the details."

Aviva sighed. She pushed Hannah through the turnstile. "Okay, but there's really nothing to tell. Just some tired guy with wavy brown hair and a stained shirt. He wasn't overly polished, and he didn't make up some obnoxious one-liner when he came to my table. Neither of us wanted to be there, so we escaped."

"Where did you go?"

They boarded the train, squeezed together as it lurched along its way. "Don't give me those eyes, Han. He offered to walk me home, but a cab pulled up instead. I got in. I don't know where he went."

"Well, you must have liked him enough to plot an escape with him."

She had liked chatting with him. It had been easy, and for the first time all night, she'd been comfortable. Aviva shrugged. "I'll admit he was the best of the bunch. But there was no plotting. He was funny."

"Funny?"

"Yeah, he got my sense of humor. He joked about being an axe murderer." She stifled a laugh.

Hannah looked at her askance. "Sounds like he has potential."

"I could be reading into it. Besides, I don't have his number."

Aviva relayed the rest of the story as they hopped off the train, exited the station, and walked the few blocks to their class. The crowded sidewalks made conversation difficult. By the end, Hannah was laughing. "You know, it's a shame you don't have his number. He sounds like someone you might like to know better. I bet you could get it from the organizer."

"After ducking out early? I don't think so."

Hannah paused in the open door of the classroom. "That's too bad."

Aviva scoffed. "No matter how charming he may have seemed at the time, he's a law student, Han. Law students became lawyers. Lawyers put in way too much time at the office. He's probably no different than any of the other guys I've dated. Furiously climbing the corporate ladder, with no time to enjoy the things around him." Like their wives and children. She'd had enough of that in her life with her dad. Coulda, woulda, shoulda. It didn't matter, did it?

CHAPTER THREE

You need a girlfriend, Jacob," his mother said on the phone to him the next morning. "Your social life is important, whether it's casual now or more serious after you finish studying."

Jacob gripped the hair at the nape of his neck. He began counting to ten. He made it to three.

"Jacob? Jacob, are you there?"

He gritted his teeth. "Yes, Ma, I'm here."

"Well, we need to talk about your priorities, and finding a girlfriend should be one of them."

He took a deep breath. He closed and opened his eyes before he spoke. "No, it doesn't. I need to study."

"Jacob, you're a brilliant young man. Any law firm would be lucky to have you. But you also need to balance things out with a girlfriend."

"I don't want a girlfriend."

"Wait. Jacob, are you trying to tell me you're gay? Because it's fine if you are, but you need to tell your mother these things."

He was going to lose all the hair on the back of his head. Did men lose hair there? He'd have the reverse "monk" look. It would be ridiculous. Especially since he was Jewish.

"No, Ma, I'm not gay. But thanks for your support."

"Are you sure? Don't be lippy with me. I'm still your mother."

He swallowed. There wasn't enough oxygen in the world for him to breathe through all his frustration. "I'm positive. I just don't have time for a girlfriend right now."

"But you would if you had one."

"Huh?"

"You'd have time for one if you had one. You'd make the time. Just like you make time for other things. Which is why I'll introduce you to the daughter of a friend of mine."

"What? No! You can't do that."

"Jacob, it's a mother's job to make her son happy."

"But I *am* happy."

"Don't try to fool me."

She was killing him. "Uh, I've kind of already met someone."

"What?"

Jacob pulled the phone away from his ear. On a good day, he could hear his mother through the phone when it sat on his lap. Right now, with her shriek, well, he couldn't hear anything, but when his hearing returned, he'd be able to hear her across the room.

"I said I've already met someone." He wasn't lying.

"When? Where?"

"Last weekend. At a speed-dating event." Actually, he'd met lots of someones, but only one had stuck with him in the back of his mind.

"Speed-dating. Hmm, we'll talk about that later. In the meantime, tell me about her. What's her name? What does she do? What's she like?"

"Her name is Aviva. She has short brown hair, a great sense of humor, smart." So far, so good.

"What does she do?"

Crap. He didn't remember. Had they discussed her job? "She's an escape artist."

His mother was silent on the other end of the phone. That wasn't a good sign.

"Jacob?"

"It's a joke, Ma."

"Is Aviva a joke?"

"No, she's real." She'd smelled of flowers.

"Stop joking and tell me about her."

He pulled his hair again. Although he'd spent more than five minutes with her, and they'd bonded over their dislike of speed dating, they hadn't discussed much of substance. Certainly nothing that would convince his mother not to meddle in his social life. He'd have to make something up. What kind of woman would his mother think was perfect for him?

"She's pretty. She lives with her parents in New Jersey. She's going to cooking school to learn to be a chef and hopes to open her own restaurant. She has a dry sense of humor and likes Rowan Atkinson, like Dad used to. She loves animals and kids. She coaches a girls' basketball team at a local Boys & Girls Club, likes to travel to exotic places and plays the piano. Jazz." Oh man. He was totally lying. To his mother. Thank goodness she would never meet Aviva.

"Well, it sounds like a lovely list of character traits, but how do you feel about her?"

He covered his eyes with his hand. "It's a little early for feelings, Ma."

His mother sighed. "When do I get to meet her?"

"Ma, I just met her."

"Jacob don't waste time. If she's as wonderful as you say, she won't stay single for long."

His mother was never going to understand. Smacking the palm of his hand against his forehead, he said he had to study, and they said their goodbyes. He hung up and sank onto the sofa. He'd barely avoided a catastrophe with his mother, all because he didn't want to date anyone right now. His mother should be pleased he was so devoted to success.

He stared at his books but couldn't concentrate now. Her voice reverberated in his head. He needed to do something to quiet it. Studying wasn't enough of a distraction, and at this rate, he'd have to redo all of his work anyway. Might as well take a break. Turning to his computer, he scrolled through one of the websites he liked to check in the rare moments he had free time. An ad for a pirate exhibit at the Discovery Times Square Museum jumped out at him. He smiled to himself. He'd loved pirates as a kid. His dad had fostered that love. This would be the perfect way to get his mind off his mother. Grabbing his keys, he left the apartment.

Worst case, it might provide him a way to make her walk the plank.

"Aunt Aviva, come look at this pirate!"

Aviva smiled at her nephew's enthusiasm as Ben dragged her through the crowded display hall of the Discovery Times Square Museum. At seven, her nephew loved everything to do with pirates. As soon as she'd heard about the Shipwreck exhibit, she reserved tickets for the two of them.

They approached Blackbeard's display. Ben made pirate noises while Aviva read his story out loud.

"Did you know he operated around the East Coast of the United States?" she asked him. "He never harmed the sailors on the ships he took."

"I read a book about him. He used his beard to scare people."

"Do you think his beard was scary?"

"Maybe if he growled a lot." Ben scrunched his freckled face into a fearsome frown and stroked a pretend beard.

Aviva laughed. "Hey, you can draw your own pirate over there."

They waited in line for a kiosk to free up, and Ben got to work. When they were done, they turned to go. Ben bumped into someone.

"Sorry," Ben said.

The man looked down. "It's—"

Aviva looked up and gasped. "I can't—"

Ben looked between the two adults. "What's going on, Aunt Aviva?"

Aviva's stomach fluttered. She absently slipped her hand over Ben's head. "We know each other. It's Jacob, right?"

"Yeah. You're Aviva?"

She nodded. "I didn't expect to see you again."

"Same." He looked at Ben. "Exploring pirates with your nephew?"

"How...oh. Yes, he's a big pirate fan."

"So am I." His face colored. Aviva smiled. He was embarrassed to admit he liked pirates. How sweet.

"What's your favorite part of the exhibit?" Jacob asked Ben.

Ben looked around the room, his face scrunched in concentration. "I think I like all of it the best."

Aviva smiled at her nephew.

"I should let you get back to your explorations." Jacob turned to leave.

"Are you two going to go out on a date?" Ben asked.

Aviva gasped. Her heart thundered and her cheeks warmed.

Jacob turned around and tipped his head toward him, one eyebrow raised. "Why do you ask, matey?"

Ben looked solemn. "Because you're being nice to her. Girls like that."

"Ben!" Aviva fought her sudden desire to escape. She fingered her chai necklace.

Jacob's shoulders shook. By the look on his face, he was trying not to laugh, which made her desire to disappear more urgent. "They do, huh?" he asked.

Ben nodded. "And they like stinky flowers too. Except, they don't think they stink." He shook his head in disgust. Aviva didn't know if she should laugh or try to melt into the floor.

"You seem to know a lot about girls."

"Girls are icky. No self-respecting pirate would let a girl on his ship."

"Hey, wait a minute, Ben," Aviva said. "Look over there at that display. It's all about female pirates."

She pointed across the room to a small, but interesting, display. "You should check out Back from the Dead Red," she added.

Ben's eyes widened. He ran to the display. Mortified, Aviva realized Jacob continued to stand with her. Apparently, it wasn't as easy to get rid of him as it was a seven-year-old boy. She wracked her brain trying to figure out whether to apologize for Ben or create an excuse to leave.

"Your nephew is cute," Jacob said, breaking the silence.

The sound of his voice eased some of her nerves. She took a deep breath. "Thanks. He's my brother's son and the first and only grandchild, so he gets a lot of attention. I usually have to beat the grandparents off with a stick to spend time with him." She was babbling.

She walked toward Ben, who was mesmerized by the display. Jacob followed. Why didn't he just leave?

"See, Ben, women were pirates too."

"Did you know she pretended to be dead, Aunt Aviva? She lived like a man, and she died in a shootout!"

"Sounds pretty violent to me," Aviva said.

"That's 'cause you're a girl."

Before she could respond to his chauvinism, Jacob interjected. "It's a pretty good thing she *is* a girl, Ben."

"Why?" Ben asked.

Jacob winked at Aviva. She raised her eyebrows waiting for his response. Maybe he should stay a little longer.

"Because if she wasn't, she wouldn't be your aunt."

Ben paused; his face scrunched. With a shrug, he moved onto the next display.

"That's not where I thought you were going," Aviva said.

Jacob shrugged. "Come on, he's only a kid. What did you expect me to say? I can't corrupt him this young."

"Good thing. I don't think my brother would forgive me. I think he wants to do all the corrupting himself."

"Probably right." He thrust his hands in his pockets. "Well, I should leave the two of you alone to enjoy the rest of your weekend. It was nice to see you again."

"You too."

Jacob walked away. Just as she was about to follow Ben into the next room, Jacob paused. He clenched and unclenched his hands before walking back to her. "Should we listen to him?"

Aviva swiveled her head from Ben to Jacob. "Listen to whom? My brother?"

"No, your nephew. He suggested we go out on a date."

Her face heated. "Well, technically, he asked *if* we were going to go out on a date. He didn't actually suggest it."

Jacob's eyes brightened. Aviva couldn't turn away. His eyes weren't brown or green. They were...the color of cognac. The noise of the people around them faded into the distance.

"True, but it would be rude of us to not give him an answer."

"It would be a shame to disappoint a seven-year-old," she said.

"That's right. He might go through his whole life feeling like he was missing something."

"That really wouldn't be fair."

"So, what do you say—want to go out on a date?"

"With you?"

Jacob looked around for a moment. "Well, there's a security guard over there, but I'm not sure he's your type."

Aviva pretended to consider. "No, not really," she said, without a glance at the guard. "Yes, I'd like to go out on a date with you."

Jacob expelled a breath. Once again, Aviva was drawn to his sweetness. He pulled out his phone. "Can you give me your number?"

His smile was a little bashful. He had beautifully straight, white teeth. It was either good genetics or a great orthodontist.

His whole demeanor relaxed when she nodded. He tapped the screen a few times. She recited her number, and he repeated it.

"Great. I hope you don't mind if we wait until next weekend. My class schedule this week is crazy, but I'll call you tomorrow to set something up."

"Oh, right, you're a law student." Her shoulders slumped. Law students were overworked.

"I am."

"Okay, fine. Call whenever you have time."

"I'll call you tomorrow. Bye, Ben! Bye, Aviva." He disappeared into the crowd.

"Hey, Aunt Aviva, can we get ice cream? I'm hungry."

"Sure thing," she said.

Jacob disappeared into the distance.

He probably won't even call.

At eight-thirty the next morning, Jacob looked at his phone. He shook his head. What the hell was he thinking? He didn't have time for a social life. He barely had time to breathe. One minute he told his mother he didn't have time to date, the next he asked Aviva out. He should forget it. He had to study. With a yawn, he made himself a pot of coffee, sat at his desk, and opened his books.

Two hours later, he pushed away with a groan. He'd told her he'd call. And he always kept his word. He'd enjoyed his conversation with her yesterday. Could he somehow find the time to make it work? Pulling up the calendar on his phone, he searched for time to spare. Classes, assignments, and study time left little room for anything else. He punched the Contacts button and searched for her number. Best to get this over with. Maybe if he got her out of his system, he'd be able to forget about her and concentrate. She answered on the third ring.

"Aviva? Hi, it's Jacob. From the Discovery Museum. And the speed dating fiasco."

Aviva laughed, reminding him of a bowl of cherries in a sunlit kitchen—bright and genuine and full of flavor. "I don't know if I'd call it a fiasco, technically. But I didn't expect you to be this prompt."

He glanced at the clock. "Well, I told you I'd call. I'm on a break now and I won't have time later. I thought you might be interested in dinner on Saturday night with a round of bowling at Bowl Rite in Jersey City afterward."

"You bowl? Somehow, I don't picture you bowling."

"Well, I don't have a monogrammed bowling ball, but I always have fun. We can do something else if you'd rather."

"No, I'd love to go bowling. Saturday is good."

"Great. If you give me your address, I can pick you up. Unless you'd be more comfortable meeting me at the restaurant."

"No, you can come to my building." She gave him the address.

That night, while he studied at the library, Aviva texted him.

What do u think?

He frowned at the distraction but scrolled down and chortled out loud. She'd texted him a picture of a monogrammed bowling ball—bright pink, with the letters of her name engraved in sparkly silver writing. Hushes from fellow students stifled him.

didn't know you were a "pink" person

didn't know you were into bowling

guess we're even now. Looking forward 2 learning more about u

The next day, he called his mom. "Can you take a picture of Dad's old bowling shirt and text it to me?"

"Jacob, I don't text."

"Okay, could you email it to me?"

"What do you need it for? Shouldn't you be in class now?"

Jacob moved the phone from his ear and took a deep breath. "It's Monday, Ma, I don't have class until eleven today. I want to show it to a friend."

"You know I'll do anything for you. I have my mah jongg group in a half hour, so I'll take the picture and send it to you when I get back."

"Thanks, Ma, love you."

"Love you too, dear."

That evening, when he checked his email, the picture waited in his inbox. The shirt looked to be straight out of the sixties, brown- and white striped with the team logo on the back, his dad's name stitched in gold thread on the front pocket. He typed a quick text to Aviva.

> will u still go out w/me if I wear this?

A few moments later, he received her answer.

> I was thinking of this 1. goes w/my ball

The shirt was pink with Betty Boop on the pocket and rhinestones on the collar.

> guess we're good

Two days later, Jacob received another text from Aviva.

> found the perfect shoes

"Holy—" He silenced himself as his classmates turned to look at him. She'd texted him a photo of bright pink bowling shoes with silver rhinestone stripes. As soon as class was over, he searched the web for vintage men's bowling shoes. He shot her a text of a pair he found.

these r mine

awesome

By Saturday afternoon, Jacob oscillated between hoping Aviva would show up in her bright pink bowling outfit and praying she wasn't a poufy pink kind of girl. She'd seemed to be joking, but you could never be sure via text. He locked his apartment, whistled as he jogged down the stairs. Time for the moment of truth.

CHAPTER FOUR

From her trajectory as she exited the elevator in her apartment building, Aviva had the perfect vantage point to see Jacob without being seen. Through some architectural magic, she could see the expanse of the brightly lit lobby and Jacob, who drummed his fingers on his leg, his gaze focused out the window.

He wasn't wearing the ugly brown and orange vintage bowling shirt, thank goodness. Instead, he wore a dark red button-down shirt with grey slacks. She smoothed her hair, fingered her necklace, and walked forward.

His face brightened. He held out his hand. "I thought you might like some 'stinky' flowers." He held out a mixed bouquet of multicolored pink roses, daisies, and yellow carnations.

Ben would be proud. She smiled. "Thank you. These are beautiful." She buried her nose in the fragrant bouquet. "Let me just run them upstairs."

When she returned, she arched her brow as they headed out the door. "No bowling shirt?"

His laugh was deep. It made her stomach flutter. Or were those nerves?

"I didn't think it would look right in the restaurant. But later...well, that's a different story."

"I like your discretion."

"I like what you're wearing. You look pretty."

She'd chosen black leggings and an off-the-shoulder, three-quarter sleeved turquoise top. Pretty for dinner and comfortable enough to bowl in, she hoped.

"Thanks. Tell me about the restaurant we're going to."

The rideshare pulled up, and he held the door for her. Once they were settled, with the driver armed with the address of the restaurant, Jacob answered her. "Battello. Obviously Italian. The food is great. It's on the waterfront in Jersey City."

He talked with his hands—large, neat, and graceful hands. He was a foodie. His descriptions made her mouth water. At the restaurant, he once again held the door for her and ushered her inside. The aroma of garlic and homemade pasta assailed her. Her stomach growled.

"Hungry?" he asked.

She thought about making some noncommittal response, but she was sick of shallow small talk and slick posturing from previous guys she'd dated. If this worked, it would be on her terms.

"I'm always hungry."

"Oh, thank God. You have no idea how annoying it is to deal with women who pick at their food."

Aviva nodded as she followed Jacob and the maître d to their table. She took the proffered menu. "My roommate is like that. I find crumbs everywhere, but little other evidence she actually eats."

"That would drive me crazy. I have to confess, though, I'm a neat freak too."

"Uh-oh, that might just be a deal breaker." She made as if to rise from the table. Jacob's jaw dropped. She laughed. "Relax, I'm just kidding."

The waiter placed a basket of bread on the table and took their order.

"So, I just told you two damning things about myself. What about you?"

"Two?"

"I like to eat and I'm a neat freak. Your turn."

Aviva swallowed a bite of bread. She glanced around the dining room before answering. With so many windows overlooking the waterfront and the bright lights of the Manhattan skyline, there was a bustle about the place. It would never be considered a soothing place to relax.

"Hmm, I don't know about damning information, but I work at Shelby Public Relations as an assistant account executive. I'm taking a writing class at Rutgers, in Newark. I have no patience for artifice. I'm not impressed by shallow things or how much money you earn." She tore off another piece of bread. "Have I scared you away yet?"

"Nope, not yet. In fact, I'll even tell you your writing class and my apartment are pretty near each other. You're in public relations? What exactly do you do?"

"I work with clients to help them get their message across in more believable ways than advertising."

"Like what?"

"I try to get articles written about them in magazines or newspapers. Right now, I'm working on a gala for a medical research client. They want to raise money to fund their cancer research."

"That shouldn't be too hard."

"Well, you'd think not, but often pharmaceutical companies are portrayed as the evil empire, putting money above everything else. My client wants to break the mold and raise money to fund research into the disease, rather than promote their own drugs as the solution."

"Interesting. Where are you holding the gala?"

"At the Liberty Science Center. What kind of law do you want to practice?"

"I'm planning on environmental law."

"That sounds rewarding. Do you have a job lined up or are you still looking?"

Jacob propped an elbow on the back of his chair. "I interned at a large firm last summer. They offered me a job starting in September, providing my grades continue as they are, and I pass the bar exam. That's why I'm spending all my time concentrating on my studies."

Aviva's stomach dropped. She wrapped her arms around her waist.

Lawyers who worked at big New York law firms were usually career-focused to the exclusion of all else, leaving no room for anything or anyone else. Certainly not her. She'd seen it with her dad as a child and even now. Work came first, family second. It didn't matter how much they needed him or wanted him; his paying clients came first. Once, as a little girl, she'd brought him her piggy bank and asked if he could take her to the park. "I can pay you, just like your clients, Daddy." He'd given her a hug and ruffled her hair, still looking at his papers. "You can't afford my rates, sweetheart. Now, go ask your mother." He'd given her a kiss and told her he'd play with her when he was finished with work.

She was still waiting.

She wouldn't get close to a guy who was like her dad. "You're lucky to have gotten a job offer so early."

"It's a great firm with a lot of potential for growth. Of course, like all big law firms, I'll put in long hours, but it's worth it for what I want to do."

Of course, it was.

The waiter arrived and placed their food in front of them—Mediterranean branzino and pignoli-crusted cod, along with tuna rollatini and a Romaine wedge. The aromas of garlic, cumin, seafood, and spices wafted from the dishes. Aviva inhaled deeply.

"Smells good, doesn't it?" Jacob asked.

She sliced the branzino. "It tastes even better."

Jacob smiled as he dug into his food. He had such a beautiful smile. She could spend the rest of the evening staring at it. With a sigh, she continued eating and talking throughout dinner.

When they were finished, he followed her out of the restaurant into the cool evening air. "You don't mind walking, do you? The weather is great."

"No, I like the exercise, especially after such a big meal."

He curled his fingers around hers. His hand was warm and solid. It made Aviva feel secure, though she hadn't known she lacked the feeling before now. She squeezed her eyes shut for a moment. He might sound perfect, but career choice-wise, he was too much like her dad.

"Whoa, watch yourself. Are you okay?"

She opened them in embarrassment as Jacob pulled her against him to keep her from tripping on the curb. So much for not falling for this guy—she was literally falling at his feet!

"Yeah, I'm fine, just a bit of a klutz, apparently." If her hand in his made her feel secure, her body pressed against his made her feel...unsettled. His chest was hard, like a marble statue, but warm. His arms were muscular. They wrapped around her like a vise, yet she felt safe. Heat radiated off him. His scent, a combination of cedar wood and spices, filled her nostrils.

He hadn't released her hand. Their intertwined fingers highlighted their different skin tones. His was a shade or two darker. She followed the contour of his arm to his shoulder where his muscles filled out his polo sleeve. The indentation between his shoulder and his biceps fascinated her.

His eyes were filled with concern and a hint of desire. She quickly looked away, focusing instead on the pedestrians enjoying the view of Manhattan across the river.

"What are you thinking?" His question drew her gaze to his, although she wished to look at anything but him.

"I'm thinking about beating you at bowling."

He raised an eyebrow. "I find that hard to imagine."

"Have you never been beaten by a girl before?"

"It's not the girl part I have a hard time with."

"Then what is it?"

"It's the pink. All the pink you texted me—the ball, the shoes, the shirt. Seems to me it would just be a distraction."

"Unless distraction is a strategy."

Jacob nodded and increased his pace. With legs much longer than hers, Aviva almost had to jog to keep up with him. He didn't seem to notice her difficulty, nor did he respond when she said, "Slow down." She reached over and punched his arm.

"Ow! What was that for?"

"For making me run to keep up with you."

He let go of her hand and rubbed his arm. "If you're as fierce with a bowling ball as you are with a punch, I may have to reevaluate my assumption of your bowling skills."

"You may just have to."

With a rueful smile, he took her hand again. This time, he walked at a much more leisurely pace. "This better?" He glanced sideways at her, the corners of his eyes crinkly from his smile.

"Much. Thank you."

They reached the bowling alley, picked up their shoes, and found a free lane.

"So, I see you decided against the throwback greaser look?" Aviva asked.

"Well, if you're not doing the pink poodle thing, I figured I'd just come as myself."

Aviva nodded. "Probably a good plan. Besides, I don't know about you, but I think that much pink would have made me ill."

"It would have affected your bowling game, and we wouldn't want that."

All around them, the crack of the ball against the pins, the sweep of the pinsetter as it pushed the fallen pins out of the pit, the cacophonous shouts of other players, swirled. But all Aviva heard was the teasing tone of his voice, its deep rumble vibrating in her chest and making her toes curl. He grabbed the bowling ball with his long fingers, bent over and let the ball loose down the lane. His arm muscles rippled; his butt clenched. Aviva resisted the urge to fan herself. Bowling was an excellent first date.

She looked at the score on the overhead screen—third frame and he was ahead, but only by a few points. They were pretty evenly matched, unless...

"You're not going easy on me, are you?"

He stopped in the middle of reaching for his ball off the rack. "No, but would it matter if I were?"

"Absolutely."

"Duly noted." He grabbed his ball and bowled his next round. Returning to her, he picked up her ball and handed it to her.

Their fingers touched, and they paused. His were long and tapered and reminded her of those of an artist.

"Do you paint?" she asked, her voice a little breathless.

His irises were flecked with gold. They appeared to glow as he stared at her. She licked her lips, suddenly dry. His gaze shifted with her movement.

"No." He moved closer, until the only thing preventing them from touching was the gold bowling ball bridging the space between their ribcages. "I used to play guitar though."

Her stomach dropped as she imagined how those fingers would strum across her body. Her breasts tingled. She felt a distinct lack of air. She pulled away and gulped a deep breath. "I think it's my turn."

She'd never thought of herself as a coward, yet, as she focused on her game, she thought she might have to change her opinion. She could fall for him. His wit and charm during dinner and their brief walk afterward crept past her defenses. His sexiness was undeniable. His intelligence self-evident. Oh yes, she was a coward. Because, despite all his admirable qualities, Jacob was pursuing a life she didn't want. One she couldn't go through again. Therefore, Jacob was dangerous.

If he were the kind of man who only judged women by their physical traits, bowling was a genius move because it gave him the perfect opportunity to observe her butt. He wasn't. He liked Aviva for more than her looks. He liked her laugh, her forthrightness, her sense of humor. Indeed, those qualities were what stuck in his brain and lasted when he couldn't be sure he remembered her name. They made him enjoy her company and opened him to the idea of spending more time with her.

He had to admit, though, as she paced toward the lane, held the ball, bent, and aimed, she had a terrific ass. Not too big, not too small and it filled out her leggings nicely. She swayed back and forth as she moved, tantalizing him. Once the ball knocked down six pins, she turned back toward him.

She had nice breasts too. The blue—or was it green—top hugged her chest enough to give it definition and hint at cleavage. He'd stared at that cleavage surreptitiously enough during dinner. He wasn't a pervert, drooling over lady parts. He was a man who appreciated a sexy woman. And she was sexy in an understated, classy way.

Their funny texts during the week hinted at a cutesy girly-girl, yet the woman he'd dined with and whom he was trying to beat in a good-natured competition, was also intelligent and perceptive. He was relieved. He'd thought her texts and photos were funny. He'd given as good as he got, but it was one thing to joke about something and another thing to live it. High maintenance, ultra-girly females weren't his type.

Aviva? Well, she might be. He could easily see himself falling for her, having a relationship with her. It was a problem because he didn't have time for a relationship. Could he find the time for her in between all his studying? Would a relationship with her jeopardize his grades?

"You're up."

He jumped off the white plastic chair, unaware how lost he'd been in his thoughts. "Sorry." He checked the scoreboard. "You're beating me."

She smiled.

Was it his imagination, or did she stand a little straighter, preen a tiny bit? Definitely not a girly-girl. In her heels, she'd only come up to his chin; now, in the ugly bowling shoes, she barely reached his shoulder. Her eyes twinkled. With her short hair, she resembled a fairy. He was tempted to search for wings.

"Yes. Yes, I am."

"I'm not sure my manliness can handle this."

"Oh, I don't know." She lowered her gaze from his face, down his body to his feet, and up again. "I think your 'manliness' will survive. Flourish, even."

Jacob's neck heated. He shifted from one foot to the other at her unexpected perusal. He reached for the bowling ball.

When he turned to her again, she was smiling.

Two could play this game.

"Oh, yes, I'll flourish." Standing next to the ball return, he raked his gaze from the top of her short-cropped, haircut, down to her chest, where he lingered for a moment. He continued past her waist and hips, down her legs to the tips of her ugly bowling shoes. When he finally returned to meet her face, it was bright red, almost matching the neon sign pointing to the snack bar behind her head. He leaned toward her, his bowling ball between them.

Her breath brushed his chin, warm and unsteady. A lock of hair fell across her forehead. He pushed it in place with one finger, one finger that drew across her smooth skin and traced her fine-boned skull. She bit her lip. He pulled away, millimeter by millimeter, though he wanted to get closer.

"But first, I'll win." He winked, walked toward the foul line, adjusted his stance, took a few strides, swung his arm, and let the ball go. It spun down the lane. At the last moment, it veered into the gutter. Jacob's jaw dropped. He shook his head, turned, and stopped short.

Aviva tapped her fingers on the table. "Interesting strategy you've got there." Her eyes sparkled. Her tone told him she wasn't being mean.

He'd liked her sense of humor before; he couldn't decide to not like it when she was teasing him.

He nodded in acknowledgment, turned, and swung the second ball. It knocked down seven pins.

Aviva grabbed her ball, patted his arm, and aimed at the pins. Strike. She didn't move. Jacob couldn't figure out why she stood still, until her shoulders began to shake.

She was laughing. At him.

She turned around. Tears ran down her face. She inhaled. "I'm sorry. I swear I have no idea how it happened."

"Sure, you don't." As his grin widened, he bit the insides of his cheeks, folded his arms, and did his best to look sad. "What a way to get a guy when he's down."

"You're not down. You just challenged the bowling gods. They don't like human challengers."

"Bowling gods?"

"Of course. How else do you think we recreational bowlers manage it?" She stepped toward him. Her green eyes were wide with fake innocence.

"Bowling gods."

"Exactly. You challenged them." At this point, they were toe-to-toe. Her floral scent wafted around him. He refocused on her words.

"As you like to say, Aviva, *technically*, I challenged you."

"Yes, but with bowling skill, so you actually challenged them too."

She looked supremely satisfied with her circuitous bowling logic. Jacob had an urge to kiss her. Her lips were full and pink and tantalizingly close. He rested one hand on her waist and clasped the other hand behind her neck. She rose on tiptoe. This close, the brown flecks in her eyes shone. Her pupils widened. He tilted his head, leaned down and softly kissed her lips.

She sighed and ran her hands up and down his biceps. Her touch made his skin tingle.

With a groan, he pulled her tighter, kissed her deeper. She tasted sweet. He was hungry for more. But they were in a bowling alley. Distractions he'd blocked out, as he focused on her lips, returned—voices around them, the aroma of fried foods coming from the snack bar, blinking lights— and reminded him how public this place was, so he pulled away.

"Looks like we're challenging each other," he whispered.

Aviva lay in bed that night unable to fall asleep. Her nerve endings were on fire, her body hyperaware of everything against her skin—her pjs, her sheets, her hair. Scenes from her date played out, image after image, as if she projected the event on the ceiling. Closing her eyes only allowed her to focus more on it, added the sounds and smells from the evening— the waxy aroma of the bowling alley, his spicy aftershave, the deep timbre of his voice. Her heartbeat increased. Heat pooled low in her belly as she remembered their kiss.

If his kiss was any indication, this man epitomized sex on a stick. Sex in a bottle, sex on the floor, sex of any and all kinds. He made her want to do things she'd never wanted to do before.

Desire was dangerous. Because his dreams were nothing like hers. Her stomach clenched. She remembered her father, or rather, his absence—from birthday parties, dinners, school events. She couldn't relive that.

Her body, however, was a traitor. It wouldn't let her forget how it felt to be in his arms or against his lips. It protested never seeing him again.

When they'd finished bowling, he'd brought her home and stood outside the door with her. "I had a great time with you, Aviva, even if you did beat me."

"Yeah, that was an unexpected surprise. A nice one, though."

He leaned in to kiss her. She kissed him back, tasting, exploring, pushing for more. When they pulled apart, they were breathless. She held onto him for a moment until her legs no longer felt like jelly.

"Would you like to do it again sometime?"

She pulled her head back.

He stammered. "Uh, I meant go out, not the kiss. Although the kiss was great. We could do that too..."

She bit her lip to keep from laughing at his awkwardness.

He shook his head. "I'm making a mess of this. What I meant was, can I see you again?"

She stared at the ceiling now and swallowed. She should have said no. Should have said she didn't think it would work out.

Instead, she'd said, "Yes."

She turned and punched the pillow. She wouldn't go out with him again.

CHAPTER FIVE

Aviva plopped her school bag on the chair next to her in the Rutgers University Dana Library.

"So, how was your date?" Hannah asked.

She sank into the chair across from her friend. Before she answered, she took a long drink from a mocha latte. "It was good."

Hannah stared at her in silence. When Aviva didn't elaborate, Hannah rolled her blue eyes. "That's all you're going to tell me?"

"What else is there to say?"

"Did you seriously just ask that question? For the first time in, like, forever, you went out on a date with a guy who had potential—it wasn't some obnoxious set-up by your roommates—and all you have to say is 'it was good'?"

Aviva swirled the latte with the stirrer. The liquid created a vortex in the center, which, for some reason, reminded her of the ball return last night. "Okay, technically, it was more than good. I really like him. We're definitely attracted to one another. But I'm going to end it."

"Why?"

"He's a law student."

"You say law student like they're dirty words."

"Han, there's no point in getting serious with him. He's going to devote all his time to studying and his job."

"Did he say that?"

"He didn't have to."

"So, you didn't ask him."

"You mean like, 'please sir, can you spend some time with me?' No, I didn't ask."

Hannah rolled her eyes. "Have you talked about his career plans?"

"He wants to work for a large firm."

"Lots of law students take large firm jobs to pay off student loans. Did he talk at all about his study habits?"

Actually, he *had* talked about paying off law school loans. "He studies all the time."

"Yet he called you anyway, right?"

"Yeah, when he said he would."

"So maybe you're jumping to conclusions about him."

Aviva stirred her coffee again. She watched the liquid spin. "Maybe."

"Did you have fun last night?"

She couldn't hold back a smile. "Yeah."

"So, don't write him off yet."

Aviva's phone beeped. "It's him." She read the text.

"You're smiling."

"He wanted me to know he had a good time, even if I did beat him." She texted him back.

"You didn't just break up with him, did you?" Hannah asked.

"Well, technically, we're not dating."

"Aviva!"

She laughed. "No, I didn't. I told him I had fun too, and I liked winning."

Hannah shook her head. "You really have no clue how to do this, do you?"

"I won't throw a game just because my opponent is a guy. If he can't handle it, that's his problem, not mine." She looked at her phone. "He texted again. He has to study but he'll talk to me later."

"Good, now see what happens."

Aviva's skepticism must have shown on her face because Hannah reached for her hand. "Not everyone is like your dad."

"I know, but that doesn't mean I won't be prepared."

"Alright, just give him a chance. Now, speaking of prepared, we need to write this assignment."

As they pulled out their books, Aviva thought of Jacob. He said he'd talk to her later. She didn't know when later was, but she wouldn't wait around, even if so far, he'd kept his promises. Experience had shown her not to expect too much.

Jacob stared at the page in his law book without seeing words for the fourth time that day. He rubbed his face, took a drink of coffee, and remembered dinner with Aviva—how her lips sipped from her glass. He cleared his throat, adjusted the alignment of his book and his computer, and lined up his highlighters. With a deep breath, he read the chapter.

This time, he made it through three paragraphs before he forgot what he read, and his mind drifted to Aviva's text. She liked beating him. It had made him smile, but his smile wouldn't last long if he failed this class. He stretched and looked around the library. Everyone else's heads were buried in their books.

This was why he didn't have time for a relationship. No matter how physically attracted he might be, he shouldn't see her again. There wasn't enough time in his life right now. Wrong place, wrong time. With a shake of his head, he forced himself to concentrate.

Three hours later, when it should have only taken two on the outside, he finished his assignment. He packed his things and headed to a sandwich place on the corner for lunch. All around him, couples sat at tables and held hands. How did they do it?

Picking up his sandwich, he munched while staring blindly at the wall. Aviva was already a distraction, and they weren't even in a relationship. He paused. If that was true, maybe he just needed a little more time to get her out of his system. Not a full-blown relationship, but another date. Or two. Could he do it? Was Aviva worth it? There was something about her that he couldn't get out of his mind. Maybe seeing her again would allow him to refocus on his studies or figure out what to do next. He still had fifteen minutes before he had to go back to studying. He dialed Aviva's number and waited while it rang. At the sound of her voice, he started, but realized it was her voice mail.

"Hi, Aviva, it's Jacob. Just taking a break from studying. I'll try to catch you later."

Well, since he hadn't been able to talk to her, he might as well go back to the library. As he finished his sandwich, his roommate, Adam, approached. "How's the studying going?"

"It's a little slow."

Adam plunked down at the table across from him. "Is she hot?"

Jacob snorted. "Why do you always assume it's a girl?"

"Isn't it?"

Jacob pulled his collar away from his neck. "Well, yeah."

Adam laughed, and Jacob told him about his date.

"So, you just saw her last night, and you've already texted and called her?"

Hearing his friend describe his actions made him wince. "Yeah, I may have overdone it."

"You think? What about the three-day rule?"

Jacob snorted. "Rules are stupid, especially the arbitrary ones. I don't see why I can't let someone know right away if I had a good time. I don't like games."

"You may not like them, but they're there to keep you from sounding desperate. You have to project the right image. Has she responded?"

"She answered my text this morning, said she had fun beating me at bowling."

"I don't suppose you let her win?"

Jacob rubbed the back of his neck. "Uh, not exactly."

Adam shook his head. "So, not only are you talking to her too soon, but you lost to her in a game. You sure she's into you?"

"Yeah." Of course, she was. She'd texted she'd had fun. She was the one who said she liked beating him.

Adam shrugged, popped in his earbuds, and headed out the door. Jacob stared at the far wall and replayed last night's date in his head. Had he imagined how much she liked him? She'd seemed to enjoy herself. Except, at dinner, she'd looked...uncomfortable. When they talked about the type of law he wanted to practice, she'd suddenly grown quiet. He was attracted to her. He thought she felt the same way. Maybe he wouldn't have to worry about making time for her after all.

A clap on his back made him jump.

"Hey, Jake." It was his classmate, Lori.

"Hey. Join me?"

She sat and opened her sandwich. "Hold on." She answered a text. "Sorry, boyfriend. Ugh, he's driving me crazy."

"How do you do it?"

"Do what?" she asked.

"You're the top student in our year, you're editor of *Law Review* and you have a boyfriend. Plus, a part-time job. How do you make time for all of it?"

She laughed. "It doesn't always work, and right now, honestly, it's not. A lot of it is balancing things and focusing on priorities. Studying is my priority. My boyfriend is second. Sometimes that causes conflicts. But I work ahead and make the most of my time. I'm determined. Why?"

"I met this girl..."

"Ah, that explains your distraction the other day."

"Really? I could have been distracted about a million other things."

"You? You're never distracted. Look, a relationship takes practice, but don't miss out on someone because of books. Set a routine, keep to a schedule, put her on your calendar just as you would any other assignment." She looked at her watch. "Sorry, gotta run. Good luck!"

He stared at the space she'd vacated. Relationships were distracting. He knew that. Lori only managed hers by removing all spontaneity. He didn't want to "schedule" a date with Aviva like he scheduled study groups. But if he didn't, he couldn't guarantee he'd be able to see her, and she'd turn into a distraction, one he couldn't afford.

That night, Aviva stared at her phone, her finger hovering over the Send button. Jacob had called earlier, and she'd let it go to voice mail. She didn't want to encourage him. The problem was, every time she decided to tell him she wasn't interested, a memory of how much she enjoyed being with him stopped her. She hadn't stopped thinking of him all day. It would be rude not to respond. She hit Send.

sorry I missed ur call. Day got away from me.

That was polite but didn't encourage him. With a sigh, she pulled out nail polish and painted her nails. A minute later, the phone buzzed again. With a groan, she read his text.

NP. I was studying too. Movie?

Now what was she to do? Did she want to go to a movie with him? Of course. But should she? No way. Well, she couldn't answer right now—her nails were wet. She needed to break it off with him. Be honest. Explain that her dreams and his were polar opposites. As much as she enjoyed his company, there was no point in pursuing this.

She blew on her nails and waited for them to dry. She couldn't send him a breakup text. And if she called and he was in the library or something? She didn't want to do that either. But she didn't want to lead him on. Ugh. She flopped back on the bed. Going to the movie would enable her to see him. She could break up with him in person.

k

Aviva turned off her phone for the night. She stared out the window at the street below. Streetlights cast the pavement a yellowy orange, stretching long shadows on the cement. While cars and pedestrians continued to traverse the main streets on a pretty regular basis, her street, which was a few blocks from the main thoroughfare, wasn't as busy. Hoboken might be a mecca for young professionals, but this part of town slowed late at night.

She was doing the right thing. Despite Hannah's attempts to convince her Jacob wasn't like her dad, it was stupid to start something with a guy whose dreams were so different from hers. Leading him on was a mistake. They were going to the movies on Tuesday, and she'd break it off with him.

CHAPTER SIX

Between the time they made plans and the moment she left for the movie theater, Aviva half-dialed Jacob numerous times to beg off their date. Each time she started, her boss walked into her office. Or the phone rang. Or her roommates interfered. Or whatever stopped her from telling him over the weekend stopped her again.

The door to her room burst open. Maddy, her other roommate rushed in. "I have the perfect man for you, Avs," Maddy gushed.

"What?" She'd been reading. She cleared her head to focus on her roommate.

"Man. You. Perfect. His name is Phil. He's an artist. He's the brother of my friend's roommate. He just broke up with his girlfriend. I think you'd be perfect for each other. You know, since Erica's speed dating idea didn't work."

An artist? That was new.

"Come on, you said you're tired of professional guys. This guy is an artist. He's probably starving. What possible excuse could you come up with now?"

Aviva smiled. "I'm kind of already seeing someone, but..."

"What?"

The shriek made her ears ring. She winced.

Maddy sank onto the bed. "Tell me everything."

"His name is Jacob. I met him speed dating. But I don't think..."

"So, it worked?"

"Sort of." She wouldn't tell her they'd both ditched the event. "We went out to dinner, and we're going to the movies." She was just about to add it was the last time they'd see each other, when Maddy flew across the bed. She knocked the breath out of her as she grabbed her in a hug. "I'm so happy for you!" She paused before she left the room. "I'll just tell Phil you're no longer available."

"Wait!"

But Maddy had left. The door clicked shut. She'd get his number Tuesday, after she broke up with Jacob.

On Tuesday, Aviva approached the movie theater where Jacob stood outside waiting for her. Her steps slowed. She fiddled with her necklace. How should she greet him? Should she hug him? That might be lame. Kiss him? That would be misleading.

His face brightened when their gazes met. He took the decision out of her hands when he pulled her close to him. Tipping her chin, he placed a whisper-soft kiss on her lips. If she could have melted into the ground, she would have. His lips were firm, his grip on her arm secure. His fingers on her chin, gentle. Spicy aftershave floated around her. Her pulse increased as warmth infused her belly.

When he pulled away, she forced herself not to whimper. Women who were about to break up with a man didn't whimper after a kiss like that. Technically, women didn't break up with men who kissed like that.

"Hi, I hope you don't mind I just did that," he whispered.

She should mind, or at least brush it off, rather than lead him on. But her traitorous body still felt like liquid. "I wondered if you might...or if I should kiss you first." Apparently, her mouth had a mind of its own.

His grin lit up his face. He wrapped his arm around her. "How was your day?"

"Long and frustrating. Yours?"

"Went to class, turned in a paper, studied. The usual. Why was yours frustrating?"

She pulled away. Did he want to know or was he being polite? His gaze was focused on her. Not on her lips he'd kissed, or her breasts, but on her eyes. He stood there patiently waiting for her to respond, like he had all the time in the world, like he didn't care if they missed the movie.

She relaxed her shoulders. "My boss is trying to organize a major fundraiser for our client—that one I was telling you about at dinner. Let's just say she doesn't handle stress well and her stress is making me crazy."

She nodded toward the theater entrance. They headed that way, Jacob continuing to ask questions about her job.

"She adds additional deadlines to projects so we make sure to meet the client deadlines, which wouldn't be so bad except the closer we get to a deadline, the more of a perfectionist she gets. More deadlines, more annoyance, and more time at work, because, in her eyes, you don't leave until you're completely finished."

He steered her toward the movie doors. They found seats. "Wow, your boss sounds difficult."

"She is, but she's also an amazing mentor, so I have to put up with her temperament in order to learn from her. Days like these can drive me crazy. I'm sorry, I didn't mean to hog the conversation."

He grasped her hand as the lights dimmed. "Don't be," he whispered. "I love listening to you."

She shivered, but whether it was from his words or the touch of his hand, she didn't know. When the lights came back on after the movie, she blinked in the brightness.

Jacob turned toward her. "Did you like it?"

"Yeah, it was really funny. I'm glad you picked it."

"You can learn a lot about a person by what makes them laugh."

"Oh really?" She rose from her seat but made no move to exit the aisle. "Like what?"

"Like you laughed when the woman made snarky comebacks to the man, which means you've got a pretty intelligent wit. You didn't laugh nearly as often at the physical comedic elements, so slapstick probably isn't your thing. You leaned forward when the hero and heroine showed chemistry on the screen, so deep down, you're a romantic."

Aviva's face heated. "Wait a minute, the chemistry didn't make me laugh, so why did you notice?"

He brushed a lock of hair off her face. "I notice lots of things about you."

She ducked and turned to leave the theater. He followed, holding onto her hand. Once outside, he pulled her close to the building, away from the movie-goers who teemed around them.

"Are you in the mood for a bar or a dessert place?"

"I'd love a dessert place."

He led her three blocks to Dahlia's Delights. "Are you ready?"

She was about to break up with him. She didn't think she'd ever be ready.

He held the door. She walked in and stopped dead. The sweet shop was bubble-gum pink. Every-where. From the walls to the chairs to the lamps hang-ing from the ceiling. She gasped. He led her farther in, away from the doorway. "I don't believe you." Laughter bubbled in her chest. She bit her lip to keep it inside.

He grinned. "When you picked all those pink bowling items, my mind zoomed in on this place. I thought it would be perfect for our second date."

He'd already been planning their second date.

"What if I'd said I was in the mood for a bar?"

He shrugged. "Then it would be our third."

Her heart stuttered in her chest. She took another look around as he led them to a free table. In the center of the shop was a counter filled with confections. Along three walls were small tables with white linen tablecloths, pink napkins, spotlighted by pink glass hanging lanterns. The chairs were pink tufted leather, and the large window in the front was framed with white lace curtains. Even the floor was part of the color scheme, with large black and white marble squares studded with smaller pink diamonds.

"Not to sound sexist, but I'm surprised you'd want to be seen in here."

"You haven't tried their desserts."

A waitress stopped by carrying large white menus with pink writing. Aviva spent the next few minutes deciding among numerous sugar-laden concoctions. Once Jacob chose the lemon meringue pie and Aviva ordered the chocolate decadence cake, he cleared his throat.

"So, call me crazy, but I thought you were avoiding me."

Aviva had taken a sip of water. At his unexpected, and correct, insight, she choked. Jacob rushed to her side and patted her back. When she'd recovered, she wiped her eyes on her napkin, took another sip to soothe her throat, and placed her glass on the table. She wiped the condensation with her fingers and dried her fingers on her napkin.

"From your reaction, I think I might have been right." His brown eyes were serious, his jaw clenched. He leaned forward, arms folded on the table. His knuckles were white.

"You were."

"Did I do something wrong?"

"It's nothing you did."

"Well, if I didn't do anything, what is it?"

Aviva swallowed. "You're a law student. You're planning on working for a big law firm, which means lots of hours working, studying, and focusing on your career. I admire your ambition, but I don't see a lot of room for me in there."

His expression softened. He reached for her hand. His thumb made circles against her wrist. She shivered. "I actually wondered the same thing. In fact, between the time I texted and called you, I'd resolved not to see you again because I didn't think I had time for both you and my studies. Before I met you, my priorities were to do whatever I had to do to pay off my school loans so I can take care of my mother. She made a lot of sacrifices for me. I want to pay her back. I'm study-ing and making good grades so I can get the job to do that. But I like you. I'd like you to be one of my priorities, too."

Listening to his words, watching the care and concern showing on his face, made Aviva's insides warm. Was this where they got the term, "my heart melted"? Because if so, hers definitely did. As a child, she never remembered regret or sadness on her dad's face. She remembered an empty space where he was supposed to be. Remnants of arguments between her parents filtered through her brain—her mother asking him to stay home, her dad saying no. He'd never made them a priority. Yet here, across the table, was a man who had known her a little more than a week and already wanted to make her one.

"I'd like to be one of your priorities."

His face lit up. The crease between his eyebrows disappeared. "Good."

Could it really be this easy? She squeezed his hand.

The waitress showed up with their desserts.

Pulling away, Aviva made room on the table for the most heavenly looking chocolate dessert she'd ever seen. A three-tiered tower of chocolate, the bottom tier was dark chocolate piped with white chocolate flowerets, the middle tier was milk chocolate with a dark chocolate crumb topping, and the top layer was white chocolate with milk chocolate ganache. She spun the plate around and raised and lowered her fork several times.

"I'm not sure where to even begin! It's like a work of art. It might be a crime to eat it."

Jacob paused, one eyebrow raised, his fork in the air. "I have no such difficulties."

His lemon meringue pie was the tallest piece she'd ever seen. The meringue was peaked to rival the Taj Mahal and faintly browned to perfection. Its shiny cast glowed. The lemon filling was a perfect pale yellow, creamy, and soft.

His fork speared the first piece and approached his mouth, the mouth that had recently kissed her.

Her lips became wet.

Lips that had met hers softly, insistently, molded around the piece of pie on the fork.

She licked hers.

Eyes that had darkened from cognac to chocolate brown, as he leaned toward her, closed with bliss.

She trembled.

His throat worked as he swallowed, his adam's apple bobbing, the cords in his neck tightening.

She watched, transfixed.

"My friends and I come here to celebrate birthdays occasionally. My apartment isn't far away, but I haven't been here for a few months. Every time, I swear I'm going to order something else. Every time I'm unable to get past this pie."

She grabbed her fork, squeezed it, and focused on her dessert.

Jacob reached across the table for her hand. She willed herself to feel nothing, but her nervous system was a traitor because the second his fingers contacted hers, goose bumps ran up her arm, across her neck.

Her body flooded with warmth. Her mouth dried. She raised her water glass with a shaky hand.

When he removed his hand, the sudden emptiness overwhelmed her. To distract herself, she took a forkful of the dark chocolate layer cake, the molten chocolate inside oozing onto the plate. She dipped the cake into the chocolate and put it in her mouth. Chocolate flooded her senses. If it were possible to have an orgasm from eating chocolate, she would have pulled a *When Harry Met Sally* moment. Right in the middle of the restaurant. In front of everyone. Her stomach trembled with aftershocks. Her eyes widened. "Oh. My. God. How do you not come here daily?"

Jacob leaned back and laughed. He lowered his chair to the floor and returned his focus to his pie. "It's difficult, but there's a little thing called studying that keeps me busy."

"You should have blindfolded me on the way, because now I know where this place is, I'll always want to come back."

"Yeah, because that wouldn't have been creepy at all."

Laughter burst from her lips. "You said you aren't an axe murderer. Technically, you never said anything about not being creepy."

"True." He tipped his head toward her in acknowledgment.

When she'd scraped her plate clean enough that she'd have to lick it in order to get anything else off of it, she groaned. "I think I may have to join my roommate at the gym tomorrow morning after this. Which kills me, but it was worth it."

"Do you dislike your roommate, or the gym? Or both?"

Aviva rested against her chair. "I have two roommates, Erica and Maddy. I've known Erica since I was a kid. She's the gym nut. She works out every day before I even get up, and I get up at five-thirty. I like her, don't get me wrong, but we used to be a lot closer than we are now. Since our parents are friends, I need to be careful. Maddy is the flighty one. She wanders around from one thing to another, never really finishing anything. She's sweet and harmless and drives me crazy. Technically, they both do when they try to set me up. But the gym?" She shuddered. "No, I hate the gym."

"Why do you hate the gym?"

"I'm not sure. Everyone there seems to be able to lift more and run longer than I can. I feel like they judge me. I'd much rather take a long walk in the park, anyway."

"So...your roommates set you up?"

Was he uncertain? "Constantly. Which, I suppose I appreciate, but they set me up with the same guys, or the same types of guys, no matter how many times I try to tell them I'm not interested."

"Well, see, I've helped you out." His eyes twinkled.

She blushed. "You've done me a *mitzvah*. Thank you."

"Actually, you've done me one as well."

"I have?"

"Yeah, because my mother—her name is Karen—was just about to set me up with someone, God knows who. Then I met you. So, I could legitimately tell her to not bother."

"Nice!"

"She's great, you know, my mother, but pushy. She speaks her mind. I remember she told my English teacher he was an idiot because he had us watch *Romeo & Juliet* instead of reading it. When she wants something, she goes after it."

"That's not necessarily a bad thing. At least she's up front about it."

"True." Jacob rested his arms on the table. "What about your mom?"

Aviva smiled. "My mom is my biggest cheerleader. I think she alone is responsible for whatever self-confidence I have. I tell her everything. Well, almost everything. It used to get me in trouble with my friends back in high school—you're never very popular if you tell your mom what your friends are doing—but it's made us close. I wouldn't change it. She commiserates with me whenever I tell her about my roommates' set-ups."

"My dad was the same way. He died ten years ago."

"Oh, I'm sorry." Aviva placed her hand on his arm.

He covered hers and squeezed. "Thanks." He cleared his throat. "Are you ready to go?"

"I'm not sure I can move, but yeah."

The cool air was a welcome relief after the rich dessert. Aviva took several deep breaths.

"You okay?"

"Yeah, just appreciating the air after all the food."

"Why don't we walk a little?"

Jacob took her hand and walked with her toward Broad Street. Despite the number of people around, Aviva was in a bubble. Her heightened senses focused on the two of them. Cars breezed by, car doors opened and closed, passersby spoke a multitude of languages, but all Aviva heard was the brushing of fabric as her sleeve rubbed against Jacob's. Their fingers entwined. She shivered. He gripped her hand tighter, looked toward her and smiled. Was it the streetlamp that lit the sidewalk, or was it his smile? She didn't know, but she'd bet it was his smile. On the corner, a vendor selling candied nuts and pretzels hawked his wares, but the only scent Aviva smelled was Jacob's aftershave, a light, spicy fragrance she was learning to recognize as unique to him. She inhaled.

"Feel better now that we're walking?" he asked.

"Actually, I'm kind of amazed at myself. I didn't think I'd be able to move after I ate the entire piece of chocolate cake, but here I am, one foot in front of the other."

"You're definitely amazing."

His eyes burned. Their cognac-color deepened to mahogany as he stopped her under the streetlight. He was going to kiss her. Her pulse quickened. Her mouth went dry. When he moved her against the lamppost and brought a hand to her cheek, her skin warmed at his touch. He stepped closer to her. She slipped her hands beneath his jacket, feeling his solidity. Leaning down, his gaze became drowsy with desire. Her knees weakened. His hand slid behind her neck, drawing her forward, while the other stroked her waist. She whimpered, rising on tiptoe. She wanted his mouth on hers now. His lips parted in a ghost of a smile, right before they met hers.

The barriers of clothing and skin overwhelmed her. She couldn't get close enough. Her nerve endings tingled. His lips tasted like lemon. Suddenly, her life as a chocoholic seemed meaningless. What had she missed?

Him.

She slipped her arms out of his jacket, up and around his neck. He gripped her tighter. When she opened her mouth to sigh, he slid his tongue inside. Her tongue met his, and they danced, neither one giving up control, neither one stopping.

Moments or hours later, Jacob pulled back, his breath harsh and uneven, like hers. "Wow." He ran a hand through his hair as he braced himself against the lamppost.

Aviva expelled a shaky breath. She straightened her jacket. "Yeah. Wow." Had she been about to break up with him?

Pushing away from the lamppost, he checked out their surroundings. "I'm sorry. I shouldn't have done that here."

She grinned and took his hand. "I didn't complain."

With a nod, he walked with her toward the corner and called for a rideshare. Aviva bit her lip. Did he regret their kiss?

With his other hand, he drew her close. "Just to be clear, it's not you, it's the place. You deserve better than some street corner."

She expelled a breath, looked at him and smiled. "Thank you, but anywhere you are is good for me."

His nostrils flared, but the car arrived. He swore under his breath. "Timing. Come on, get in. I'll take you home."

During the ride to her apartment, they were silent, legs touching, hands gripped tight. Should she invite him upstairs? Did he expect it? Would he kiss her again if she didn't? She didn't think she could live without another kiss from him.

The car pulled up in front of her apartment. He told it to wait and followed her out. Her feet dragged as they approached the front door of her building.

"Well, this is me."

His lips curled with amusement. "You're much softer than all this glass and concrete. I have it on personal experience."

Her cheeks heated. She shook her head. "You're terrible."

"You didn't seem to think so a few minutes ago."

She opened her mouth to protest, but he drew her against his body. "Would you like a refresher?"

Desire pooled low in her belly. "Definitely."

With a quick look around, he brought her into the shadow provided by the large planter framing the doorway. Cushioning her head with his hand, he backed her up to the wall of the apartment building and claimed her mouth with his. No longer tentative, his lips slanted on hers. He opened his mouth. His tongue pressed against her lips, asking for entry. She complied. Everything amazing about their last kiss came back for a second round.

Her breasts pressed against his chest. He pulled away enough so his other hand could fit between them. He rubbed his thumb back and forth across their tips. She gasped as sensations flooded through her. She tilted her hips. He froze for a second, before he removed his hand from her breast and grabbed her butt. Pressed to him, she felt his hardness. It made her want him more.

Voices to her left brought her out of the moment. She peeked over Jacob's shoulder to see her roommate leave the building. She rested her forehead in the crook of Jacob's neck. They remained together while their hearts slowed, and their breathing returned to normal.

"Whoa," she whispered.

"Yeah." He stepped back, cradled her face in his hand. "Hell, I want to stay, but I want to do this right.

I think we need to slow this down a little. Timing, you know?"

She stared into his eyes and saw desire, the same desire she felt. His face was strained, as if pulling away required more effort than he possessed.

"Yeah. I don't want to tumble into bed with you by mistake. I want it to be because we're both ready."

"Me too." He kissed her forehead. "I can't wait to get there with you."

CHAPTER SEVEN

Jacob turned on his computer in his room the next day, his off-key whistling filling the silence. Last night's date with Aviva had been fantastic. He'd never experienced such a connection with someone this quickly. Her honesty? Even when it hurt, it was attractive, because she was honest about her fears and desires. He could deal with anything if he knew about it. Maybe he could even deal with his time constraints.

He clicked the email icon as his phone rang. "Hello?"

"Hello, dear, it's your mother."

He leaned back in his desk chair, watching the new emails appear on the screen. "Hi, Ma, what's up?"

"What's up? Is that how you talk to me?"

He rolled his eyes. "Sorry. How are you?"

"That's much better. I'm not some hooligan on the street, you know. I was calling to see how your chef is."

Chef? What chef?

"Jacob don't give me the silent treatment. I'm interested in the girls you meet."

Oh, holy hell, she meant Aviva. Jacob tried to remember what he'd told her, other than the lie about her career as a chef. He came up blank. Shit. Time to stall.

"Sorry, Ma, I didn't mean to give you the silent treatment. I was distracted."

"What's more important than talking to me?"

He glanced at the emails. One from the law firm where he interned last summer, where he planned to work after he passed the bar exam. Smith, Kane & Associates. He clicked on it.

"Uh, Smith Kane just sent me an email." He skimmed the body of the message for relevant details. "They've invited me to hear one of their partners speak on environmental law at a seminar Friday evening."

"Wonderful, dear. You're going, right—even though it's Shabbat? Of course, I wanted to invite you to dinner Friday night, but I can change it to Saturday in this case."

There went his weekend and any attempt he might make to see Aviva. His heartbeat sped up. Breathe. "Yes, I'm going to the seminar. I'm not sure about Saturday. I need to study."

"I know you do, but you have the rest of the week-end to study. You haven't stopped by in a while. I want to see you. I'm sure you can afford to take a little time off to visit me."

He knew better than to argue the point. At least she was off the Aviva topic. He rubbed his chest. "Of course, Ma. What time?"

"Come for dinner, around five-thirty. Bring your chef friend with you. I'd love to meet her."

His feet slipped off the chair pedestal and crashed to the floor. No way. Not happening. "Uh, I don't think it'll work this time, Ma, but thanks for the invitation. I'll tell her you invited her. I'm sure she'll be sorry to miss it."

"How do you know she's going to miss it if you haven't even asked her yet?"

"Because I saw her last night. She talked about this huge party she's catering as part of her coursework. It's fancy. According to her, some well-known actors and socialites will be there. It's supposedly a great way for her to get her name out there for when she completes her classes."

"Humph. Sounds like her career will take a lot of her time. Make sure she makes some for you. You'll have to bring her by another day. Now, I'll let you reply to the law firm. You don't want to keep them waiting."

Jacob rolled his eyes. "You're right, Ma. Thanks. I love you. I'll see you Saturday." He rubbed the bridge of his nose. Timing sucked. Last night, he'd had an en-tire conversation with Aviva, promising her she was one of his priorities. One phone call, one email, and his priorities got screwed. He had a ton of schoolwork he needed to complete as well. He had a job offer from a major law firm. He had to continue to court them in order to keep it. He had a mother who loved him. He owed her the respect she deserved, which meant he couldn't ignore her. All those things took time. Time was the one thing he was short of. How would he fit Aviva in when those other three things took up the extra he'd planned to devote to her?

He examined his schedule. After going out last night, and having the seminar on Friday night, he needed to study the rest of this week. There was no way he could take her to dinner on Saturday. No matter how badly his mother wanted to meet her, they weren't at the point in their relationship where they met each other's parents. Not to mention the lies he'd told his mother. Lies he'd have to straighten out before she could meet Aviva. He'd have to fix things on Saturday before the situation got out of hand.

So, when could he get together with her? His last serious girlfriend had been back in college. They'd broken up when she'd gone to grad school and he to law school. Sure, he'd dated since then, but no one he'd considered seriously. Until Aviva. Should he even bother to try, or should he just quit? No, wait. He took a deep breath. Hasty decisions were usually the wrong ones.

He typed the reply to the law firm as he contemplated what to do. If he cancelled their tentative weekend plans, would she think he was reneging on his promise to make her a priority? Or would she understand the demands on a busy law student? He didn't know.

As if on cue, his cell phone beeped. It was a text from her. He closed his eyes, offering a silent prayer.

I really enjoyed last night.

me too.

I may have to work this weekend.

He caught his breath.

too bad. how come?

fundraiser. maybe a study date?

Just like that, the muscles in his shoulders relaxed.

great. sunday?

perfect

He tossed his phone on the desk, looked at the ceiling in relief. He wouldn't need to make any excuses. Sitting straight, he entered everything into his calendar. Four days. He wouldn't see her for four more days. He frowned. Waiting this long wasn't what he wanted either. This was exactly why he'd said he didn't want to have a relationship.

But that was before he'd met Aviva.

Aviva couldn't concentrate. She was supposed to be researching information on ancient Greece, Hippocrates, and medicine for her client's medical research fundraising gala at the Liberty Science Center.

But all she could think about was Jacob. She wanted to see him, except with all the work she had to do, there was no time. Kind of ironic after they'd had a long discussion about him making time for her. Luckily, he'd just agreed to a study date on Sunday. Even so, she picked up her phone after almost every page of material just to see if he'd texted again.

He hadn't.

She scrolled through the information on her computer, pausing every few minutes to check her phone.

At that moment, her boss walked in. Tall and thin with blonde hair in a simple, yet sophisticated ponytail, and a navy pencil skirt and jacket, Meryl perched on Aviva's desk. "Problem?"

Aviva dropped her phone. "Yeah, uh, no…not with the research." She brushed hair behind an ear, smoothed sweaty hands on her black skirt. Turning to the computer, she clicked the article on ancient Greek symbolism. "Apparently, there were symbols associated with healing the sick and medicine, as well as the god Apollo. I'd like to do a little more research. It might provide a theme for the gala." She placed the cursor at the top of the article.

Meryl leaned over, adjusted her glasses, and placed a hand on Aviva's chair. "Mmm, interesting. Finish your research, write up your analysis for me, and have it on my desk tomorrow." She turned to leave but paused at the door. "Oh, and Aviva, try to not spend so much time on your phone, please. We have a lot to do to prepare for this gala. When you're in the office, I need your attention focused on work."

The next afternoon, Aviva came up for air. Meryl was reviewing her color and symbol choices for the gala, while Aviva worked the guest list. They needed the right mix of society, investors, industry bigwigs and press. She'd crosschecked her list of invitees nonstop, arrived at work early, and stayed late. She hadn't seen her roommates or Jacob, and she needed a break. From the sound of their last phone call, he did too.

They'd spoken last night before bed. Aviva needed to hear his voice and called, rather than texted. She'd thought she'd go straight to voice mail, but he'd picked up. He'd sounded stressed. He'd asked her about the fundraiser, and she'd told him about her research. By the time they hung up, he sounded a little better. He texted her this morning saying how nice it was to talk to her. Warmth spread through her body as she reread his text.

ur call made my day

She checked the time. About five-thirty. She picked up the phone and dialed Meryl.

"Hi, do you mind if I run out to get dinner? I'll be back to put in a few more hours before I go home."

"Sure. I can manage for an hour or two."

A grin crossed her face as she hung up. She didn't know what drug her boss was on today, but she hoped she stayed on it. Meryl hadn't been this reasonable in weeks. She texted Jacob.

where r u, and what's ur
fav milkshake?

A moment later, he responded.

library. strawberry

law school?

yeah y?

can I bring u dinner?

absolutely!!!!

She grabbed her purse and flew out the door. A restaurant, whose claim to fame was the best milkshakes, was right around the corner, but the line was out the door. Thirty minutes later, she rushed to the Journal Square PATH train station. The trains were late. By the time she exited the station it was raining. She rushed, wet and bedraggled, to the law library, more than an hour after she'd first texted Jacob.

He stood in the doorway with an umbrella. At the sight of him, she burst into tears.

Jacob hugged her. "What's wrong?"

"I wanted to do something nice for you because you sounded stressed yesterday, but the line was long. The PATH train was late. Now it's raining, and I used almost all of my dinner time getting here," she sobbed. "I wanted to see you."

He took the bag from her hands, brushed away her tears and led her to a bench. "It was sweet of you to do this. I'm sorry you went through all of that for me. Sounds like I'm not the only one who's stressed. Tell me about your day."

He listened as she told him about her work on the fundraiser.

"And my boss is being really understanding all of a sudden, which makes me suspicious."

"Why?"

"Because she's usually pretty stern. This time she told me to take an hour or two for dinner. She never tells me to take time off."

"Well, maybe she appreciates all you're doing."

"That would be nice. How about you? How was your day?"

He caught her up on his studies and told her about tomorrow's seminar with the law firm.

"That's where you're going to be working, right?"

"Yeah. I've interned with them for the past two summers."

"And you like them?"

"They've got a great environmental law practice."

He collected their garbage. "It was great of you to bring me dinner. And the milkshake hit the spot." He kissed her.

She would have liked to kiss him longer, but there were people around and she needed to return to work. When he pulled away, she glanced at her phone. "Oh my gosh, I'm going to be late."

He caressed her shoulder. "Relax, I'll call you a rideshare. You'll be back to work, dry, in twenty minutes." Jacob walked her out and waited for it to show up. "Thank you again. You have no idea how great you just made my day."

She kissed him again, pulling away reluctantly. "Well, we have to eat, right? I wanted to see you, even if I did show up looking like this."

He stepped away and looked her up and down. Her cheeks heated at his perusal. She resembled a drowned rat. "You're just about perfect to me."

Aviva was speechless. Was this guy for real? Although her hair was short and dried quickly, it probably looked like it did most mornings—like a porcupine— as a result of the rain and having run her fingers through it to try to give it some kind of order. Since she hadn't expected it to rain, she'd left without a jacket, never mind an umbrella. Her clothes were splotchy, soggy, and clingy. Okay, he probably didn't mind the clinginess, but still. She'd cried all over him. Her eyes were probably puffy and red. This was his idea of perfect?

She found her voice. "You have an odd idea of perfection, but I'll take it."

He chuckled. The sound rumbled in his chest as he squeezed her against him. He handed her into the car, and it pulled away. Perfection was hard to live up to, but living up to his ideal didn't scare her as much as she expected. When she could no longer see him, she leaned back in the seat. Regardless of the difficulties during the past two hours, the look on his face when she showed up, the happiness in his voice, made it all worth it.

She'd been wrong. The next time she talked to Hannah, she'd have to tell her. He wasn't like all the other guys she'd dated. He was better.

CHAPTER EIGHT

Jacob raced to Newark Penn Station. When the train stopped, he caught a rideshare to his mother's house in Livingston. After last night's seminar, he'd spent time with some of the environmental law group's lawyers, studied for a few hours and gone to bed late. An early morning wakeup left him groggy, but he had a lot of work to do. This dinner with his mother wasn't good for his study regimen. He'd learned a long time ago, though, his tiny mother was a force of nature. Sometimes, it was better to go with the flow.

Entering the elegant retirement community, he gave the security guard his name and waited while the man checked the visitor log. After being waved through, the driver drove to his mother's building. He said hello to Harold, the handyman, who gave him a quick rundown of the news. He buzzed upstairs to his mother and waited for the elevator. It was modern and sleek, but the doors squeaked as they closed. The noise never bothered him before, but now it set his teeth on edge. Or maybe it was the thought of spending the evening with his mother.

He shook his head as the elevator rose to the fourth floor. He wasn't being fair to her. His mother was great. She'd always supported him as a child, raised him well. Since his father died, she'd shown strength of character he admired more than anything. Sometimes, though, she was a lot to take.

As he walked down the silver-carpeted hallway, he tried to adjust his attitude. It wouldn't do for his mother to notice something in his voice or posture. The evening would be ruined before it began. He had enough time to roll his shoulders and take a deep breath before his mother opened her door.

"Hello, dear. It's good to see you!" She wrapped him in a bear hug, took his hand and led him into the condo. "Come in, come in. Relax."

He followed her down the beige-tiled hallway into the kitchen. From the delicious smells wafting from the oven, he identified roast chicken and garlic potatoes. "Mmm, smells great, Ma."

"Thanks. I'm sure it's nowhere near as good as your chef friend can make, though." She pulled out a tray of roasted asparagus. Jacob grabbed an oven mitt to help as he tried to force his stomach to unclench.

"I wouldn't say that, Ma. Here, let me do it."

She handed him a serving bowl and tongs. He removed the asparagus from the tray.

"So, tell me, how are your studies going?"

"Well. There's a lot this time of year. I'm never able to get ahead of it."

She nodded as she carried the bowl into the dining room.

"Why are we getting fancy, Ma? We can eat here."

"My son comes to dinner; we eat in the dining room."

He shrugged. "Okay. Want me to set the table?"

"Yes, please."

Since it was the two of them, he placed the settings on the end and the side of the table, rather than across from each other. His mother brought out the potatoes.

"So, you're not ahead of your studies, but you're not falling behind?"

"Don't worry, I know, Ma. Nothing will keep me from doing well."

"Your chef friend understands?"

He cringed at his mother's description of Aviva. He didn't want to perpetuate a lie, but he also didn't want to discuss too much about her. Again, he had to figure out a way to correct her without making her think he lied to her. Which he had.

"She's not my chef friend, Ma. Her name is Aviva."

"That's right, she's Jewish." A smile lit his mother's face. He caught a glimpse of what a beautiful woman she'd been when she was younger. Not that she wasn't attractive now, but her smile gave her an inner glow that radiated.

"Yes, she's Jewish."

"She'll have to come to Shabbat dinner soon."

"I think you're getting ahead of yourself, Ma. We just started dating. It's a bit early to meet the parents, don't you think?"

His mother handed him the carving knife and put her hands on her hips. "Excuse me, but you don't have time to waste dating random girls. If you like her enough to fit her into your busy schedule, it's serious enough for me to meet her."

He'd carved brisket and turkey and chicken long enough that he could do it in his sleep. Which was a good thing, because the only thing he could focus on was his mother's desire to meet his girlfriend.

Was Aviva his girlfriend? Well, they'd gone out enough for it to be true. He liked her enough for it to be more than true. They hadn't discussed it, but he wasn't sure if one needed to specifically discuss it before declaring it. He'd sound like an idiot, but he guessed he could ask her the next time he spoke to her. *Are you my girlfriend?* He shook his head in exasperation. *Yeah, that doesn't make me sound like an idiot.*

But his immediate concern was his mother. She wanted to meet Aviva. He needed to clear things up regarding the information he'd told her. The only thing he remembered talking about was that she was a chef. For the moment, he'd gotten her off calling her his "chef-friend"—reminding his mother of her name was useful for that—and would be an easy mistake to correct later. But what else had he told her?

"Okay, Ma, I'll make sure she comes to dinner. I don't know exactly when, though, since we both have busy schedules."

"Get it on the calendar so we know it will happen." She served him food. He picked up her plate as well. "Now, tell me about this speed dating business. Is that the only way for you to meet a girl?"

Apparently, this entire dinner would focus on his girlfriend. Wonderful. He stifled a sigh. "They're popular, now, Ma."

"But is it safe, Jacob? I just read an article in the newspaper about a young man who was robbed by a girl he met on the Internet. You can never be too careful."

Jacob took a deep breath, followed by a forkful of chicken. So much for speed dating. Now what? "I'm very careful. There are rules and security measures when you sign up. Adam did it with me." That was the truth.

"Oh, okay. How is Adam?"

Although he wondered why Adam's involvement suddenly made something legitimate, Jacob continued to eat and filled his mother in on Adam's life, providing far more information than she probably cared to hear. But it was better than a discussion about Aviva. That conversation, and fixing the mess he'd made in the beginning, would take longer than he originally realized and more time than he currently had. Because his mother, as great as she was, held grudges. If she knew he'd lied to her, even by mistake, she'd remind him of it whenever she felt wronged by him. He'd eventually have to straighten things out. Sooner rather than later. Until he figured out a plan of action, he hoped distraction would work.

When they finished dinner, Jacob rose to clear the table.

His mom followed him into the kitchen. "How was your seminar last night? Do they usually do such things on Shabbat?"

"It was interesting. Last night was the first time they told me about one on a Friday night. I'm not sure why they chose to do it then, but I'm glad I went." He told her about the people who gave the seminar, the attendees, the conference room where it was located, and the information it covered. "Afterward, they took us out for drinks at a nearby bar."

"That was nice of them to do. Do they have many Jews in the firm?"

He swallowed. "I'm sure they do, Ma. It was a good chance to get to know some of the junior partners better. I worked with one of them last summer, but the other three were new to me."

"Maybe if they had enough time to go out for drinks, you'll have some free time when you work for them."

Jacob exhaled, rolled his sleeves, and loaded the dishwasher. "I doubt it. They were all headed back to the office when I left at ten."

"Are you sure this is the best place for you to work? It can't be healthy to put in such long hours."

"It's the same with all big law firms, Ma. I want to work there." His chest lightened at the thought of a future with them. "They have a fantastic environmental law practice. After I put in a few years there, I can have my pick of anywhere. Trust me, it will be worth it in the end."

"What does Aviva say?"

He gripped the edge of the sink and shut his eyes a moment. "She knows I have limited time, but she also knows I'll make time for her. She understands. We discussed it."

"Oh, you 'discussed it.'"

"What do you mean?" He folded his arms across his chest.

His mother fiddled with the dishtowel. "I didn't know you were at a point in your relationship where you discussed those kinds of things."

He sighed, stepped toward her, and gave her a hug. "Ma, we discuss our time constraints all the time since both of us are busy. I told her I'd make sure to make time for her. Just like I make time for you. Don't worry, I promise you'll see me."

She looked at him. "I know I'm probably being silly. You have a life to live. I want you to enjoy it. I just don't want you to run yourself completely ragged, either." She stood on tiptoe and planted a kiss on his cheek. "Don't think I don't recognize your stalling tactics."

"What stalling tactics?"

"The ones you're using to distract me from your new girlfriend."

Jacob's neck warmed. He pulled at the collar of his shirt. "Ma—"

"Don't Ma me, Jacob. I recognize the signs. I'm your mother. I created those signs in you. Or maybe your father did. Regardless, I'll go along with it for now. I understand the relationship is new. But one of these days," she shook her finger at him, you'll have to satisfy my curiosity."

He hugged her again. "I can't get anything by you, can I?"

She fixed him with a stare. "No. You can't."

"So, this is the girlfriend."

Aviva looked up from her laptop. Jacob was scowling at the guy who'd walked into the apartment. He was tall and lanky, wearing gym shorts and earbuds, and holding coffee. He scanned her with frank interest. She met his green-eyed gaze with a smile.

"Hi, I'm Aviva."

"And she's obviously more polite than you," Jacob added. "Aviva, this is Adam, my roommate."

"Don't believe everything Jake tells you, unless it's good. In which case, assume he's downplaying my strengths."

Aviva laughed at Adam's smooth mannerisms. "How about I reserve judgment for now?" He appeared different from Jacob—more laid back and cavalier. He reminded her of a goofy puppy.

Adam turned to Jacob. "I like her."

"Great, my life's complete. Now leave." Jacob frowned, but rather than obey, Adam pulled out a chair and sat.

"Whatcha studying?" Adam looked with interest at Aviva's laptop screen.

"Adam," Jacob warned.

"Jake."

Jacob crossed his arms. Aviva was curious about his reaction to his roommate. They'd discussed roommates briefly when they'd first met, but Jacob seemed intent on getting rid of Adam today. Aviva didn't know why, but she was curious to find out.

"I'm taking a writing class. I have a paper due tomorrow."

He picked up her thesaurus and flipped through it. "Cool. You guys want to get lunch?"

"We ate already," Jacob said, through clenched teeth.

"Thanks for the offer, though," Aviva added. "We're kind of in a groove now. If we stop, it'll be hard to get going again. At least for me. But maybe another time."

"Okay. I'm gonna grab a bite and watch the Yankees game."

Aviva pulled her Yankees T-shirt away from her body.

Adam grinned. "Awesome, another pinstripes fan." He turned to Jacob. "Dude, you're outnumbered."

Jacob shrugged. "It's okay. I'll survive."

"Yeah, until the next subway series." Adam saluted. "See you later, Jake. Aviva, nice to meet you. We'll have to watch a game soon so I can find out all about you."

Aviva waved. As Adam left the apartment, she leaned forward. "What was that about?"

Jacob shook his head. "I have no idea."

"Actually, I meant you. Why didn't you want Adam to hang around?"

He raked his hands through his hair, tapped his pencil on the table before he answered. "I don't know. He's my best friend. I didn't want him to give you a hard time."

Aviva walked around the table. Pulling out the chair next to Jacob, she sat and took his hand in hers. "I'm really good at taking care of myself, you know. I can handle Adam."

He played with her hands. Aviva focused on the different texture of his skin against hers. His fingers were long and flexible. She wondered again what they'd feel like on her body.

"I'm sure you can. It's just..."

"Are you jealous?" She'd never been with a guy before who got jealous. She wasn't sure how she felt about it.

His head shot up. His neck and face flushed before he looked away. Aviva put her hand on his arm.

"I shouldn't be," he said.

"But you are."

He nodded wordlessly. "Damn. I swore I'd never be that guy."

"What guy?"

"The 'jealous' guy. You're not mine. I don't have the right to say who can talk to you or not." He frowned. "Why are you laughing?"

Aviva pressed her lips together before speaking. "I don't mean to. I just think it's sweet you're jealous, especially since you clearly don't want to be. For what it's worth, I'm not interested in anyone but you. Does this mean you want us to be exclusive?"

"Yes. I didn't realize I'd get to this point so soon, but I do."

"Good, so do I. But it doesn't prevent either of us from being friends with, or friendly to, guys and girls. We both have friends. We should be able to see them. It will be a lot easier to do if we're introduced to each other's friends and even sometimes do things together."

Jacob rubbed the back of his neck. "Yeah, you're right. I've never had that rush of jealousy before when Adam was around a girlfriend of mine. He probably won't let me forget it, either."

"He's your friend. Friends bust each other all the time. It's our right. But seriously, you have no reason to be jealous of Adam and me. I'm interested in you, not him. He calls you Jake?"

He shrugged. "His choice, not mine." He kissed her. It was short, but tingles ran from her spine to her toes. As he pulled away, he rubbed noses with her. "I'll have to figure out what my deal is. But I promise I won't be the guy whose girlfriend can't have guy friends. I won't be suspicious or crazy, okay?"

She took his lower lip between her teeth and pulled gently. "Okay."

He pulled at her waist. She climbed onto his lap. His arm wrapped around her and drew her close. As she leaned into him, his heart beat against her. Resting on his shoulder, she breathed sandalwood and spice. Peace settled over her. He liked her. He wanted to be with her. He wanted to give her space too, despite the fact he wasn't particularly good at it at this moment. But he was willing to work on it. She smiled against his neck.

"What?" he asked.

"I like you."

"I like you too. But you've got to sit over there," he pointed at the chair across the table, "so I can finish studying. Because I'll never get this done with you on top of me."

She wiggled against him. He groaned. With a laugh, she returned to her seat. "So, I'm a distraction, huh?"

He nodded.

"I'll remember that."

"Aviva, how is the guest list coming along?"

Aviva looked past her computer to Meryl, who stood in the doorway of her office on Monday morning. "It's all set. Do you want me to email it to you?"

Meryl's blood-red lips stretched into a smile as she nodded. Expensive perfume wafted around Aviva. Her boss approached her. "Wonderful. Have we gotten the invitation designs from the stationer yet?"

"No, do you want me to give Stephanie a call?"

"Please. Tell her we need to get the choices to our client by end of day tomorrow." She turned around, back ramrod straight in her Oscar De La Renta cobalt pencil dress. Before she exited the office, she spun around. "Oh, I wanted to thank you for your extra work the past few days. It hasn't gone unnoticed."

Aviva's cheeks warmed. "Thank you."

Meryl nodded. "Make sure you clear your calendar for the night of the gala. You should definitely plan on being there. And feel free to bring someone if you'd like."

Aviva tried to quiet her racing heart as Meryl walked away. This was the first time she'd received so much praise. She didn't know whether to be excited she was finally making her mark or scared about all the attention. Pride bubbled inside. She closed her eyes. An image of Jacob from yesterday flashed. It was the one of him looking sheepish when she caught his jealousy over Adam. She opened her eyes. Spinning around in her desk chair, she suppressed the shriek of glee that bubbled in her chest. Things were finally going her way. She would revel in the happiness for as long as it lasted. If her boss praised her, she wouldn't fear the "what ifs" that could happen later. If her boyfriend—she could call him her boyfriend now—tried not to feel jealous, she wouldn't feel stifled but rather would appreciate how much he cared about her. Things were looking up. Now all she had to do was turn in her final paper tonight. And ask him to the gala.

After spending the rest of the day tracking down the invitation samples and doing a last review of the guest list with Meryl, Aviva raced out of the office at five to get to her class. Hannah met her at the door to the classroom with a soda and a muffin.

"Here, I thought you might be hungry. You didn't leave your desk all day."

"Han, you're a lifesaver. My stomach is growling."

"I figured as much. We've got five minutes before class starts."

They found a bench outside the classroom.

"You look very happy," Hannah said.

"I am." Briefly, she filled Hannah in on yesterday's study date and today's work successes. As she finished the overview, their professor walked past them into the classroom.

"Do you have time after class?" Aviva asked.

"Even if I didn't, we can't leave it like this," Hannah said.

An hour and a half later, they handed in their papers and left the building. "Come to my apartment for a little while?" Aviva asked, as they stepped onto the sidewalk.

"Are your evil roommates at home?"

Aviva swung around, her bag banging against her leg. "I don't know why you don't like them. They're harmless."

She shrugged. "They just bug me with their superficiality. Anyway, spill. I want all the details from yesterday."

Aviva went into further detail about her conversation with Jacob.

"I can't believe I don't find his jealousy creepy," Hannah said. "That's not usually my thing, but somehow, it sounds sweet the way you described it."

"It really was," she said. They turned into her building and headed for the elevator. "It's like he stood outside of himself and judged his feelings as he described them. He didn't want to be jealous."

"Is this Adam jealous worthy?"

"I don't really know him well enough to say. Why, are you interested?"

"I don't know. Maybe. Is he single?"

"I really know nothing about him." They walked into her apartment and turned on the lights. "I guess no one's home. I'll talk to Jacob and find out. I think he was with him on the speed dating disaster, but I don't know if he met anyone he liked."

"Get some more information about him. You know, I'd like to meet Jacob one of these days, too."

They sank onto the sofa, and Aviva kicked off her shoes. "Ahhh." She wriggled her toes. "So good to get out of those things. Heels look great, but after an entire day, my feet kill me. I'd like you to meet him too. I want your opinion about him."

"Okay, let's set something up."

They pulled out their calendars and compared dates.

"I have to check with Jacob, because his time is crazy, but maybe we can get together this weekend sometime."

"I'm free, just let me know."

Hannah grabbed her bag. "I really should go. I've got a big day tomorrow. Client meeting all day."

"Yuck. Text me when you get to your apartment."

"Okay, 'Mom.'"

Aviva shut the door behind Hannah and thought about their upcoming plans. Would Jacob want to meet her friend? Would Hannah like her boyfriend? There was only one way to find out.

CHAPTER NINE

Jacob's phone rang as he stepped out of the shower the next morning. "Hey, sweetheart, I was just thinking of you."

A voice cleared on the other end. "Is this Jacob Black?"

Jacob froze at the sound of the male voice. He wrapped a towel around his waist. "Yes, who is this?"

"Jacob, I'm Stuart Rose from The Croft Firm."

His chest tightened. He cleared his throat. He'd called a lawyer "sweetheart." He walked into his bedroom and shut the door. "Uh, hi, sorry about that. What can I do for you?"

"Well, we wondered if you'd be interested in interviewing for a position in our firm for after you pass the bar exam."

Jacob groped for his desk chair. He sank into it. "That's very nice of you, but I already have a job offer."

The man on the other end chuckled. "Yes, I know. But we've heard good things about you from your professors. We're interested in meeting you."

"Is that even ethical? I mean, I've interned with my firm for two years. They're counting on my working for them. I'm not sure it would be right to meet with someone else. Not to mention, it would be a waste of your time, too."

"Well, Jacob, your work ethic is one of the things that makes me want to talk to you even more than just your grades or recommendations from professors. Look, you don't have to commit to anything except meeting me for a drink. Let me tell you about my firm. If, after we meet, you still aren't interested, fine. But I'd like the chance to at least meet you. If not for now, for the future. You never know what will come down the line."

They made plans for the next evening. Jacob remained where he sat for several minutes after he hung up the phone. Another law firm was trying to recruit him even though he had a job offer from one of the most prestigious firms in New York. They'd heard about him. How did that happen? He'd have to remember to ask Stuart tomorrow night.

Why was he going? It wasn't like he had any spare time these days. He was going to make plans with Aviva tomorrow night. Maybe he could still see her after drinks with Stuart. How long could it take to listen and say a polite no?

"So, this guy called you, out of the blue, and wants to interview you for a job you haven't applied for?" Aviva sat in the break room, taking a few last bites of her sandwich. She adjusted the phone against her ear. Her boyfriend was in demand, and it filled her with pride.

"Pretty much. Weird, huh?"

"Very. But flattering too. I mean, he must have heard some pretty good things about you to offer the interview."

"Yeah, I guess. But I need to find out more. I don't want it to be one of those 'too-good-to-be-true' things, you know. Plus, it will affect you."

"Why?" Curiosity made her fidgety, and she pushed away from the table and leaned against the heater to look out the small window. There wasn't much to see, but it offered a glimpse of sky and light.

"Because I'd intended to see if you wanted to come over tomorrow night. Now I have to cancel."

"Well, technically, you can't cancel something you didn't ask, so..." His deep chuckle made warmth flow in her belly. She gripped the phone closer. "Besides," she continued, "I was actually about to call you and suggest something."

"What?"

She took a deep breath. "I told my best friend, Hannah, about you. She'd like to meet you. Adam wanted to get to know me better, too. So, I wondered if maybe the four of us could do something..." She clasped her necklace. Adam made Jacob tense. Although they'd talked it out, she wasn't sure if he'd be amenable to the idea.

"I think it's a great idea," he said after a moment.

"You do?" Her skin tingled. She let out a breath she hadn't realized she held.

"Yeah, I do."

"I wasn't sure if you'd be okay with it."

"This week is tight, but do you want to try for Thursday? There's a garage band coming to a coffeehouse near you guys. They might be fun to listen to."

"Sure. I'll check with Hannah and let you know. If they're busy, maybe you and I can still get together?"

"I hoped you'd say that."

Aviva hugged herself, looking forward to seeing him and introducing him to her best friend. She and Jacob were both busy, yet they really were making each other a priority. She smiled with satisfaction.

"Good luck with the interview. Let me know what happens."

Jacob walked into the sushi bar. He paused to let his vision adjust to the light. Located in the Newport section of Jersey City, the restaurant offered spectacular views of the waterfront. It was easily accessed by the PATH train station, something Jacob appreciated. As he stood there feeling a little nauseated, a man in his forties—thinning hair slicked back and a suit minus a tie—approached.

"Jacob?"

Jacob nodded.

The man stuck out his hand. "Stuart. Join me."

He followed Stuart to a table by a window and sat in a red leather chair. A waiter appeared. Jacob looked at Stuart.

"Please, order whatever you'd like. I'm having a beer. I've ordered us a sushi sampling platter."

"I'll have a beer as well, thanks." He clenched his hands in his lap, trying not fidget.

"Let me get right to the point. The Croft Firm is a boutique law firm here in Jersey City, which specializes in environmental law. Every few years, we look to add one or two fresh-out-of-law-school lawyers to our firm. Usually, we pull from interns we've worked with, but occasionally, we go to other sources. Our firm has three partners and five junior lawyers. You'd be our sixth. We only take environmental clients. Our lawyers do everything and work with a client from the beginning through the end of the case, or, if we're on retainer, continue to work with them on non-court matters."

The waiter returned with Jacob's beer and the sushi.

"How did you hear about me?"

Stuart leaned back and smiled; his hands folded on his stomach. "Your professor is a friend of mine.

Periodically, he feeds me names of students he thinks are promising. Yours was just given to me."

He leaned forward. "I'm flattered, but I'm not sure I can help you. Like I said, I already have a job offer."

"I know, but I think if you check us out and give my offer some thought, you might find you could be happy with us. I know you've accepted an offer from a big New York firm, but at our law firm, you'll jump right in on important issues. You won't just do grunt work. What you've studied in law school will be able to be directly applied as soon as you start. You'll do research, but also much more."

Jacob looked out the window at the water below. What Stuart said piqued his interest. "I have to admit I'm intrigued."

"Good. I'd like you to come to our office and meet the rest of the staff. We're like a family. We like to make sure the chemistry is right. At that point, we can discuss particulars, like salary, benefits, etc."

Jacob's eyes widened. "I haven't said yes."

"I know, but you haven't said no either." He paused, a glint in his eye. "Give it some thought. Call me to set up the appointment." He slid his business card across the table.

Jacob rotated it through his fingers. "I'm still not sure how I feel about this. I like to honor my promises."

Stuart leaned forward. "Did you sign an employment contract with them yet?"

"No."

"Then you still have freedom to make your own decision. Do you have a girlfriend? Boyfriend?"

Jacob smiled. "Girlfriend."

"Okay, talk it over with her. Talk to your professor. Think about it for a while. Call me next week."

The two men shook hands. Jacob left the restaurant gripping the business card. It was a lot to think about.

CHAPTER TEN

Hannah and Aviva walked into the coffee-house. "Are you sure this is a good idea?" Hannah asked.

Aviva stopped scanning the crowd. She faced her best friend. "What do you mean? I thought you wanted to do this."

Hannah fidgeted. She curled a lock of auburn hair around her finger. "I did...I do...I don't know. I'm nervous."

Aviva gave her a hug. "Relax. You're meeting my boyfriend. Adam is just a bonus." She craned her neck and finally spotted Jacob and Adam in seats toward the back of the dim room. When they reached the table, the men rose. Jacob leaned over and gave Aviva a quick kiss on the lips. Her cheeks heated. She was grateful for the indirect lighting.

"Hey." Her voice was breathless.

"Hey," he replied. He angled toward Adam. "You remember Adam, right?"

With a smile, she nodded. "Hello, again."

"What, no kiss for me?"

Jacob stiffened.

She arched a brow. "You haven't earned it yet." Out of the corner of her eye, she watched Jacob relax.

"This is my friend Hannah," she continued. "Hannah, this is Jacob and Adam."

"Hi, Hannah, I'm glad to finally meet you." Jacob leaned forward to shake her hand. "Aviva talks about you all the time. Don't worry about Adam. He's obnoxious but harmless."

"I'm also able to speak for myself, Jake. Hi, Hannah, hope you didn't mind before. I'm all talk."

"I don't mind at all." She smiled. "I'm really here to check out Jacob, so you're good."

Adam winked. He pulled out her chair. "Come sit next to me. I'll give you all the dirt you need."

"What do you think you're doing, Adam?" Jacob settled Aviva next to him. He crossed his arms.

"Just doing my best-friend duties."

"Yeah, don't worry about us." Hannah grinned.

Aviva stroked Jacob's arm. He turned to her. His forehead was creased, his jaw clenched.

"What can I get you to drink?" He flagged down a waitress, who raised an eyebrow, pencil poised, at Aviva.

"I'll have a mocha latte," she said with a quick glance at her watch, "but make it decaf."

Everyone else ordered. Adam and Hannah returned to their conversation.

"Tell me about yesterday's interview," Aviva said.

As Jacob told her about the conversation, the coffeehouse filled with people—students, professors, and young professionals—all gathered to hear the band. The stage was located in the center of the coffeehouse, with tables scattered around it. Brown walls, beige and brown brick, brass wall sconces and leather chairs made the place feel warm and homey.

"So, what do you think about his offer? Are you going to go meet the rest of the firm?" Aviva asked.

Jacob leaned back in his chair. He fiddled with his coffee mug. "I have an appointment to talk with my professor tomorrow. I want to know why he recommended me and what he thinks of the firm."

"He recommended you because he thinks you're effing awesome," Adam interrupted.

Jacob smiled. "Well, besides that. I haven't decided yet."

"I think it's great they want you," Aviva said. "It's always good to have options."

"Hannah, you've been quiet," Jacob said. "What do you think?"

She turned to Jacob and played with her hair again. "Well, Aviva told me a little about it. I think it's worth checking out. It's better to pursue all your options than to have regrets later for not trying something."

"Oh, an adventurous woman," Adam said. "So, does that mean you're up for anything?"

She glanced sideways at him. "Depends on who asks and what they offer."

Jacob and Adam burst out laughing, while Aviva high-fived her friend. Hannah was an enigma. She could be shy and subdued one moment, flirty the next. It was one of the things Aviva liked about her. Not to mention, it was always a surprise to those who met her for the first time. Aviva loved to witness those moments.

"Adam, my friend, I think you've just met your match." Jacob shook his head. He reached for Aviva's hand.

The four of them chatted while the band warmed up. They listened to a few tunes. The musicians were talented. Everyone nodded and tapped along with the guitar players. When they took an intermission, the foursome turned to each other once again.

"So, Adam, where are you going to work after the bar exam?" Aviva asked.

"My father's law firm in Morristown. I offered this guy here a spot, but he's all 'I want a high-powered firm,' so I'll be on my own."

Aviva's stomach tightened. She focused on easing her tension. Adam was Adam. Jacob wasn't into the high-powered law firm lifestyle. He wanted it as a temporary means to an end. She refused to rise to the bait, even if Adam didn't realize he was baiting her.

"Come on, Adam, you guys don't have an environmental law practice. It doesn't make sense for me to work there."

She smiled at him as he straightened Adam out. She was learning to trust him. It felt good.

Once again, when he wasn't able to get a rise out of Jacob, Adam changed the subject. "So, Hannah, do you work with Aviva?"

"We're at the same PR firm, and we went to college together."

"Cool, what kind of PR do you do?"

"My current client makes technology products for chefs and culinary schools."

Jacob choked on his drink; his face contorted in a grimace.

"Are you okay?" Aviva asked.

He cleared his throat, pushing his coffee away. "Yeah, sorry, it just went down wrong."

"That's interesting," Adam said. "What kinds of products do they make?"

"A lot of the computer components in high-grade ovens. You know, so your cookies don't burn."

"I love cookies," Adam declared.

Aviva laughed, along with the rest of the table.

"Yeah, keeping him fed is a full-time job," Jacob added. "Now if only he'd learn to do dishes."

"But why would I do that when I know you'll take care of it?" Adam leaned toward Aviva. "Aviva, did you know your boyfriend is somewhat of a neat freak?"

"Yeah, he told me early on."

"It didn't scare you away?"

"Nope."

Jacob kissed her. Hannah said "Aww," while Adam shook his head.

"It's a little too sweet over here," Adam said.

"But I thought you liked sweets," Hannah said.

"Only as a food group," he said.

"Don't let my clients hear you say it. They'll give you an entire lecture on food groups."

"But will they give us samples?" Aviva asked.

"I'll ask them the next time they come in, Avs," Hannah said, sipping her coffee.

Beneath the table, Jacob's leg entwined with hers. She raised her head to meet his gaze. The warm brown of his eyes met hers. Inside, something clicked into place. He picked up her hand and held it, his thumb drawing lazy circles around her wrist, his fingers inter-laced with hers.

She rubbed his palm with her thumb. His glance smoldered.

"Ahem."

They turned toward Adam. "Sorry to disturb you two, but anyone hungry? For food, I mean."

Aviva wanted to hide under the table as her cheeks heated, but everyone else's laughter was infectious. Once she joined in, she couldn't stop.

She shook her head and took a deep breath. "I would love something to eat, Adam, thanks." Turning to Jacob, she raised an eyebrow. "What do you recom-mend?"

Adam snorted, Jacob's eyes bulged, and Hannah gave her a high five across the table. "Nice one, Avs."

She nodded. "Thank you."

The band returned from their intermission. During the second half, the guy on bass guitar played a solo. Adam whooped when it was over.

When the musicians finished, Adam spoke. "We never ordered food. Anyone hungry?"

Jacob and Aviva looked at each other and shook their heads. "Not really."

"I am," Hannah said.

While she and Adam made plans to eat, Jacob leaned forward. "Want to go for a walk?"

Aviva nodded. "Let me just make sure Hannah doesn't mind if I leave."

He grinned. "I think she's pretty well set."

Adam shifted his chair around, so he sat closer to Hannah. Their knees touched. He was focused on her, nodding to whatever she said.

"I still want to check."

Jacob held out his hand to Aviva and pulled her toward him. "For all of his obnoxiousness, Adam is a nice guy. His bravado is just a front."

She clasped her arms around Jacob's waist and rested against his shoulder. Hannah looked comfortable and happy. Adam looked besotted.

"I believe you, really. But I don't like to leave my friends in the lurch. Han?"

Hannah turned her head. "Yeah?"

"We're going for a walk. Need anything?"

"No, I'm good. I'll talk to you tomorrow. Jacob, it was nice meeting you."

"You too, Hannah. Adam, see you later."

"You bet. Aviva, take care of him."

She smiled. "You, too." She shifted her gaze between Adam and Hannah, and Adam nodded.

Aviva and Jacob wrapped their arms around each other and walked outside. Spring in Hoboken was mercurial, and Aviva shivered at the unexpected chill. She leaned into Jacob, who hugged her tightly.

"You're not too cold?"

"Not with you," she said.

They strolled down Washington Street, peeked in shop windows still lit for the evening, listened to the mélange of eclectic music as they passed bars, and smelled the variety of food odors emanating from a multitude of restaurants. They paused in front of a T-shirt shop and pointed out some of the funny sayings. When they got to a used bookstore, they turned to each other with identical looks of desire.

"Want to go in?"

"Sure."

Together, they meandered the aisles, pulling books they'd read or wanted to read, discussing likes and dislikes. Aviva ran her hands over the spines of the books in the literature section. The smell of vellum and leather pleased her. She inhaled deeply. Shakespeare, Brontë, Conrad. She passed her favorite authors and walked to where Jacob browsed.

"Faulkner?"

"Yeah," he replied. "He's my favorite author. You?"

"I don't really like him. I prefer Shakespeare and Joyce."

"Good choices. Someday I'll have more time to read them."

Even if you work at a big firm? She swallowed her question and they continued into the Biography section.

As they passed by the R's, Jacob grabbed her hand. He dragged her into an empty corner. Backing her against the shelf, he took her face between his hands and kissed her. His lips ravaged hers and she wrapped her arms around his neck, loving the feel of his skin. Warmth pooled in her belly. His lips were firm, yet gentle. His thumbs caressed her ears, while his fingers played with her hair. She couldn't get close enough to him. She whimpered in frustration.

He pulled away, rested his forehead against hers. "I've wanted to do this all evening."

"I'm not sure what Roosevelt would think if he saw us make out in front of him." She pointed to a shelf of books about the former president.

"I think he'd try to get in on the action."

Aviva was about to respond when a sound in the next aisle interrupted them. They froze. He opened his eyes wide, she smiled, and he drew her to him. She buried her head in his shoulder and stifled a laugh. Looking up briefly, she spotted an older woman passing their aisle. Aviva waited a few extra moments before she spoke. "I'm not sure I'm up to this sneaking around."

He stroked her collarbone. Goose bumps ran along the back of her neck. "So why sneak?" He tipped his head and kissed her again, long, and deep. Their tongues danced, a fire burning deep in her belly.

She didn't want to stop, but the fire burned hotter and brighter. She pushed him away and stepped to the side. "I can't do this here."

"Then let's go somewhere else," he said.

She leaned in, took his bottom lip between her teeth. She didn't want to hide out in the stacks, but she couldn't stand to be away from him. His hands cupped her bottom. She rose on tiptoe, rubbing her hips against him. He groaned and held her tighter. Electricity zinged up and down her body. His breath feathered her neck, making her shiver with longing.

"We have to stop," she pulled away.

He grabbed her hand and pulled her out of the bookstore. The cool air slammed into her, making her gasp. Her senses picked up everything, yet she felt woozy. The wind sent chills down her spine; her clothes irritated her skin; his hand heated hers. The hum of car engines grated on her ears. She shook her head to clear it.

"Let's go to my place," she said.

He stopped to look at her. His eyes burned with desire, his jaw tight. "Is that okay?"

She nodded. They walked along the crowded sidewalk hand-in-hand. Every jostle from a passing pedestrian caused her body to lean into him. Every contact made her feel like his body burned a hole in hers. When they finally arrived at her apartment, she unlocked the door with shaking hands. The place was dark, and she flicked on the lamp. The sudden onset of light blinded her. One hand in his, she held the other one in front of her as she led him toward her bedroom. Her bed jutted out from one wall. The sight of it, pillows fluffed and wrinkle free, jolted her out of her desire-fueled haze. "Um, wait."

He stopped, put his hands on her shoulders, and leaned down. He was about to kiss her. His lips tempted her, his eyes drew her in, his jaw with its five o'clock-shadow begged to be stroked. But her bed. Her bed made it all real. It made it immediate. It made it have consequences. Consequences she wasn't yet ready for.

"What?" His eyes were dazed; his chest rose and fell rapidly. The erection she'd felt earlier? It was still there. She'd waited too long to say something. She'd gotten carried away without fully processing the direction they were heading.

"I can't do this," she whispered as she pointed to the bed.

He stepped away from her and stuffed his hands in his pockets. Drawing deep gulps of air, he paced the room.

"I'm sorry," she said. "I know I should have said something earlier, but...I got carried away. I didn't think. I didn't mean to lead you on."

He frowned at her.

"I really like you," she continued. "I love kissing you. Maybe I can do more at some point, but I'm not there yet. I'm sorry."

Somehow, during her conversation, she'd ended up backed against the bed. She didn't mean to end up there. She never meant to taunt him with it. Now she had to get away from it. Except, he blocked the door. He looked at her like he was on a mission, and she was his target. Aviva edged further from the bed, her gaze switching between Jacob and the door.

"Avs?"

"Yes?"

"Stop."

She stood still, arms wrapped around her waist, trying not to tremble. She watched him walk closer and closer to her. He ran his hands up and down her upper arms. "Relax, Avs. We're not having sex. You don't have to apologize."

The weight in her chest lightened. A nervous urge to laugh bubbled in her chest. Instead, she exhaled.

"Can we sit?" He nodded toward the bed.

She sank down. He followed. This time he left plenty of space between them but kept a hand on her shoulder.

"I'm beyond attracted to you. But I'd never want to do anything to make you uncomfortable. You can invite me here without my expecting sex. We can even fool around on your bed and not have sex. But you get to set the pace, okay?"

She leaned into him in relief. "I'm not trying to lead you on," she whispered. "I'm just not ready to have sex with you. I want to know you better before I 'know' you. I want it to mean something."

"Me too. I want us to be on the same page when and if we finally decide to have sex. I don't want you to ever feel pressured into it. Why did you apologize?"

"Because you looked angry."

"I wasn't angry. I was surprised and caught up in the moment. Your 'no' made me switch gears. That's what you saw. Don't be frightened of me. I'll never hurt you."

He kissed her gently on the lips. His whiskers tickled her upper lip. She smiled against him. With a slight push, he followed her as she fell onto the bed. Legs dangling off the edge, one hand clasped in his between their bodies, she played with his hair as her lips tasted his. Her quilt lay beneath her cheek, smooth and soft. His hair was silky beneath her fingertips, his scalp warm. Need built inside her again but didn't overwhelm or frighten her.

He traced her jawbone, down her neck, across her collarbone and to her breasts. She inhaled as his fingers stroked the flesh above her bra, dipped beneath the fabric and flicked over her nipples. She arched into his hand. He laughed, his voice husky with desire.

"I love making you react to me," he whispered.

"Two can play this game." She rolled over, ran her hands down his chest. Slipping them beneath his shirt, she played with his chest muscles. She traced the line of hair until it disappeared beneath his pants. As her fingers dipped beneath his waistband, he inhaled. His stomach muscles rippled. With a laugh, she withdrew her fingers and ran her hands across the front of his pants. He hardened beneath her hands. He sucked in a breath when she dipped her hand between his legs.

"You're going to kill me," he ground out.

She climbed on top and dragged herself against him until she reached his lips. With a groan, he flipped them, so he was on top. He ravaged her mouth. Although fully dressed, they rocked against each other, matching each other's rhythm.

Her breath caught in her throat. She pulled away, panting. "Then we'll both die happy."

That night, Jacob stared at the ceiling in his bedroom. Muted traffic sounds from the street, dulled by the closed windows, provided a background white noise, which should have helped him fall asleep. Inky black sky and pale buildings showed in the muted moonlight. The sight was boring. It should have made him want to close his eyes.

But every time he closed them, Aviva appeared before him and chased sleep away. He wanted her. No, *want* wasn't strong enough. He hungered for her. He could still taste her on his lips, still feel her against his body, still smell her. His body hardened uncomfortably. Turning on his side, he stared at the wall.

More than a physical attraction, he cared for her. The more time he spent with her, the deeper his desire for her. He wanted her to be a part of his life. She'd been a huge help as a sounding board about the Croft Firm. He respected how she'd kept her opinions to herself when he discussed whether or not he should take the next steps with them. He suspected she'd prefer him to work at a small firm with better hours, but she'd limited her questions and comments to what was best for him.

What was best for him? He thought Smith Kane was, but there was something intriguing about Croft. He wasn't sure if it was ego—the idea of being pursued—or their firm itself, but a small part of him wanted to see where this led. Aviva understood. She hadn't thought he was being dishonest by checking them out, in spite of the offer from Smith Kane.

His mind drifted to the band. His hands tapped out the music on the bed. They'd been good, but being with Aviva, Adam, and Hannah had been better. He couldn't explain his earlier reaction to Adam, but tonight his jealousy had evaporated. The four of them had a great chemistry together. He'd laughed more than he had in months. Hannah was great, and Adam seemed to like her. When Aviva interacted with Adam, it clarified things for Jacob. She didn't treat Adam the same way she treated him. Her feelings for each of them were crystal clear. While she seemed to like

Adam, she was able to cut through his bull and brush off his teasing or give it right back.

He stifled a laugh at her double entendre. So unexpected, yet so perfect.

Perfect. She was perfect.

He sat in bed, eyes wide. He fisted the sheets in his hand. Perfect? When he was with her, he couldn't imagine being anywhere else. When she was gone, he missed her. She could make his body ache with a look. Her kisses? He couldn't imagine a sweeter way to die.

"I want to know you better before I 'know' you. I want it to mean something." Those words she'd spoken were more powerful than any others he'd heard. He could have been angry. He should have been frustrated. But he was honored. Honored she could bare herself to him that way, that she valued herself, and him, enough, to wait. To make it mean something.

Raking a hand through his hair, he fell against the pillow. He wanted to mean something to her. A lot of "something," if he was honest. He would continue to learn to manage his time and wait. Because anything worth having was worth waiting for.

CHAPTER ELEVEN

When Aviva walked into her apartment that evening, she called her mom.

"Hi, sweetheart. You're just in time to light the Shabbat candles with me."

Aviva smiled as she pulled out her own candlesticks, inserted the candles and found the matches. "Oh good. I'm glad I didn't miss it. Are you ready?"

"I am."

Together, they recited the blessing. "*Baruch atah Adonai, elohainu melech ha'olam, asher kideshanu b'mitzvotav vitzivanu l'hadlichnair shel Shabbat.* Blessed are you, Adonai our God, ruler of the Universe, who commanded us to kindle the lights of Shabbat."

"I love when we do this together," her mom said.

"Me too."

"So, how are you? You sound tired."

Aviva told her about the day at work and all the work for the event she had to do over the weekend.

"It sounds like fun."

"It is, but I'd hoped to see Jacob this weekend. I'm not sure I'll have time."

"Tell me about him. How are things going?"

"Much better than I expected." She sank onto the bed, kicking off her shoes before folding her legs under her.

"I heard Ben really liked him."

She laughed. "Yeah, Jacob totally won him over with the pirates. How are Ben and everyone, by the way?"

Her mom filled her in on the family. "Don't change the subject, I want to hear more about Jacob."

"Okay, hold on." She put the phone on the bed, tore off her work clothes and threw on her pajamas. "Hi, I'm back. I had to get comfortable." She snuggled under the covers.

"I think I love him!" her mother cried when Aviva finished her story. "Seriously, he sounds wonderful. Are you seeing him again?"

"Well, like I said, I'd wanted to see him this weekend, but now I'm not sure how much time I'll have. We talk all the time on the phone and text. I hope we can figure something out."

"I'm sure you will. Maybe sometime in the future we can meet him?"

Aviva paused. Was she ready to have him meet her parents? If she was considering sex with him, things were obviously serious. Introducing him to her parents would be the logical next step. But what would he think? Would it scare him away? She'd already told him she wasn't into meaningless sex. Was meeting her parents too serious too soon?

"It's still early, Mom, but I'll let you know."

The next day, Aviva stood by the Hoboken PATH station, searching for Jacob. Their plans to get together this weekend had been foiled at every turn. The only thing they could come up with was a free hour on Saturday afternoon to walk around Hoboken together. It wasn't perfect, but it was better than nothing.

A cacophony of voices in various timbres, accents and languages enveloped her. People brushed past her on their way somewhere or stopped short in front of her to take a picture or ask directions.

"Hey, there you are." Jacob's voice came from behind her. He grabbed her elbow.

She turned and gave him a hug. "Hi."

He kissed her, and she rose on tiptoe to meet him. Sounds and smells disappeared as she melted into him. A bump against them, a muttered curse, brought her to her senses. She pulled back.

"Not so fast." Jacob grabbed her hand. He pulled her away from the middle of the sidewalk. "I missed you." As they stood against the side of the building, his hands threaded through her hair.

His fingers against her scalp were luscious. She wished for a headache so he could massage the pain away. She slipped her hands around his back, ran them over the broad planes of muscle and reveled in the knowledge he was hers.

He leaned in close. She bit her lip in anticipation.

"So, are we going to make out here for the next hour or do you want to walk around?" he whispered.

Her mouth flew open. At the sight of his eyes filled with humor, she laughed and tipped her head against his shoulder. With a sigh, she pulled away. "Yes, let's walk."

They meandered around the waterfront with their hands in each other's back pockets. Around them, people took selfies, checked out the boats on the Hudson River, listened to music, and admired the skyline.

"Want to stop for a quick coffee?" Aviva pointed to the nearby Starbucks.

"Caffeine? You have to ask?" He pulled her across the street. They ran to the store, panting. Although the line was almost out the door of the small space, the baristas were efficient. In less than ten minutes, they'd ordered coffees and sat outside.

"So, I talked to my mother the other day," Aviva said. "She thinks you sound very nice. She hopes to meet you one day."

Jacob's face paled. Aviva rushed to reassure him, ignoring the pit in her stomach. "Relax. I told her we weren't there yet. I just thought you'd want to know, she likes you."

Jacob's body stilled. He looked at his coffee cup. She peeked at it—it was the typical Starbucks cup with a white lid, nothing interesting there. He stared off in the distance. Was the thought of meeting her parents awful? Had she somehow jumped the gun telling him?

"I didn't mean to freak you out. I'm sorry."

He wrapped his arm around her shoulders. Pulling her close, he kissed the top of her head. "No, it's not that. You just startled me. I guess I hadn't thought about the 'meet the parents' stage yet."

"I'm not saying we're there, but I hope we're heading in that direction."

"It's fine. Come on. I've got to study." He kissed her again. They headed their separate ways, but Aviva couldn't get his look of discomfort out of her mind, or his non-answer.

It was definitely not fine. Not by a long shot. Jacob paced in his bedroom. He had a ton of studying to do for finals, but all he could think about was Aviva and her mother. Her mother, who wanted to meet him.

He groaned at his reflection in the mirror. He liked mothers. Mothers generally liked him too. They found him polite, intelligent, and focused. He treated their daughters well. He groaned again.

This wasn't a good idea. It was a very bad idea. One of his worst, in fact since meeting Aviva. Because if he met Aviva's parents, Aviva would have to meet his mother. His mother, who thought she was a chef, and who knows what else, because he couldn't remember all the lies he'd told her.

A knock on his door interrupted his thoughts. He opened it.

"You okay? I heard groaning. Thought you might be sick."

Jacob shook his head. He followed Adam into the living room. "No, I'm not sick, but I've got a problem."

Adam sat on the sofa, waiting. Jacob paced the room.

"Aviva wants me to meet her parents."

"Well, it's a little soon, but okay."

"No, not right now. She knows it's too soon."

"Ooookay. What's the problem?"

"Meeting them."

"Jake, I don't follow."

Jacob sighed. He sank into an easy chair. "I know. Sorry. If she's ready for me to meet her parents, it means I have to introduce her to my mom."

"Your mom's not bad, Jake. Aviva can handle her."

"I know she can handle her. The problem is the 'her' my mom will meet."

"What?"

"I kind of made up a story about Aviva."

"What kind of story?"

"I told her she was a chef and a bunch of other details I honestly don't remember now because I never thought I'd have to remember them."

Adam let out a low whistle. "Why would you do that?"

"Because it was right after I'd met her. My mom threatened to set me up with someone. I had to cut her off, so I told her about Aviva. But since I didn't know anything about her. I made most of it up."

"So just fix things with your mom. You have nothing to worry about."

"Yeah, because she'll love hearing I lied to her."

"You'd rather tell Aviva you lied about her?"

"No."

"Well, I think you need to man up and straighten things out with your mom."

"I know, I'm just trying to find the right time and the right way to tell her."

Adam headed toward his room. He paused in the doorway. "Aviva is awesome. Don't wait too long to fix things."

CHAPTER TWELVE

"Jacob, you've been holed up studying too long," his mother said through the phone. "I'm on my way to pick you up. We're going on an adventure. I'll be there in twenty minutes."

Jacob stared at the phone. He shook his head. "Ma, I'm studying. I've got finals next week."

"I know you do, but you need to clear your head occasionally. It's not good to shut yourself in like this. Get yourself presentable, we're going for a walk."

She hung up the phone before he had a chance to argue further.

With a sigh, Jacob closed his book and "made himself presentable." His mother hated *schleppy*. He changed into shorts and a shirt. As he put on his shoes, he realized this would be the perfect time to tell her about Aviva. Because he had to study, they couldn't spend hours together, so a short get-together would be perfect. Adam was right. He had to tell his mother the truth.

He jogged downstairs just as her car pulled in front of the building. He rushed outside and opened her door. "Hi, Ma. How are you?"

"I'm good, sweetheart. It's a beautiful day. Let's go for a walk. You could use the fresh air. Get in."

"Get in?"

"You don't think I'm walking through Newark like this?" His mother wore a black velour tracksuit with matching sneakers, full makeup, and jewelry. He shook his head before climbing in. There were three things he could always count on when it came to his mother—she never went anywhere without her "face on," his happiness was her personal mission, and she hated when people lied to her. The first one was cute, the second was sweet, and the third was making him sweat. No matter how many times he rehearsed his explanation in his head, it never came out right. He gripped the door handle. He should tell her now, get it over with and be done. Only having this discussion while trapped in a car that she was driving was even less ideal than having it last time he was at her apartment for dinner. He didn't want to risk her getting into an accident. While they were walking was a much safer time—for both of them.

"Are we ready to go?" Aviva asked her sister, Sophie.

"Ben, are you ready?" Sophie addressed her son. She nodded to Aviva.

"Are there pirates on the High Line, Aunt Aviva?"

Aviva locked the door. "I don't think so, Ben, although it kind of sounds like there should be, don't you think?"

Ben chattered about pirates on their walk to the PATH train, jog down the flight of stairs and their ride to 34th Street.

"It's too bad Marc couldn't come with us," Aviva said, finding a brief moment to speak when Ben paused for air. They stood together on the train as it whizzed away.

"Yeah, he's crazy with work. I'm just glad you still had time to get together."

"I swear, if I look at one more menu option or linen color, I will scream," Aviva said.

Sophie smiled. "Just wait until you get married. The party sounds like fun, though."

Aviva agreed, ignoring the wedding talk. "Yeah, it really does. I'm glad Meryl wants me to go. Guess I should probably go shop for a dress."

"I've got some you can borrow, if you want."

"Thanks. I'll let you know. Here's our stop."

The three of them exited the train and followed the others onto the High Line. Ben ran ahead. Aviva and Sophie followed at a slower pace. Intrigued by their position above ground, Ben pointed out the people and cars below, while Aviva admired the trees and flowers blooming in the park-like setting. Always being surrounded by concrete made nature more precious.

"So, tell me about Pirate Man," Sophie said.

"Pirate Man?"

"The guy you and Ben ran into at the museum."

Laughter burbled in Aviva's stomach. She shook her head. He'd made a huge impression on her nephew during the few minutes they'd met. She started to tell her sister about him. "I really like—" A sound caught her attention. She waited but didn't hear it again. "—him, Soph," she continued. She thought she'd heard Jacob's voice a moment ago but didn't see him.

Must be wishful thinking.

"He sounds wonderful."

Aviva paused. She squinted at the man ahead. The man, sitting on the bench with an older woman, looked like Jacob. She blinked.

"He's here."

"What? Where?"

"Right there." She pointed to the bench. "I'm going over to say hi. I'll be right back." After their conversation about meeting her family, she didn't want to drag half of them with her to say hello.

Her face split into a wide grin. She hadn't expected to see him for a few days. She missed him. Turned away from her, he couldn't see her approach. She decided to surprise him. Tiptoeing closer, she slid her arms around him from behind, leaned in cheek-to-cheek and gave him a hug. "Hey, there."

He jumped. Aviva peeked around to make eye contact, stomach fluttering.

"Uh...hi. What are you doing here?" His face flushed, and his movements were jerky.

That wasn't the kind of greeting she'd anticipated. "My sister and I are walking the High Line with my nephew. You remember Ben. You met him at the pirate exhibit."

A brief smile stretched his cheeks before it disappeared. "Yeah, I do." He stretched, as if to look for him but stopped short. He turned to her. "I didn't expect you to be out today."

"Me neither. But if I look at one more catering option for the gala, my head will explode."

"You're planning a gala?"

Aviva looked at the older woman who sat next to Jacob.

"Yes, for my pharmaceutical client. Hi, I'm Aviva, Jacob's girlfriend."

"So, I gathered. I'm Karen, Jacob's mother. It's nice to meet you. Jacob tells me you're a chef." The woman held out her hand to Aviva.

"Ma!" He placed a hand on Karen's shoulder as if to pull her away.

Aviva shook Karen's hand. A chef? She looked in bewilderment between Jacob and his mother. "Um, no, I'm not a chef. I work in PR."

"But you're going to cooking school," Karen held onto Aviva's hand.

"Ma!" Jacob's eyes were wide, his ears bright red.

"No...I'm taking a writing class at night." What was she talking about? She frowned at Jacob. He hadn't mentioned his mother's mental faculties being impaired.

Karen dropped Aviva's hand. She turned toward Jacob, who shifted and ran a hand across his face. A small woman, Karen held herself rigidly straight. She looked formidable. This was not how Aviva had planned to meet Jacob's mother.

"What about Rowan Atkinson?" Karen asked, facing Aviva once again, shooing Jacob away as he started to interrupt. "Do you like his humor?"

What in the world was this woman talking about? "I'm sorry, I'm not familiar with it. I tend to prefer snarky comebacks and sarcasm if that helps." Jacob was no longer looking at either of them. He sat there, eyes closed, lips pressed together. She felt as if she were in the middle of a play. The wrong play. She was the lead but didn't know her lines. And she'd shown up naked.

"From your size, I'm guessing you don't coach a girl's basketball team at your local Boys & Girls Club, either," Karen said, looking her up and down.

Aviva stood tall. She pushed her shoulders back. Was this some fantasy that Karen expected her to live up to? And why wasn't Jacob intervening? "No, I don't. I'm confused. There seems to be a misunderstanding here."

"You're right, there does. Apparently, the woman Jacob told me he's dating has your name but none of your character traits."

Aviva didn't know what to say. Jacob was no help at all.

Finally, he met her gaze, a pleading look in his eyes. But the more she looked at him, the angrier she got. She gritted her teeth and narrowed her focus. His posture was stiff, his jaw clenched. His eyes were wary. He looked as if he'd like to be anywhere but here, with anyone but her. Which was fine because she didn't want to be here either.

"I think you two have a lot to talk about." Her voice sounded strangled to her ears. "I need to catch up with my sister. It was nice to meet you, Karen, although I apologize for the strange circumstances." She looked around for Sophie, trying to figure out a way to escape.

They were ahead at one of the concession stands. They wouldn't see her signs of distress. She took a step away.

"Somehow, I don't think you're the one who needs to do the apologizing, Aviva," Karen said. "But before you go, do you mind if I ask what you told your sister about Jacob?"

Aviva shrugged. She shook her head at Jacob. "Everything, really. How we met, what he does, how much I like him…" Her voice caught. She cleared her throat. "She already knows he likes pirates, since my nephew hasn't stopped talking about him since we ran into each other at the pirate exhibit." She'd told her sister everything about him. Why hadn't he done the same with his mother?

Karen's eyes softened a moment before she flared her nostrils and folded her arms across her chest. "How interesting. Did you hear her, Jacob? She told her everything. If I had to guess, I'd bet she told the truth."

Aviva nodded. "I don't lie." She never would have thought Jacob did, but apparently, she was wrong.

Karen placed a hand on her shoulder and softened her voice. "I'm sorry you had to witness this, Aviva. I don't blame you for this. I'd love to have a chance to get to know you better, dear. The real you."

Jacob turned red. "Aviva, I'm sorry."

His voice wrapped around her, but instead of filling her with warmth as it usually did, it made her icy cold. Her head pounded, and her throat felt thick. She didn't want to talk to Jacob right now. She couldn't. "Goodbye, Karen."

Trying not to run, she caught up with Sophie and Ben.

"That was fast. I figured we'd lose you for the rest of the time," Sophie said as they continued to walk.

"No, I'm back."

"Everything okay?"

"No."

"You lied to me, Jacob. How could you make a fool of me like that?" She glared at him as he rose.

"I'm sorry, Ma. It wasn't intentional." He paced in front of the bench. Aviva was going to kill him.

"Really? You told me information that wasn't true. You answered questions with more information that wasn't true. Seems to me that's pretty intentional." Her eyes flashed.

Jacob ducked his head. "It just slipped out." How the hell was he supposed to fix this?

"Don't compound your problems here. Your words 'slipped out' of your mouth no more than Janet Jackson's nipple 'slipped out' of her costume. It took effort."

Even now, Jacob's face heated at his mother's imagery. "Ma, I can't believe you're talking to me about a nip slip."

"See, that's the difference, Jacob. I talk to you about everything."

He'd fallen right into her trap. "I'm sorry." Would Aviva accept his apology?

"Sorry you got caught, or sorry that you did it?"

He was smart enough to know which way to answer. "Sorry I did it."

"Hmmph. What I want to know is why you thought you needed to lie to me in the first place. I thought we had a better relationship."

"We do, Ma, but you pressured me. I didn't want to deal with it."

"So, you should have said something to me about it. Not invented a pretend girlfriend. If you're going to do that, you might as well just buy one of those inflatable dolls."

Jacob spun toward her. "I have said something to you, Ma. Multiple times. Yet you still try to set me up on dates."

She touched his arm. "Because I love you. I want you to be happy. I don't want you to only have a professional life. You need a personal life, too."

"Yeah, Ma, personal. As in, it's personal to me."

"Which is why I don't question you too much about it when you're in a relationship."

"I'd rather you left the relationship—even the getting to the relationship part—to me."

"Well, it's a moot point now, since you apparently have one with this woman."

"Aviva, Ma. Her name is Aviva."

"At least you were honest about that. Will you tell me the real facts about her, or will I have to ask her?"

Some people's nightmares involved showing up naked somewhere important. Others involved spiders or clowns. His involved his mother questioning his girlfriend. Except, he wasn't asleep.

He raked a hand through his hair and sat on the bench. "She's in public relations. She has an older sister with a seven-year-old nephew who lives somewhere in New Jersey. I'm not sure where her parents live."

"I can believe this?"

"Yes, Ma, you can believe this."

"She seemed pleasant."

"She's very pleasant." When she wasn't angry with him.

"I hope she's more than pleasant if you expect to continue this relationship. How does she feel about your working?"

"She's not a fan of the long hours required by the law firm, but she knows it's important to me. I've told her, hopefully shown her, she's a priority, so it's been a little better recently." Of course, now that she knew he lied to his mother, his long hours were the least of his problems.

"But she knows you have to study."

He rubbed the back of his neck. "Yes. Her job demands a lot of time as well, so she's almost as busy as I am. She was very supportive of my checking out Croft."

"Good. I want you to invite her to Shabbat dinner, Jacob."

"I know."

"She's mad at you."

"I know that too." He didn't need his mother to tell him that.

"You plan on fixing things?"

"Yes." *If she lets me.*

"When?"

"Soon." The thought of talking to her made his throat go dry.

"Not 'soon,' Jacob. Today. If you care about her, you need to fix this before it festers and turns into something bigger. Trust me on this one. Fix this today."

"Okay, I'll call her." As soon as he gave her time to calm down. From the look on her face, it might take a few hours.

"You will not call her! You need to fix this in person. She needs to see your face when you apologize. Your father and I were married for forty years. We never let things stew. We always apologized in person, no matter what we had to do."

"Fine, Ma, I'll talk to her in person." As much as he hated to admit it, his mother was right. Dammit.

"You should go now."

CHAPTER THIRTEEN

Sitting on the floor of her living room later that night, photos of the venue, menus, and linen choices displayed around her, Aviva stared into the distance. Her head pounded and her chest was tight. She couldn't get Jacob out of her mind, and every time she thought about him, her thoughts jumbled around like scenes in a kaleidoscope. The only thought that remained constant was this one—he'd lied.

This was the second time she'd met someone in his life. The second time his response was odd. The first time, when she met Adam, he explained away his feelings with jealousy. She believed him. This time, he'd lied to his mother about her. Who did that and could she ever believe him again? Her stomach twisted and she rubbed it, trying to ease the pain.

He'd lied to his mother. His mother. He'd left Aviva to be cross-examined. The only times he'd tried to talk, he tried to interrupt his mother, as if he didn't want her to find out anything else about her. How many lies had he told? He hadn't tried to clarify anything. Or apologize. He'd remained silent unless pressed. He hadn't introduced her. He sat there stiff and unyielding. She fiddled with her necklace. What made him lie about her to his mother? She paced the room before sitting down again.

What was wrong with her that he didn't want to introduce her to the important people in his life? The color swatches on the floor jumbled together as her eyes glazed over. What the heck was she getting herself into?

If today was any indication, maybe he didn't have a good relationship with his mother. Maybe he was afraid for the two of them to meet. She inhaled and tried once again to see things from his perspective. Okay, a part of her could understand his nerves. She had them too. But she had such a good relationship with her mother; she wanted to date a man who could understand that kind of relationship. Still, a poor one didn't explain his lying to her. She clenched her fists at her sides.

What was wrong with him? What kind of a man lied to his mother about something as important as the woman he was dating?

She couldn't have a relationship with a liar.

Aviva remembered his reaction to her conversation about her mother wanting to meet him. He hadn't wanted the meeting to happen. Did he have a problem with all mothers, or had he been afraid his mother would find out the truth?

She groaned. Maybe he didn't like her as much as she'd thought. She knew she turned him on; every time they touched, he couldn't get enough of her. But she wanted way more than sex from a guy. If that was all she wanted, she would have done it with him already. She wanted Jacob to like her for things other than her body.

She needed to confront him, drag everything out into the open. The thought of it made every bone in her body ache. Her emotions ricocheted from anger to embarrassment to confusion to hurt. This was the man she was dating?

Her head pounded. She rested it against the sofa as her thoughts spun in circles. Nothing made sense. Every time she tried to concentrate on work, memories from today intervened and prevented her from getting anything done. Aviva closed her eyes, but images of Jacob's face taunted her.

A knock at the door jolted her. She rose, biting her lip. Why the heck couldn't her roommates remember their stupid keys? Looking through the peephole, she gasped.

Jacob.

She slid the chain out of the lock and cracked the door. "How'd you get inside?"

"I followed someone in."

So much for building security.

"Will you let me in?"

"No." She wasn't ready to talk to him.

"Please, Aviva. I owe you an explanation for earlier."

"Yeah, you do." He owed her a hell of a lot more than an explanation.

"So, can I come in?"

She should tell him to leave. End the relationship right now. Forget about him. Except...she needed answers, and he was the only one who could explain. Once she had an explanation, she could tell him to leave. She let out a huff and backed away from the door. He came inside. She led him into the living room. Her stuff was everywhere. With another sigh, she bent to pick up her piles.

He kneeled next to her. "Here, let me help."

"Don't touch anything." Her voice was sharp. Good.

He jerked away, walking to the window. He clenched and unclenched his fists.

When she finished cleaning up, she stared at his back. His navy shirt stretched across his broad shoulders. At one time, she'd wanted to lean into him, wrap her arms around him. Now, she wished he would walk out her door. Forever.

She kept her mouth shut. If she opened it, she was afraid of what would pour out. He needed to explain. He needed to talk first. He owed her.

Whether he heard the silence or saw a lack of movement reflected in the window, he turned, his hands thrust in his pockets. "I don't exactly know what to say."

"How about the truth?"

He pushed away from the window. "I've never lied to you."

"Lying about me isn't any better."

He swallowed. "I know. And I'm sorry."

"Sorry for what?" She wrapped her arms around her waist.

"Sorry for what I did today. For lying to my mother about you."

"I don't understand why you did it. Are you that embarrassed by me? Do you wish I was the girl you invented?"

He rushed toward her, stopping feet away. "No, Aviva. I made a mess of things." He took a deep breath. "Okay, let me start from the beginning. I lied to my mom because she caught me off guard. She wanted to set me up with someone. I'd just met you. You popped into my head as a perfect way to foil her plan. But she asked me questions about you I didn't know so I made things up."

"But why did you say those things specifically? Are those what you want in a girlfriend? Am I somehow not good enough for you?"

"No, yes. Wait." He held up a hand. "They're not what I want in a girlfriend, and you are more than good enough for me." He sat gingerly on the sofa, as if he thought she'd push him off.

Tempting, but she restrained herself.

"They're what I thought would keep her off my back. I didn't expect to see you again, so it didn't seem like a problem."

"But you are seeing me. Why didn't you fix things?"

"I wanted to straighten things out, but the time never seemed right. Lying to my mom was a big deal. I needed to have the time to talk to her about it."

Aviva rubbed her arms, chilled. "And did you?"

"Yes, after you left, I explained everything to her."

Yet he never explained things to her. Aviva rose and walked around the room.

"Tell me what you're thinking, Avs."

Her stomach clenched at the name coming from his lips. "You're obviously close to your mother. Yet you still lied to her. How do I know you won't lie to me?"

Jacob followed her. "Aviva, my relationship with my mother is a complicated one, but I swear to you, I'm not a liar. I made a mistake. I compounded it by taking the easy way out. I'd never lie to you."

She spun around, put more distance between them. "You don't talk to me either."

"Sure, I do."

"Jacob, telling me about your day is not the same as telling me what's in your heart. You listen to me when I'm upset or stressed, but when I ask about your day, you tell me what you did. You talk about the job descriptions at Smith Kane and Croft, but you don't tell me why you make the choices you do. You don't tell me how you feel about me, other than show me how attracted to me you are. It's flattering, but shallow. If I knew how you felt, I'd understand what happened on the High Line. Instead, I'm left to wonder. Believe me, you don't want to know what goes through my brain when I wonder."

He pushed his hair off his brow. "Okay, first, I'm pretty sure even if you knew what was in my heart, you still wouldn't understand what happened today. Second, I always want to know what's going through your brain, even if I'm not good at relaying what's going through mine. Third, and most importantly, I'm sorry."

Aviva looked into his eyes. She saw remorse and embarrassment there. A part of her thawed. She'd had the same problems with her roommates. Granted, they weren't family, but she understood the pressure to date and handling pressure badly.

"Here's my problem," she said. "I don't like the lying, regardless of the reason. I don't like how it made me feel. Not to mention the position you put me in! What would have happened if your mom and I met before you'd explained?"

"It never would have happened."

"That's not a good enough answer."

His shoulders slumped.

"That's why you didn't want to meet my mom, isn't it?"

"Yeah."

"I can't be with someone who doesn't tell the truth, whether it's to me or someone else."

"You won't have to worry. It won't happen again. My mom knows you're blameless. You don't have to worry about her opinion of you either."

Aviva wrapped her arms around her waist. She wanted to believe him, she did. She bit her lip. But could she? "How do I know you told me the truth just now and not what you want me to hear?"

Jacob flinched. He raised his chin. His brown eyes hardened.

She had every right to doubt him.

As if he heard her thoughts, he relaxed.

"I deserved that." He raked a hand through his hair again. "You're right. I tell a lot of people what I think they want to hear. I'm great at listening to people, but I'm not good at sharing my feelings."

He cupped her elbows. They were inches apart. She could smell his soapy, spicy scent, feel his breath on her forehead. If she let herself, she could melt into him and be taken over by desire. But she couldn't let herself. Not right now.

"Okay, if it's true, tell me your feelings," she said

"About what?"

She swallowed. "About me."

"You know I like you."

"Yes, but technically, *like* isn't a feeling."

"How isn't it a feeling?"

She sighed. "It's an opinion. It doesn't tell me how your liking me makes you feel."

"Seriously?"

She nodded. "Yes. If I'm going to believe you, I need to know what you tell me is what you feel, not what you think I want to hear. So, you need to tell me how you feel about me."

He turned away and spun back again. "You're difficult, you know that?"

"Surprisingly, you're not the first to tell me that."

He shook his head. He looked around the room, as if he expected someone to pop out from the shadows.

She followed his gaze. "Don't worry, my roommates are out tonight. We're alone."

"You know, I can think of other ways to spend our time alone, Avs."

"So can I. Because we always fool around. That time I told you I wasn't ready to have sex with you? I won't be ready until I know your feelings. So please grant my request and tell me how you feel about me."

"That was a request? Remind me never to be on the receiving end of your demands."

She remained where she was, waiting.

"Okay, my feelings. I care about you deeply."

"How?"

"How deeply?"

"No, how do you care about me deeply?"

"Aviva, you have to help me out here. I want to answer your questions, but I have no idea what you mean." He held up a hand. "Before you ask, no, I'm not trying to tell you what you want to know, but I need to at least be on the same page as you."

He looked lost. She took pity on him. "Okay, how do you know you care about me deeply?"

"Because you're the only person I think about. Because when I'm not with you..." His eyes widened. "...something is missing." He grabbed her hand and placed it over his heart. "Right here. Something is missing when you're not with me. I'm terrified I'm going to mess things up with you and not have time to make this work, and the thought of being without you leaves me empty."

Her fingers curled in his shirt. She stood on tiptoe to caress his cheek. "That's feelings. Now I know you're being honest."

"I always will be. I promise. Will you give me another chance to prove it to you?" He leaned down. His lips brushed hers. Warmth pooled in her belly as her breasts pressed against his chest. They stood together, like dancers in a choreographed waltz at the moment right before he swung her out and away from him.

"Yes." She didn't want to move. She wanted to get closer. Swaying her hips, she ran her fingers through the hair at his nape. He needed a haircut, but she loved the feel of the silky strands on her skin. He tipped his head farther, kissed her harder. She parted her lips for him. His tongue delved inside. Her tongue met his, continuing the dance of their bodies. Their noses touched. Her neck heated. He let go of her hand, grabbed her bottom, pressing her to him. He was hard. She began to rock. Their breaths came faster.

With a groan, he pulled back. "We can't do this," he said.

"Why not?"

He whipped his head up, pupils dilated with desire, mouth red. "Because you said you weren't ready yet."

She ran her hands down his chest, dipped her fingers behind his waistband. His stomach trembled at her touch. "I said it had to mean something. It does. I'm ready."

"Are you sure?"

She nodded.

She didn't think his irises could get any darker, but they were almost black with desire. He wanted her. He cared about her. She'd created the desire. She'd helped him recognize his feelings for her. The power was as much of an aphrodisiac as oysters. She couldn't stand to spend one more moment apart from him. She took his hand and led him to her bedroom, tripping over her feet in an effort to get there quickly.

Once inside, he leaned her against the closed door. He kissed every inch of her, starting at her hairline. He traced kisses over her eyelids, behind her ear, down her neck, across her collarbone. She shivered as he moved lower, stopped to kiss each breast through her shirt and ended at her belly button. His hands gripped her hipbones as he kissed her through her jeans. She bucked. He drove her crazy.

When he rose, she led him to the bed and pushed him onto it. He growled but lay there. She climbed on top of him. He raised his hands to grasp her waist, but she pushed them on the bed. She trailed tiny kisses across his forehead, along the bridge of his nose. He pursed his lips to kiss her back, but she maneuvered out of his reach. She kissed his neck, trailed her lips across his Adam's apple.

He was wearing too many clothes.

Reaching under his shirt, she stroked his chest and flat stomach, his muscles jumping beneath her hands. She undid his belt and shorts. She trailed kisses lower and lower, listening to him hiss as she made it below his waistband.

With a sudden move, he flipped her over, pinned her beneath him, pulling at her shirt and shorts with feverish movements. Only when they were skin to skin did he slow down.

"You're beautiful," he whispered, as he rose above her. He feasted his eyes on her body.

The cool air chilled her, reminded her they were apart. She raised her hips to try to meet him.

"Easy," he chuckled. "Do you have anything? I didn't bring condoms with me."

She fumbled in the drawer of her nightstand and handed him the packet. After he'd put it on, he lowered himself on top of her. His body was warm, hard, and heavy. She shifted under him to get comfortable. He inhaled, making her smile.

"Tease." He bent forward to kiss her breasts.

She scratched her nails along his back. She rocked her hips with him, and he hardened against her. His mouth grew more insistent. Their breathing increased in tandem. She stroked his backside.

When he raised his head, she pushed him. She straddled his hips, reached down, and cupped him in her hands. He threw his head back as his hips bucked.

"Avs, oh God, Avs," he panted. "I can't...I can't...I c-c-can't..."

She rose. He flipped them over once more and slid inside her. He paused while she accustomed herself to him. When she nodded, he thrust, their bodies moving as one. He kept his gaze focused on her. Aviva was unable to look away. His eyes closed. His lips parted. Tightness spiraled between her legs. Pressure built until she had no choice but to close her eyes. She rode the wave as it grew bigger and higher, until stars burst behind her eyelids. As she came down, he drove into her faster and faster. He shouted her name. Afterward, they lay together, limbs entwined.

His breathing slowed in time with hers. Awareness of her surroundings returned—the ticking of her bedside clock, their sweat slicked bodies, the wrinkled sheets beneath her back. She buried her face in his shoulder, unwilling to lose their intimacy.

He raised his head, a twinkle in his eye. "You know, if you'd just told me I needed to confess my feelings for you before we had sex, we could have saved a lot of time."

She punched his shoulder before laughter burst from her. "I don't know. I think this was worth the wait."

He took her face in his hands. "Definitely."

"So, how are things with Jacob?" Aviva's mother asked the next day. "Sophie told me you ran into each other on the High Line."

Aviva's face heated as she held the phone to her ear. She couldn't possibly tell her mother about the makeup sex. No matter how close they were, there were some boundaries that couldn't be crossed.

"Much better."

"Oh good. Sophie mentioned there was a problem, but Benjamin was around so she didn't go into details."

Aviva filled her in on their fight. "He's promised to be honest with me from now on, because I can't be with him otherwise."

"Absolutely not. But at least he's owning up to his mistake."

Aviva shifted the phone against her ear. "We had a long talk, and he understands and agrees with me. As for the rest, well, he's not good at sharing his feelings, but hopefully he'll improve with practice.

Her mother laughed. "Good luck with that, *bubbelah*. Most men wouldn't recognize their feelings without a nametag. I know your father certainly wouldn't."

"Jacob's not like that, Mom. I mean, he knows how he feels, he's just not good at expressing himself.

But he's willing to try. And that's all I can ask for right now."

"I'm glad you worked things out. You know, I've found prioritizing things helpful when I deal with your father."

"Mmm." Aviva didn't like to make any comparisons between Jacob and her father. But perhaps her mother was right. Jacob needed to be honest with her and learn to express his feelings, but she also needed to respect his time commitments. "I'll consider it, Mom. Thanks."

"I'm not suggesting Jacob is just like your father, Aviva."

"I know." She hoped her mother was right.

Jacob stood outside the unassuming brownstone on a well-manicured, residential-looking street in Jersey City. He wiped his sweaty palms on his slacks. The windows reminded him of hooded eyes. He couldn't believe he'd agreed to this.

Stuart Rose's business card sat on his desk at home, daring him to act. He wasn't sure if the dare was to throw it away or call, but finally, he'd decided to call for a follow-up interview, if only to get it out of his system and be able to concentrate on more important things, like finals.

Finals. He should be studying. His stomach churned, but he took a deep breath in through his nose and out through his mouth until the nausea passed.

Jacob heard Stuart's smile over the phone. They'd set up the meeting for today, despite the ton of work he still had left to do. A light breeze lifted the hair on his forehead. He turned toward the sun. At least this interview enabled him to spend a few minutes enjoying the weather.

Squaring his shoulders, he jogged up the steps and opened the forest green door. Stepping into the foyer onto a cork floor with a large woven mat, he took a moment to orient himself. A wall of greenery faced him. It set the tone for the obviously environmentally friendly office. To his left, French doors separated the foyer from a reception area. Straight ahead was a carved stairway. Next to the stairs, a long hallway. On his right were bamboo pocket doors. The place resembled a California tech firm more than a law office.

Out of the corner of his eye, he saw motion. He turned. A woman behind a desk in the room with the French doors waved to him. He entered.

"Hi, you must be Jacob, right?"

"Yes, that's right." He shook the redhead's outstretched hand.

"Hi, I'm Ann. We've been expecting you. Sit there. I'll call Stuart."

He sat on a modern, yet comfortable green and blue sofa. On the table in front of him, also made of bamboo, sat several magazines and a law review or two. A shadow slid across the table.

"Stuart will be right with you, but he asked me to have you fill out this form." Before Jacob could argue, she smiled and held up a hand. "I know, Stuart said you haven't accepted the offer yet. That's fine, but we do need this information from you, regardless. If you end up here, it will save time later." She handed him a tablet. Jacob filled out the information.

Ten minutes later, Stuart appeared. "Jacob, great to see you. Sorry for the delay. I was on the phone with a client. We have a mediation next week. They had a few questions. Come, let me show you around. You've already met Ann. Those doors there lead to the copiers, printers, etc., which we use sparingly. Our entire office is environmentally friendly, which is important with the types of clients we represent. We figure you can't talk the talk if you don't walk the walk."

He led them out of the reception area and down the hallway next to the stairs. "Down here are the mailroom, kitchen and dining room. Everyone is encouraged to stop for meals. Whether you eat here or go out is your choice."

They walked into the dining room. Stuart introduced him to the lawyers who were eating there. They chatted a few moments and continued on their tour. Back in the foyer, Stuart brought him over to the pocket doors. "This is our conference room." Furnished in environmentally friendly materials, the room was light and airy, with floor to ceiling windows and lots of plants. Screens descended from the ceiling for presentations. There was every technology feature available. Several lawyers and paralegals worked in the room. Again, Stuart introduced Jacob to everyone.

"Middle of finals, right?" asked one of the younger guys.

"Yeah, I should be home studying," Jacob said with a grin.

"You're at Seton Hall. Do you have Platt this semester?"

"I do."

The lawyer rattled off his number and Jacob entered it into his phone. "Call my cell if you need help while you're studying. His exams are tough, but I learned a few tricks I'd be happy to pass on."

"Thanks!"

Jacob followed Stuart out of the room, marveling at the friendliness of everyone he'd met. "We don't usually need more than one conference room for our meetings, but worst case, there's plenty of room in our law library if someone needs to hold a meeting. I'll show it to you next."

They jogged upstairs to a small foyer that was a replica of the one downstairs. Only one doorway led off of it. Stuart walked to it. "This is our law library."

Jacob entered. His jaw dropped. Floor-to-ceiling bamboo bookshelves alternated with floor-to-ceiling windows that circled the room. In the center was a large table with computer tablets. Around the table were comfortable upholstered chairs.

"Everything you need should be here. If it's not, any of our other lawyers can tell you where to find it."

Jacob wandered around the room. The books and magazines arranged on the shelves were a lawyer's dream. His heart raced as he thought about daily access to this room. For a small law practice, it was amazing.

"Wow, this is...I don't even know what this is," Jacob said.

Stuart nodded. "It's astounding. I know. But the key to our practice is knowledge. You can't have knowledge without resources. Want to meet the rest of our practice?"

Jacob nodded. He followed Stuart up the flight of stairs. "These top two floors are offices for all of our attorneys. We don't distinguish between types of offices. Everyone needs one. Everyone gets one. We're not big on titles for title's sake. We value our attorneys for their knowledge, work ethic, and how well they get along with others. Come, I'll introduce you to a few."

For the next half hour, Jacob met a variety of lawyers, some who had been with the firm for years, others who had joined the firm within the past twelve months. They all took the time to tell him about their experiences and ask him questions. Every one of them sent their contact information to his phone. In a daze, he followed Stuart into his office and sank into a chair.

"It's a bit overwhelming, I know." He passed a computer tablet to Jacob. "This is what we'd like to offer you. It's not as much money as the large firms, but the experience you'll get here is unlike those large firms as well. Take some time to think it over, figure out your law school loans," he smiled, "and let me know what you think about it. I know you have finals, so let's talk once you've had a chance to breathe."

He leaned forward. "Wow, I'm impressed by what I saw today and by everyone I met. This is an amazing firm."

Stuart leaned back in his chair. He grinned. "Glad you like it. I know you have contact information from practically everyone here. Feel free to call or email any of them with questions. They'll be honest with you. We don't want you here under false pretenses. We'd rather tell you something you don't want to hear, and have you turn us down, than have you start work here and be unhappy." He held out his hand. "I'll walk you downstairs. It's been a pleasure showing you around. I hope you give us serious thought."

As Jacob left the office, he shook his head trying to clear it. He had a lot to think about.

CHAPTER FOURTEEN

The following day, Jacob met Aviva in Jersey City for coffee after his first exam.

"How'd it go?" She bit into her muffin, then took a sip of coffee.

Her lips moved, and he imagined their feel against his. Clearing his throat, he focused on her question. "The exam? It went okay. I actually was given some good advice from one of the attorneys at Croft yesterday, which helped me. I felt prepared."

"I forgot you went there. What was it like?"

He described the building and the people, trying to relay his impressions as well. He'd taken her concerns to heart.

Her mouth dropped open. "Wow, that sounds amazing. What are your feelings about the place?"

He drank his coffee as he sorted them out. He'd been impressed by the sincerity of the place. An environmental law practice that incorporated environmentally friendly materials in its office makeup. A law firm that encouraged its lawyers to stop and eat lunch every day. Lawyers who offered him assistance with his finals. The obvious respect and camaraderie shared by the partners and the newer lawyers. It was different from Smith Kane.

Smith Kane possessed the prestige Croft didn't. It offered the salary to enable him to pay off his law school loans almost immediately and help his mother. It had already offered him a job and provided educational seminars for him to learn what he couldn't learn in law school.

Sure, its hours were legendary. He probably wouldn't last there more than two or three years max without burning out. He'd do grunt work. He wouldn't have much chance to interact with the senior partners or the clients. From all the burnished copper and polished wood, he doubted the office was environmentally friendly. But others had done it. He was familiar with the firm.

"I can't describe it with feelings. It's a job. But I know the positives and negatives. While I won't decide until after finals, I think I'll still probably end up with Smith Kane."

Her face fell, and she smoothed it out. A part of him appreciated her attempt to hide her feelings about his career, to let him decide. Another part of him wasn't sure what to make of her reaction.

"Well, it's probably wise to wait until finals are over in order for you to have time to fully consider your options, but why, right now, are you thinking this way?"

He placed his coffee on the arm of the bench. He twisted it in circles. "Part of me is convinced I shouldn't let Smith Kane down. They invested time and money in me, both during the summers for my internship, and with all the seminars they've run and invited me to. I feel disloyal for considering anyone else."

"That's admirable." She placed her hand on his arm.

The slight pressure of her tethered him to the here and now. It helped keep his thoughts from splintering in a million different directions.

"But would you really be the only intern they hired who turned them down?"

He looked into her jade green eyes, so serious and concerned. "Probably not. I'm sure it happens on a regular basis. They probably wouldn't care nearly as much as I think they might. I'm just not sure how I feel about backing out of a decision."

Aviva rose and dumped her coffee cup in the trash, before returning to straddle his lap. He rested his hands around her waist, while she balanced herself with her hands on his shoulders. Their foreheads touched. He reached up to kiss her. Her lips were sweet with a hint of coffee flavor. When they separated, she brushed hair off his forehead.

"I think it's admirable to be honorable," she said. "But I also think in this type of situation, you have to do what's best for you and your career. I mean, as much as I'd love for you to work at Croft, where it seems like you'll have more time to spend with me, if you think you'll be better off working at Smith Kane, you should. But just make sure you choose them for the right reason."

She slid off his lap and held her hand out to him. They walked to the corner, where he pulled her in for a last kiss. This one he dragged out. He tantalized her lips with his, applied pressure in small increments. When she opened her mouth to take a breath, he groaned. He wanted to taste her. His tongue entered her mouth and met hers. His muscular arms grabbed her close. He massaged the back of her head, letting his fingers run through her short locks. Their noses bumped. She smiled against him.

"We have to stop," she whispered.

"Why?"

"Because we're standing on a street corner." As if to back up her claim, a car honked. Jacob pulled away, groggy. A cab passed. He wasn't sure if it was the one with the offending horn or not. With a deep breath, he tried to clear his head and calm his libido.

"I have to go this way." Aviva pointed east.

"Yeah. I have to go home."

"Will I see you later?"

Jacob shook his head. "I've got papers to write and exams to study for. I don't think I can manage it tonight. But we can always talk or text."

"Okay." She leaned in for another quick kiss. With a wave, she walked down the street.

He watched her retreating back with her swaying hips and perky pace. The last thing he wanted to do was spend time apart. Maybe the Croft firm was the better plan. At least he'd get to see her more.

Meryl greeted her when she entered the office the next morning. She swallowed, did a quick mental check to make sure there was nothing she'd forgotten.

Coming up blank, she plastered a smile on her face. "Good morning, Meryl. How are you?"

"I'm well, Aviva, you?" Before Aviva could answer, she continued. "When you get yourself settled, come into my office so we can go over your choices for linens, menus, and such. When the mail comes, let me know if we've gotten any RSVPs."

"Okay, give me a couple of minutes. I'll be right there."

She dropped everything on her desk, found her notes for her selections and did a quick search of her email to make sure there were no emergencies. Gathering her things, she headed to Meryl's office.

Meryl looked up when Aviva knocked. She motioned her in. "Sit down." She pointed to a chair across from her desk. Aviva sat on the edge, pile in her lap. Meryl shuffled through papers and tapped on her keyboard. "I want to discuss the menu first."

Depositing her pile on the chair next to her, Aviva flipped through until she found the menu. "Okay, I've got it."

"I loved your suggestions," Meryl said. Aviva's stomach eased. "I do think we have to make a few changes, but I really like your direction. Let's start with appetizers and work our way down."

For the next twenty minutes, they finalized their choices for passed hors d'oeuvres, cocktail stations, a three-course dinner, and dessert. With a satisfied smile, Meryl entered their suggestions into the computer.

"I think Russell will love it," she said. "Moving on, let's look at music. I'm not sure classical is the way to go. It seems a bit stodgy to me."

"Well, the gala is for people of a certain age." Aviva was interrupted by Meryl's snort.

"God, you're young," she said with a grin.

Aviva laughed, and they discussed other options.

Meryl again typed into the computer before refocusing on Aviva. "For lighting, you suggest reds and golds?"

"Yes, I wanted to transport us back to the ancient Greeks and Hippocrates, the father of modern medicine." She explained the meanings behind the colors, and Meryl nodded.

"I hadn't thought about it that way, but I think the room looks more inviting with your lighting. Not to mention, I love the hidden meaning you convey. I think Russell will too. Great job."

Aviva's chest swelled. She busied herself looking for her linen suggestions while she absorbed Meryl's compliment. As she waited for Meryl to catch up, she pulled out the sheet of swatches.

"Tell me about your choices here."

Another five minutes, and Aviva had finished everything she'd put together.

Meryl nodded. "That's perfect. Do you have everything to put together in a presentation book for Russell?"

"Yes. It's all right here."

"Great. I'll forward you my part of the report; you put it all together. We'll present it to Russell when we meet later this week. Oh, and add all the Greek symbolism and how it relates to his company. He'll love it. Aviva? Great work."

Aviva left Meryl's office sure she flew. There was no way someone feeling this good could be expected to stay on the ground. Not possible.

All of her hard work was paying off and best of all, her boss appreciated it.

Was this what Jacob was looking for in his job, too?

At her desk, she hugged herself to keep her feelings in check. She needed to share with someone. Looking around, she crossed off her roommates from her mental list. There was an element of jealousy that wouldn't make it worth it. She picked up the phone and dialed Hannah.

"It's Hannah. Leave a message."

With a sigh, she left a quick message and hung up. She wanted to call Jacob. More than anything else, she wanted to share this with him, to show him she understood his drive. But she didn't want to share it over the phone.

r u busy

She watched her phone send the text and waited for his response.

swamped, y

Her heart sank. He'd already missed lots of study time by coming over to her apartment the other night and going to Croft yesterday. She couldn't make him take more time away to tell him her news.

just wanted to say hi

hi ☺

go back to studying we can talk later

k bye

Aviva spent the rest of the day assembling Russell's presentation binder. On her way home, her phone rang. She raced to answer it, thinking it was Jacob. When the name "Hannah" popped on screen, she swallowed a sliver of disappointment.

"Hey, Han."

"Sorry I couldn't call or stop by your office earlier. I was at client meetings. What's up?"

"I had the most amazing day today." She spent the rest of her commute home telling her about what happened.

"That's great! Did you tell Jacob?"

"No, he's too busy. I don't want to bother him."

"You don't sound good. Everything okay?"

Aviva sighed. "Yeah, it's just I really wanted to talk to him."

"Avs, it's the end of his last year of law school. He's got to study."

"I know. I'd better get used to it. It'll probably be ten times worse when he's working."

Letting herself into her apartment, she began to fix dinner. Her roommates had left notes they were out, so it was just her. With an omelet, salad, and bread, she kicked off her shoes and ate in front of the TV. As she changed channels between a home renovation show, *The Bachelor,* and baseball, her phone rang.

"Jacob!"

"Sorry about before. I have about five minutes before I leave to meet a study group. How are you?"

She muted the TV. "Busy with work, but good." Remembering what her mother said about prioritizing, she kept things simple. There'd be time to talk to him after finals.

There was silence for a moment. "That's it?" he asked. "Just good?"

"How are you?"

"Tired. But finals will be over next week. I just have to make it through until then. You're sure you're okay?"

"Why wouldn't I be?" She tried to keep her voice light.

"I don't know. You wanted to talk before."

"It's not a big deal. My presentation went well. Go to your study group."

"Okay, I'll talk to you later."

She hung up the phone but didn't unmute the TV. She hadn't told him about her day. It wasn't a big deal. Well, maybe it was to her, but in comparison to his finals, it wasn't. She couldn't take up all his time with mundane things. Like him, she had to prioritize.

The next day, Aviva's phone rang as she was on her way to work. The number wasn't familiar, and she let it go to voicemail. When she walked into her office, there were a million things to do to get ready for the meeting with Russell at the end of the week. By the time she was able to check her voicemail, it was lunchtime.

"Hey, Aviva, it's Scott Korbel from college. I'm in New York City for work and thought it would be fun to catch up. Give me a call if you want."

Aviva's heart raced as she hit redial. The phone rang several times, and she prepared to leave a message.

"Scott! I'm glad to hear from you. I'd love to get together. Call me so we can set something up."

Her phone rang again a moment later. She assumed it was him. "Hi!"

"Wow, you sound happy," Jacob said.

"Oh, I thought it was someone else."

"Um, is that a bad thing? That it's me, I mean."

Aviva laughed. "No, not at all. Sorry. Hi, how's studying?"

"I'd much rather spend time with you."

"We'll have time together once you're done. Don't worry, it's not much longer."

"Thanks, I just needed to hear your voice. Dammit, I have to run."

"Bye."

Biting into her sandwich, she swallowed when her phone rang again. This time, she looked at it first. It wasn't Jacob. "Hello?"

"Aviva? It's Scott."

"How are you?"

"I'm terrible at keeping in touch."

"You are. But I'll forgive you if I get to see you."

"Well, I'm in town for three days. What's your schedule like?"

"Crazy, but for you, I'm wide open. What works?"

"Any chance you're free for drinks tonight?"

Aviva checked her schedule. She'd probably have to work late tonight, but maybe she could get away for a drink, and they finalized plans.

The rest of the day flew by. Aviva finished her work and headed to the bar. It was a dive bar, but she and Scott had frequented plenty of them during their college years. She felt right at home. They'd made it something of a personal quest, to find the best dive bars around. She smiled as she entered. Scott waved to her from a booth. He rose as she approached. He gave her a huge hug.

He was as tall as she remembered, broad and beefy. He'd always reminded her of a lumberjack. No business suit or silk tie could eliminate her first impression. He smelled woodsy too.

"Gosh, it's good to see you again."

He released her and sat. She slid into the booth across from him. "What are you doing here?"

"I'm meeting with a mediator and a client today and tomorrow. I fly back to Chicago the following day. But I couldn't stop without seeing you. It's been too long."

After ordering beers from the bar, they caught each other up on their lives and laughed and joked like old times.

"So, you're dating a lawyer?"

Aviva shook her head at the gleam in his eyes. "Yeah, can you believe it? I swore, after my dad, I'd never do something like this. But here I am wondering when he'll be done with finals in order for us to see each other."

He raised an eyebrow at her. "You okay?"

She sighed, tipped her head from side to side. "He's busy right now. I don't want to bother him with little things, but I end up not talking to him about anything because what's not little in comparison to finals?"

Scott reached across the table and took her hand. "Don't shut him out. Don't doubt your importance to him. He likes you, right?"

"Yeah. He said I was one of his priorities."

Scott grinned. "Then respect him. Give it time."

"You're right." She took a sip of beer. "How's your love life?"

"I'm seeing a guy named Andrew. He works for my firm. Things are going well."

"Wow, that's almost marriageable for you." She winked at him.

"Yep, just about. But we're not rushing into anything yet."

"Probably wise. Keep him as a sex toy until you're really sure of him."

Scott roared. The other people in the bar turned to look at them.

Aviva waved. "In all seriousness, you sound happy. I'm glad."

"You have to visit me in Chicago, Avs. Maybe I'll even let you meet him."

"Oh, I'm honored. Just think of all the stories I could tell him…"

"On second thought, scratch that. I'll just visit you."

"Mm hmm. I'm really glad you called, though. We have to keep in touch better."

They finished their beers, and Scott waited with her while she scheduled a rideshare.

"Good luck with your lawyer boyfriend. Let me know how it works out."

"I will." Aviva waved as the car pulled away from the curb.

Everyone told her to be patient. But patience wasn't her strong suit.

CHAPTER FIFTEEN

Aviva heard the buzz of her phone while dry-ing off from her shower. She dripped across the floor and stared at a text from Jacob.

what r u doing today?

meeting w/Russell re the party

free for lunch?

She stamped her foot before she rolled her eyes at her childish reaction.

no r u free for dinner?

no, study group for exam

She threw her phone onto the bed. She didn't have any right to be angry. No matter how busy he was, he always texted her to let her know he was thinking of her. And she was busy too, especially as this gala approached. But every time their schedules didn't mesh, she got a pit in her stomach. What would happen when he studied for the bar exam? Or worse, worked for that crazy, workhorse law firm? Maybe she should end it now. The sour taste in her mouth gave way to chills and dizziness. For a moment, she thought she was coming down with the flu.

Aviva didn't want to end it with Jacob. She didn't want to give up yet. To be fair, he did exactly what he said he'd do. He made her a priority. He had time at lunch, so he suggested seeing each other. He could have used the time to take a nap or run errands or do laundry or any number of other things. Instead, he chose her.

Instead of being angry, she should be grateful. She frowned at herself in the mirror, not liking who she was becoming more than her actual reflection. With a sigh, she dressed and went to work. At the office, she and Meryl did their last-minute prep for their meeting with Russell. When the receptionist buzzed his arrival, they walked into the conference room.

"Russell, good to see you," said Meryl. "Wait until you see what we have to show you. Would you like coffee or something to eat?" She pointed to the black lacquer sideboard, where a platter of fruit and pastries sat, along with a coffee and tea setup. Everyone helped themselves. They sat around the black lacquer conference table.

"Aviva and I will walk you through everything." With the press of a button on the remote control, a screen descended from the ceiling. An image of the Governors Hall appeared, lit up during the day.

"This is what the gallery looks like currently," Aviva said. "For your gala, it will look like this."

Meryl clicked a button. The room was transformed with tables and the cocktail area. Another click of the button and the colored lights Aviva suggested appeared.

"Your tables will look like this," Aviva added.

Meryl clicked the remote. The tables were set with linens, china, and centerpieces.

"A quartet will play background music," she added; music filled the room. With a final click of the remote, the lights in the gallery dimmed so you could see exactly what the room would look like.

Russell gasped. "Phenomenal," he said, his voice low with awe.

"Wait," Meryl said. "We're not done. We'd like to explain our reasons for what you see."

With that introduction, Aviva took over, describing their choices and the meaning behind their color scheme.

"That's fascinating," Russell said when she was finished.

Aviva's face warmed at the praise. She nodded at Meryl.

"You obviously put in a lot of time on the research. I'm amazed we can convey our message with such subtlety just by choosing certain colors."

"You know, this gala is to raise money for your medical research," Meryl said. "The best way to do it is to make sure every message your patrons receive makes them want to support you. You want to appeal to their emotions as well as their reasoning."

"Well, I'm thrilled at what you've shown me." He rose, but Meryl reached out a hand.

"Wait, we're not finished yet. We still have the menu to go over. Speaking of food, do we want to order in lunch?"

Everyone nodded. Aviva left, wishing all the while she could be meeting Jacob instead. Swallowing her disappointment, she returned with menus. After they placed their orders, Meryl displayed their proposed gala menu onscreen.

"The science center offers a number of choices." They discussed the food options until their lunch arrived and took a break to eat.

"Aviva, I'm impressed by what I've seen today," Russell said. "Tell me about yourself."

She thrust her shoulders back as she figured out what to tell him. "I'm from Connecticut and went to college at UConn. I have an older sister in New Jersey with her husband and my seven-year-old nephew. My parents still live in Connecticut."

"My daughter looked at that school. It's great, but she wanted something a little smaller. Do you live in New Jersey too?" he asked.

"Yes, I have an apartment in Hoboken I share with two roommates. One of them is an investment banker, the other is a production assistant."

"I remember living with roommates," he said with a laugh.

For the next few minutes, they traded crazy roommate stories. Meryl joined in. Aviva was shocked to learn Meryl, who never showed up to work in anything other than a designer outfit, was into grunge bands in college.

When they finished lunch, Meryl drew their attention to the binder in the center of the table. "Russell, make sure you take this with you. It contains photos, linen samples, the menu, etc. so you can discuss it at your office. We have about a month before we have to get some of those decisions to the science center, so if you could let us know any changes you have within the next two weeks, we would appreciate it."

Russell shook their hands. "I will, although I doubt there will be anything significant changed. Thank you both for all of your hard work."

They walked him out. As the elevator doors closed, Meryl gave Aviva a hug. "I can't believe how happy he was. I've never seen him loosen up or show as much pleasure in something. It's all you. I can't even take credit for it. You totally rocked this."

Aviva wasn't sure what shocked her more, Meryl's hug or her lengthy praise. "Thank you. I really enjoyed putting it together."

"Well, it showed. You've got a great future here. I hope you realize that."

Aviva swallowed. "Thank you, again."

As she headed to her desk, she looked at the time. More than anything, she wanted to share this with Jacob, but he was busy. She couldn't bother him. With a sigh, she cleaned her space and counted the minutes until they could be together again.

Aviva woke to the sound of her alarm combined with rain spattering her windows. She groaned. She hated rain in the city. Never mind how the romantic comedies portrayed it, rain in any metropolis was messy and sooty. No matter what she did to try to stay dry, she was never successful.

Instead of taking the PATH train or subway, she decided the best way to stay dry was with a rideshare. When the car pulled up, it splashed her, of course, but she didn't want to go to the trouble of ordering another one, so she climbed in and planned to leave a review.

She turned her head to look out the window, but the car swerved. She fell to the side. Her head knocked against the window. She cried out as they were smashed from behind and spun around. Or maybe it was her? She couldn't tell because it was as if she were on one of those spinning teacup rides at an amusement park. Another jolt and her body listed the other way. Make it a bumper car ride. Meryl wouldn't be okay with her missing work to play at an amusement park. With a screech and a crunch, the car came to a halt. An oppressive silence blanketed her. She needed to get out, but she couldn't find the door. Pain throbbed everywhere. She whimpered. Why couldn't she get out of the car? She was going to be late.

The door opened. The smell of oil and burnt rubber permeated the interior. And Old Spice aftershave. Had they crashed into a delivery truck? That would be a fun mess to clean up. Sirens squawked too. Man, they were loud.

A man's voice interrupted her thoughts. "Are you okay?"

Why was he climbing into her car? Didn't he know it was hers? She frowned as his hands groped for her seatbelt. What was he doing? Wait, he asked a question. What was it? Oh, yeah, she remembered now.

"Um, I think so." At least, she thought she said it.

He didn't pay any attention to her words. He'd undone her seatbelt and put something around her neck. Aviva wasn't sure she liked a strange man touching her, but she didn't have the energy to protest. The man seemed to have a lot of hands. They were everywhere.

She couldn't follow them all, but suddenly she was lifted out of the car, laying on something hard.

The man and some other people spoke in a foreign language. No, it wasn't a foreign language, it was English, but it was technical. Or maybe medical? They attached things to her, ignored her hands trying to push them away. She heard whimpering. Who was that?

"Shh, it's going to be okay. We're loading you into the ambulance now."

Ambulance?

"My name's Rick. Can you tell me your name?"

"Aviva."

"Hi, Aviva. You've been in a car accident. You're pretty banged up, so we're going to take you to the hospital."

"Where's my bag? I can't leave it in the car."

"It's at your feet. Don't worry. Everything will be okay. Just relax."

She wanted to protest, she didn't want to go to the hospital. She needed to go to work. But she was so tired.

When she opened her eyes, she was in a hospital. No matter how fuzzy her mind, she could tell by the bright fluorescent lights, the antiseptic smell, and the nurses' pages over the loudspeaker. She turned her head with care. After a while, the pain subsided, and the room stopped tilting. Monitors kept track of all kinds of things. The lines and numbers were confusing, but as long as nothing was flat lining, she assumed she was fairly okay. With a deep breath, she turned her head the other way. The room tilted again. Still, lots of pain and nausea, but this time, bags hung from metal posts. Great. Bags meant needles.

"Oh, hi, you're awake. My name is Susan. You're in the hospital. You've most likely got a concussion, and you have some lacerations and bruises. We're getting ready to send you to x-ray in a few minutes to check out your arm and get a CAT scan for your head. Otherwise, you're okay."

Aviva closed her eyes again. She tried to relax. They flew open a moment later. "I have to call my boss. Where's my bag?"

The nurse reached for it and handed it to her. "Let me help you."

She dialed and handed Aviva the phone.

"Meryl Kreptke."

"Meryl, it's Aviva."

"Aviva, where are you?"

"I'm sorry. I was in a car accident. I'm at the hospital." She mouthed "Which one" to Susan, who mouthed back, "HUMC."

"Hoboken University Medical Center."

"Oh my God. Are you okay?"

"I think so. I might have a concussion. I have to get my arm x-rayed."

"You poor thing. Take it easy. Let me know how you are later, okay?"

"Okay, I will."

The nurse took the phone and bag and put it in underneath her bed. As she finished, a technician arrived to take Aviva to x-ray.

"Hopefully we'll have a room for you when you're done there," Susan said.

The fluorescent lights slid by as the technician wheeled her stretcher down the hall. The elevator was huge, but the stretcher bumped over the doorjamb. Her arm ached at the movement. Downstairs, they waited outside of the x-ray room for about twenty minutes until the room was ready. Once her x-ray was complete, the technician took her for a CAT scan. By the time everything was finished, more than an hour had passed. Aviva was exhausted.

"Your room is ready. I'll take you to it now. A doctor will be up later to go over the results with you."

The technician wheeled her to the fifth floor and into a double room. The other bed was vacant. Aviva exhaled. Privacy. A nurse came in and got her settled, placing her bag next to her on the table. Monitors were hooked up again, the IVs placed next to the bed.

"My name is Nancy. Press the call button if you need anything." She left the room.

Aviva lay against the pillow, listened to the relative quiet for the first time all morning. Less woozy than before, but still not right. Her entire body ached. Her vision was off a little. She was nauseated. She took deep breaths and tried to relax.

A knock on her door startled her. Aviva winced as she turned toward it. "Hannah, what are you doing here?"

"I came as soon as Meryl told me. Are you okay? Why didn't you call?"

She pulled a chair to the bed and sat next to her. She stared at Aviva, examining every inch of her. If Aviva had the energy, she'd have blushed at the attention.

"I just got into this room. I'm sorry. I remembered to call Meryl to let her know I wouldn't be in, but they took me to x-ray and…"

Hannah grabbed her hand. "No, I didn't mean to make you feel bad. I just didn't want you to have to go through this alone. Did you call your mom, or would you like me to do it?"

Aviva sighed. "Oh, no, I didn't. I'd better do it now. Can you hand me my phone?"

Hannah gave it to her. Aviva dialed. At the sound of her mom's voice, her eyes filled with tears. She gave a quick update of what had happened. After reassuring her she was okay and she didn't have to race to the hospital, she handed the phone to Hannah.

"Hi, Mrs. Shulman. Yes, I'm here. No, she actually doesn't look too bad." Hannah smiled and winked at Aviva. "Yes, I'm staying. Of course. Definitely. Okay, bye."

She handed the phone to Aviva. "So, your mom wants me to stay with you as long as you'll let me. She'll come but has to wait for your dad to see if he can get away from work. If you notice, I didn't suggest she force him to, but I really wanted to."

Aviva rolled her eyes. "I know your feelings about my dad, Han. I appreciate the loyalty. But he's busy. I'd never expect him to come. I love my mom, but really, she doesn't need to be here either. Neither do you, by the way. I'm fine."

"Avs, you were just in a car accident. Let me stay, at least for a while," she held her hand up to prevent any protests, "and keep you company if nothing else. You shouldn't have to be here alone. By the way, did you call Jacob?"

"No, I don't want to bother him."

"Bother him? Avs, did you not hear the part about being in a car accident? You have to tell him."

"No, I don't. Not now anyway." She lay against her pillow and closed her eyes, hoping Hannah would take the hint.

Hannah settled into the chair and rummaged in her purse.

Expelling a breath, Aviva let herself drift. Moments later, or maybe longer—it was hard to tell—she heard her name spoken. She opened her eyes. Nancy, her nurse, stuck a thermometer in her mouth and a blood pressure cuff on her arm. She gave her some medicine for pain.

"Your arm is broken. The orthopedist will be in soon to cast it. The neurologist will be in to go over your CAT scan results. Until then, get some rest."

Aviva resisted the urge to tell her she had been resting until she was disturbed. No one liked a cranky patient. Instead, she smiled and closed her eyes again.

Her rest was again disturbed by the orthopedist's arrival. He sent Hannah outside and examined Aviva's arm. "Based on the x-ray, it's a clean break and won't require surgery. My nurse is going to set it for you and give you care directions. When you're discharged, follow up with your own doctor. If you need a referral, let my nurse know." He shook her good hand and left.

"I'm Bridget. I'll be setting your arm. It shouldn't be too painful but let me know if it hurts."

Aviva watched with some trepidation as Bridget got to work but as promised, there was little pain. Once set, the pain lessened, although her arm was heavier. When she finished, Bridget left. Hannah returned…with Aviva's mother. This place reminded her of a three-ring circus. Her mom's finely lined face was creased with worry.

"Mom, I thought I said you didn't need to come out here."

Her mom leaned over, long greying hair brushing against Aviva's cheek. She planted a gentle kiss on her forehead. "And leave you here alone? Sweetheart, sorry, but that's never happening. Dad will be here when he can. He's tied up at work with an important client. I think he has a meeting or two as well." She shrugged and pulled a second chair closer to the bed.

Aviva told her as much as she remembered about the accident, Hannah talked about work, and her mother asked questions. Eventually, Aviva stopped talking and listened. She was getting ready to fall asleep again when the neurologist came in. He allowed the women to stay while he examined Aviva. "You have a concussion. You'll stay overnight so we can monitor you. It doesn't look too serious, but we'll perform periodic tests just to be sure."

Hannah and Aviva's mom rose. "We're going to get some coffee. I'll call the Rabbi to have him add your name to the prayer for healing list tonight for Shabbat services," Aviva's mom said. "We'll be back in a few minutes. Do you want anything from the cafeteria?"

"No, I'm not very hungry." On cue, food was delivered. She started to laugh, but the noise and movement hurt her head.

"Do you need help with eating, sweetheart?"

"No, I'm fine, Mom. Thank you. Go get your coffee. Don't worry about me. Really."

Her mom leaned over and kissed Aviva's head. "Alright, I know you don't want me to hover. But if you need anything, call my cell. We won't be gone long."

When they left, Aviva picked at her hospital food. She flicked through the channels on the TV over the bed. Shoes squeaked outside the room and muted voices played over the intercom. She'd been glad for the reprieve, but now they were gone, she was restless and bored. She was tired and hungry but didn't want to sleep or eat.

Checking out the daytime TV programs, she wondered how anyone could bear to stay home and watch them without their brains turning to mush. She was ready to throw her remote at the screen when her mom and Hannah returned.

Her mom walked into the room. "So, Hannah tells me Jacob doesn't know you're here."

Aviva raised an eyebrow at Hannah, who showed a vested interest in *The Price is Right*. "Mom, he's in the middle of finals."

"Don't you think he'd want to know what happened?"

"I'll tell him, but not right now. I don't want to disturb him."

"Sweetheart, you're his girlfriend. He'd want to know now."

"He'd want to pass his finals. I'll still be here when he's done. Well, hopefully not here," she gestured around the room, "but I'm fine. It'll be okay."

Her mother pursed her lips. "Didn't he say he'd make you a priority?"

"Yes, but not over his finals, Mom. He doesn't get a second chance with those."

"I think you're selling yourself short. Maybe it's time you made him a priority too."

"What are you talking about? If I could, I'd spend every minute with him. He knows that."

"I'm not talking a physical priority, sweetheart. I'm talking more intimate than that. Sharing your feelings with him. Making him the first one you want to share things with and following through."

Aviva's face heated. She gritted her teeth. Her mother wasn't aware of all the times she'd wanted to tell Jacob something and didn't because of his studying. But it sounded as if she knew. How did she do that?

"We're fine, Mom."

Aviva closed her eyes, hoping her mom would take the hint and end the conversation. From the sigh across the bed, Aviva assumed it worked. But rather than fall asleep, she lay there with her eyes shut, a thickness in her throat. Should she have called Jacob? What time was it? She'd have to open her eyes to find out. Her mother would know she was awake and continue this conversation she definitely didn't want to have. She didn't remember exactly what time Jacob's final was today, but he'd be done sometime in the afternoon. The problem was, when? Would her news impact something later in the week?

Creaking and footsteps made her crack her eyes open. The chair where her mom sat was empty. Only Hannah was in the room.

"She's gone," Hannah said. "She went to call your dad."

"Thanks. Sorry about being a brat before."

"I don't think you were being a brat, but I do think you're wrong."

"But—"

"Just listen, Avs. Switch places for a minute. If Jacob was in an accident and didn't call you, how would you feel?"

Aviva didn't answer. She sank lower in the bed.

Hannah nodded her head. "You should call him. Or text him. Or do something to let him know. Regardless of his exams, he'd want to know."

"I'll think about it."

She patted her leg and rose. "I'll let you rest. Anything you want me to report to the office?"

"No but tell Meryl I'm sorry to miss everything. I know how much work there is and—"

"Relax, it will all get done. You need to rest so when you do go to work, you're able to function. I'll talk to you tomorrow."

Hannah left. Aviva looked at her phone. Three o'clock. Should she contact Jacob? Before she could make up her mind, her mom returned. "Dad sends his love. He'll try to be here tonight."

"It's not necessary for you guys to uproot your lives like this. Really, I'm fine."

"I know, but I still want to be here for you. However, I'll go out for a little while and give you some time on your own. Do you want anything from your apartment?"

"Oh, yeah." Aviva gave her a list and told her how to find everything, including the key in her purse.

With a wave, her mom left. Aviva turned off the TV and listened to the silence in the room. The throbbing in her head receded and the dizziness was gone.

The silence was a relief. She needed to decide about Jacob. She couldn't get over the guilt of disturbing him, when there was nothing he could do for her anyway.

Her phone buzzed. She reached for it.

> hey, done for the day.
> how r u?

She swallowed. It was now or never. But there was no way she could put this in a text. She dialed his number and waited for him to answer.

"Hey, Avs, I'm glad you called. I've been dying to hear your voice all day."

"Hi. Did your exam go okay?"

"You don't sound right."

Her throat tightened. Tears threatened. He could tell something was wrong by the few words she said.

"Aviva? What's wrong?"

She swallowed as tears rolled down her cheeks.

"Talk to me, Aviva. What's going on?"

"The rideshare I was in was in an accident. I'm okay, but I'm in the hospital."

"Where are you? I'm on my way."

She cried harder. "No!"

"Why not? Aviva, where are you?"

"I'm in Hoboken University Medical Center, but you shouldn't come here. You've got too much work to do."

He scoffed through the phone. "Don't be ridiculous. Of course I'm coming." He paused. She tried to think what to say. "I'll be there in about twenty minutes, okay?"

He shouldn't come. He should stay home and study. She wanted to tell him, but she couldn't.

"Aviva?"

"Okay."

For the first time since hearing Aviva's voice, Jacob stopped and took a deep breath. Standing in the fluorescent glow of the hospital hallway, he leaned against the wall. It was a little like swimming against the tide as a parade of doctors, nurses, and others passed him in the opposite direction. Overhead, announcements filtered through in some sort of a muted, yet audible, tone. Disinfectant wafted around him. Everyone seemed to know where they were going and what they were doing.

He didn't.

Without the rush to get here, the knowledge she hadn't called filled the spaces in his brain. Why? Why wasn't he the first, or one of the first, calls she made? If he hadn't texted her, would she have bothered to tell him? With a strong head shake, he pushed away from the wall and searched for Aviva's room. In the doorway, he stopped once again. She lay in the bed, tiny against all the bags and monitors. Her face, a mottled blue, red, and purple, was the only splash of color against the white hospital linens. He swallowed as his stomach dropped. With a steadying breath and a silent prayer of thanks, he walked in.

She turned, winced, and he strode to the bed and grasped her hand. It was tiny, or maybe it felt that way because she was vulnerable. "Hi, sweetheart."

"Hi."

Connected to the IV bags by lines and drips, she looked trapped. He cradled her hand, taking a seat in the chair beside her. "How do you feel?"

Her lips parted in a small smile. "Sore and tired."

"I'll bet. Can you tell me what happened?"

She relayed the events of the day. He must have shown his horror because she paused mid-sentence. "I'm okay, really."

No matter how bad the events sounded, she'd somehow escaped serious injury. With another deep breath and silent thank you, he nodded. "I know. It could have been much worse."

"But it wasn't. Please don't worry."

"I didn't mean to interrupt. Continue."

She bit her lip, as if afraid to tell him the rest, but he remained silent. When she was finished, he wished he hadn't asked. Images of the accident paraded through his head. Though he hadn't been there, it was as if he were an eyewitness. He stared at her until the images in his brain receded. "I'm glad you're okay." He wasn't any closer to getting answers to his questions. He needed to know why she hadn't called him, but now wasn't the time. The last thing he wanted to do was tire her out with a long conversation.

"I'm sorry you're wasting your time here," she said.

But, given the opening…he leaned forward and gripped the bedding. "Why do you think I'm wasting my time?"

"Because you should study. That's much more important than babysitting me."

He reared back. Babysitting? "You think I'm here to babysit you? Why exactly do you think I came, Aviva?"

She slumped against the pillow, picked at the blanket. "Because you care about me."

Leaning forward, he rested his hand on her leg, hoping he wasn't hurting her more. "That's right. I care about you. You're much more important than studying. I'm not here because I want to be your babysitter." He spit out the word in disgust. "You're my girlfriend."

She shifted and winced at the movement. He rose out of the chair to help, but she waved him away. "Nothing is more important than your studying, Jacob."

He shook his head.

"You've worked too hard to mess it all up now."

"You sound like my mother," he said with a grimace. "I'm in good shape for my exams. They're almost over." He cupped her face, as if she was the most precious thing in the world. To him, she was. "You're infinitely more important to me than some stupid test."

He kept his gaze focused on her, preventing her from looking away.

After a moment, tears pooled in her eyes. "I can't be." Tears rolled down her cheeks.

"Why not?"

"Because if you don't do well on your exams, it affects your future. If it's my fault, I'll have to live with the guilt."

He wanted to wrap his arms around her in a hug, but her damaged body wouldn't allow him to. At the same time, he wanted to shake some sense into her until she put herself on a higher footing.

"Do you remember when I said you're a priority for me?"

She nodded and swiped at her tears.

"I am capable of balancing multiple priorities. I'm not perfect. Sometimes things will get skewed one way or the other, but in this case, when it's a matter of your health versus my exams, there's no contest. I need you to trust I can do this. If for some reason I can't, I need you to understand it's not your fault. Okay?"

Her sigh reminded him of a balloon deflating. He didn't know if he'd convinced her or worn her out, but she nodded and squeezed his hand, and for now, it would have to be enough.

CHAPTER SIXTEEN

The next day, Aviva sat in the hospital-issued wheelchair in the lobby. Jacob hadn't left her side since yesterday afternoon.

Not when her mom came back and lit the Shabbat candles with her. Across a hospital bed was not how she'd envisioned the first meeting of her boyfriend and mother to go, but go it had. When her mom found Jacob sitting with her, her joy had filled the room. The two hit it off immediately, chatting for an hour, while Aviva watched and dozed.

Not when Hannah returned last night. She gave Jacob a hug, leaned over, and hugged her as well, before sitting in the seat Jacob vacated. Aviva expected him to make excuses and leave. Instead, he'd crossed his arms, leaned against the wall, and continued his conversation with her mom.

Not when the nurse announced the end of visiting hours. Her mom left with the promise her dad would visit today. Jacob frowned but remained silent. He'd moved into the waiting room and camped out on what Aviva supposed were very uncomfortable sofas. As soon as visiting hours began today, he'd been in her room, looking tired and stiff, but refusing to leave.

She couldn't help but smile. What kind of man had she found?

When the nurse announced her release, Jacob and her mom conspired like generals planning the *coup de grace* in a battle. They'd ignored her protestations and called her roommates, her dad, and even her boss, making plans for tonight and tomorrow.

Now Aviva and Jacob sat in the lobby waiting for her parents. Although her father had never made it to the hospital yesterday, he arrived in time to transport her home. Watching him get out of the car, Aviva wondered how she'd ever compared the two men.

Jacob was nothing like her dad.

However, he *was* a busy law student, and he needed to get back to his studies.

"You don't have to do this, you know," Aviva said to Jacob.

He didn't bother to answer. He wasn't an intimidating guy, but his frown made her shrink. His brow furrowed, and he fisted his hands.

"Sorry," she whispered.

He took a deep breath, turned, and caressed her cheek. Before he could speak, her mom entered the lobby.

"Dad's outside. I don't want to keep him waiting. He has a conference call he has to get back for."

Jacob sat with her in the backseat of the car. She didn't remember the accident, but the ride made her jumpy, with the lane changes and traffic. After she flinched for the second time, Jacob reached for her hand, stroking it with his thumb. His hand was warm and firm, a lifeline. She gripped it for the rest of the ride.

Once inside her apartment, her mom got her settled while her dad stood by the door and checked his phone. Her roommates made her food. Jacob refused to leave her side. Again.

She'd never seen this stubborn side of him and didn't quite know what to make of it.

"Hey, sweetheart, Mom and I are going to head home. I have a client call in a couple of hours I need to prep for." Her dad leaned over the bed, where Jacob had forced her to lie down, and kissed her gently on the forehead.

She hugged him, grateful for his presence. "I'm okay, Dad. I know you're busy."

A noise on the other side of the room made her look up. Jacob's face was impassive.

Her dad squeezed her good arm. "That's my girl. Leslie, we should go."

Right before her mom followed him out the door, she hurried to Aviva's bedside. "We really like him," she whispered. With a wave at Jacob, she left the room.

Her roommates poked their heads in the doorway. "We're going out. Do you need anything before we leave?"

She shook her head.

"Okay, we'll be really quiet when we come home. Glad you're back."

Once everyone left, the silence bore down like an anvil. The air conditioner whirred as it kicked on, cooling off the room. Her breathing echoed in her ears. Jacob still leaned against the far wall, arms crossed, staring. He was dressed more casually than usual, in faded jeans and a black T-shirt. The thin fabric showed off his flat stomach. The sleeves emphasized those amazing biceps. Although focusing on one thing still gave her a headache, it was worth it to look at him. If only he didn't look ominous.

"What's wrong?" she asked.

"Other than the fact my girlfriend is lying injured in her bed? Not a thing." He pushed off the wall, sat on the side of the bed, and took her hand. "You should try to get some sleep. Is there anything I can get for you?"

"No, I'm fine. Go home. You need to sleep too."

"I can sleep here."

Aviva's pulse pounded. Possibilities filled her head. She patted the other side of the queen-sized bed, but he shook his head.

"I'll stay here tonight," he said, "just not in your bed."

"You really don't have to. My roommates will be back if I need anything."

He raised an eyebrow. Any further arguments died with that one look.

"Smart girl. Do you want to wash up or anything?"

"No, I really don't."

He left the room, returning moments later with a pillow and blanket. He spread them out on the floor. She rose on her elbow with a grimace. "Wait, you're sleeping on my floor?"

"I want to be close by if you need me." He turned out the light, silencing her opposition with darkness. But she had to try one last time.

"Not even the sofa?"

"Go to sleep, Aviva."

Who would have thought she'd find her knight in shining armor asleep on her floor?

Jacob lay in the dark, his body shaking.

The floor was hard, despite the wall-to-wall carpet beneath him. A draft blew from somewhere. His pillow no longer had a cool side to it; he'd punched and turned it multiple times to get comfortable. Aviva's breathing evened out as she sank deeper into sleep.

A dull throb began behind his temples. His jaw ached from clenching it. His pulse pounded in his ears. That SOB father of hers. Every time Jacob closed his eyes, he saw his face—thick white hair, sharp blue eyes, hawk-like nose, thin lips. What kind of father didn't sit at his daughter's bedside in the hospital? What kind of a father left her at home to go to work? On a Sunday. No wonder Aviva was gun shy about his spending time with her.

For what seemed the gazillionth time, he tried to fall asleep.

"You sure you don't want to sleep here?"

Aviva's sleepy voice startled him into a sitting position. In the darkened room, the only thing he could see were her eyes glittering in the blue-black light.

"Why aren't you asleep?"

The bed shifted. She gave small whimpers of pain. "I was, but everything hurts now."

"Let me get you some pain medicine."

This was why he'd stayed. She needed someone to help when the pain got bad in the middle of the night. Someone like him.

He went into the bathroom and found the pain meds and a cup of water. Helping her to sit up, he put his arm around her shoulders, holding her while she swallowed. The knot that had formed in his chest when he'd first heard about her accident loosened. His chest warmed as she leaned against him. He buried his face in her hair. Its softness tickled his cheek. He closed his eyes against a prickle behind his lids. He could've lost her. He exhaled a shaky breath, for what seemed like the first time since he'd heard about her accident.

His fingers covered hers as he reached for the cup again. Her delicate bones beneath his fingers awakened some long-buried ancient protector response in him, coupled with an overwhelming desire for her. His pulse raced.

She reached around with her good arm and cupped his neck. Her touch was killing him. Her fingers stroked his hairline, sent shivers down his back. He brushed light kisses along her jaw, tasting her. Her uninjured skin tantalized him with its softness. Their noses touched. In the darkness, her eyes were almost black, with a mossy green rim. Fatigue and pain shown in them. They tamped down his lust.

"Do you want me to rub your back?" he whispered. Confusion made her eyes narrow. He smiled. "Lie down."

She winced, so he helped her maneuver onto her side. He knelt by the side of the bed, stroking her hair away from her face. As a child, his mother had rubbed his back when he couldn't fall asleep. He channeled that memory, swirling his hands against Aviva—light enough to be gentle, firm enough not to tickle, platonic enough not to make her think he wanted to have sex with her.

Which he did, but not at this moment.

Her breathing deepened. He continued his motions, hoping to ease her tension and pain. Beneath her oversized cotton T-shirt, her spine was evident through the soft fabric. Her ribs expanded as she took a deep breath, let it out, and settled into a more even rhythm. After a few minutes, she slept. Jacob continued to rub her back for another five minutes until she slept deeply. Then he returned to his pallet on the floor and finally fell asleep.

Whispered voices and muted sounds pulled him awake. He stifled a groan. His eyes were gritty, his mind sluggish. He'd swear he'd only fallen asleep a minute ago, but the clock showed it was morning. Early morning. Three hours of sleep wouldn't help much today, but he'd have to make do. He rose, shuffled to the bathroom then slipped out of the bedroom, without waking Aviva.

Her roommates were in the kitchen making breakfast.

"How is she?" Erica asked.

He reached for the mug of coffee she offered, held the steaming liquid to his nose, and breathed in the rich aroma.

"Sleeping." Blowing on it, he took a taste and swallowed, waiting for the caffeine to kick in. He supposed it would be unreasonable to expect an automatic jolt, but he paused anyway. Eyelids still droopy, brain still sluggish. He sighed.

"Good, she needs it," Erica said. "I can stay with her for the morning if you want."

"Yeah," added Maddy. "I can take the afternoon off. Would that help?"

"That would actually be fantastic. I've got a paper I need to turn in today. Then all my finals are finished. I can get here tonight."

Maddy moved through the kitchen. "Don't rush. Whenever you get here is fine."

As the roommates scattered, Jacob wondered why Aviva's parents weren't involved in this equation. If he lay injured, his mother would set up base camp next to his bed. She'd refuse to leave until satisfied he was completely back to normal. He shook his head at the image of his mother dressed like a drill sergeant flashed. On second thought, maybe her parents were onto something.

Jacob worked out the day's schedule in his head. He'd have a lot of catch-up today, but he could do it if he put his mind to it. He poured a cup of coffee for Aviva and returned to her bedroom. She stirred. When he closed the door behind him, she woke.

"Hi." Her voice sounded like a like a screechy door.

"How do you feel?"

She moved with care, adjusting herself into a sitting position. "I think I'll live."

He handed her the cup and sat next to her on the bed. "I'm glad." Leaning over, he placed a gentle kiss on her forehead. "Erica will stay with you this morning, Maddy this afternoon. I'll be back as soon as I turn in my paper."

She reared back, gasped, and closed her eyes. Jacob held her hand, watching her color turn from gray to rose. After a moment, she opened them. "There's no need for everyone's schedules to be upended. I'm perfectly fine on my own."

"Don't be stubborn, Avs. You're still sore. You need help."

"I'm fine!" She pushed off the bed and swayed.

Jacob held her steady and ignored her glare. He was more concerned with her ability to focus. After a moment, she was able to do both. He considered it progress.

"I'm fine." She tottered toward the bathroom.

"Do you need help?"

"In here? You? No."

He fisted his hands and tried not to take offense. She was tired, sore, getting over a trauma...she was female. A light bulb went off. He hurried out of the bedroom.

"Erica? Maddy?" Their doors opened, and they popped their heads out. "Can you help Aviva? She's in the bathroom."

Both women hurried past him. Muffled voices assured him they took care of her. He rubbed the back of his neck and stifled a yawn. All he wanted to do was lie down. Aviva definitely didn't want him around right now. He walked into her bedroom, his steps slow.

"Aviva? I'm going to go home to get some things done. I'll call you later."

Erica popped her head out the bathroom door. "We've got this, don't worry."

CHAPTER SEVENTEEN

"He's gone." Erica opened the bathroom door wider.

Aviva let out a sigh. "Okay, now it's time for you to go too."

"Maddy's leaving, but I'm staying."

"This is ridiculous. I don't need babysitters. You both have things you need to do. I'll be fine here."

"I'll hang out here this morning," Erica said. "The more you argue, the less stuff I get done."

"You're annoying, you know that?"

"Too bad. Now say good-bye to Maddy. I'll get you some breakfast."

She started to open her mouth to protest, but Erica's glare convinced her to shut it. She appreciated the thoughtfulness, but all this attention was making her a little claustrophobic.

Opening the dresser drawer, she pulled out T-shirt and sweatpants, clean underwear, and socks. She brought everything into the bathroom and sat on the toilet seat to catch her breath. Leaning over, she turned on the shower.

I need to keep my arm dry. Never mind dry, I need to get out of these clothes.

She tried to pull them off, but the movement made everything hurt. Fighting tears, she started at the knock on the door.

Erica peeked around the door. "Want some help?"

With a silent nod, she stood as Erica helped her undress and wrapped her arm in plastic.

"Call me when you're done."

The warm water pelted her back. She winced, but seconds later groaned in pleasure as it melted away the myriad aches. The new bar of soap gave off a fresh, clean scent, and she scrubbed away the last of the hospital smell. A one-handed shampoo left her clean and almost brand new. She turned off the water and wrapped a towel around herself. One-handed, she was awkward and clumsy, but proud to do this alone.

"Can I come in?" Erica called.

"Yes."

"Feel better?"

"Much," Aviva said.

Erica helped her hook her bra. She put the T-shirt over her head. When Aviva was dressed, they walked into the kitchen and ate breakfast.

"Thanks for all of this," Aviva said. "I appreciate it."

"No problem. You relax. I'll get some work done I brought home for the weekend. If you need anything, holler. I'll be here."

"Oh, I should check in with work."

"Just don't overdo it."

Aviva made her bed her workspace for the day. After a call to Meryl, who was glad she felt better and passed along work she could do from home, she checked in with Hannah. Some press releases, a review of the menu, and Aviva was exhausted. She lay against the pillows and tried to sleep.

"Knock, knock."

Aviva woke with a start. "Afternoon already? I swear I only just closed my eyes."

Maddy shouldered her way into the room, a lunch tray in her hands. "I thought you might be hungry."

Aviva's stomach growled. "I am, but I could have gotten it myself."

Maddy laughed. "Erica said you'd be like this. Relax and eat. You can run a marathon when you're finished if you want."

Aviva rolled her eyes at Maddy but took the tray. Who the heck wanted to run a marathon? She ate the sandwich and fruit. When she was finished, she brought the tray into the kitchen.

Maddy looked up from the table where she was spread out working. "Feeling any better?"

"Yeah, thanks. Sorry for before."

"Don't worry about it. But you might want to get your grumps out before Jacob gets back."

She spent the rest of the afternoon working and watching TV. By dinnertime, she was crotchety and restless. Aviva didn't want to be ungrateful, but she was tired of being an invalid, tired of staying at home, and tired of not being able to do anything for herself. Erica, Maddy, and Jacob had been considerate, but she hated the constant hovering.

When Jacob buzzed to be let into the apartment building, she counted to ten. If one more person coddled her, she would scream.

"Good, you're up." He stopped in her doorway. "Want to go for a walk?"

She opened and closed her mouth, certain she'd misheard. *Did he suggest a walk? He's kept me practically under guard all day and barely let me out of bed. He must have said talk.*

"Sure, we can talk. How was your day?"

Jacob frowned. He folded his arms across his chest, crossed one bent leg in front of the other, and leaned against the doorjamb. "Better than yours, obviously, since you don't seem to hear well. I said walk, not talk. We can talk outside while we get some fresh air."

Who was this man, and what had he done with her boyfriend? She squinted at him. Same wavy brown hair falling across his brow; same cognac-colored eyes; same deep voice that sounded like it was trying to placate the crazy person. Was she crazy? There was only one way to find out.

"You really want to go for a walk? With me?" She pushed the covers away and sat on the side of the bed. With satisfaction, she noted he hadn't moved from his perch in the doorway. She stood. The room remained still, as did she.

"Well, it was either you or Adam. You're prettier."

She walked to him. "Before you wouldn't let me out of bed. You've had Bonnie and Clyde over there, guarding me all day."

His face lit up as he pushed off the wall. He took her face in his hands. His skin was warm, and his thumbs caressed her cheeks. She was consumed with an unbearable desire to lean into him and go to sleep. But she was tired of being needy. She threw back her shoulders, standing tall.

He drew her into a hug, and she allowed herself to rest her forehead on his shoulder. But, only for a moment. She didn't want him to decide a walk was a bad idea.

"We wanted to take care of you," he said. "They didn't hold you hostage. They helped out while I finished my work, so you had someone around if you needed anything."

She pulled away from him but looped her fingers through his belt loops. "I appreciate it, but I'm not used to it. It's...a lot."

"Which is why I suggested a walk. The fresh air will do you good. Some exercise will help you get ready for tomorrow, since I assume I'd push my luck forcing you to stay home again." He pointed to her bed, where her work was spread out.

She nodded. "I have to go in tomorrow. There's a lot to do."

"So, let's walk now and make sure you've got your sea legs."

The late May evening air was cool and fresh, or as fresh as Hoboken air got. A faint perfume from the flowers planted near the building wafted toward her. She took a deep breath. "This is wonderful."

"Great, let's go inside now."

"What? No!"

He laughed. "I'm just teasing. Come on." He tucked her hand beneath his arm. Because of the warmer temperatures, the sidewalks were filled with people. They jostled their way through the crowd until Jacob steered her onto a quiet side street. "You okay?" he asked.

She inhaled deeply. "I feel like I've been locked up for days."

"Let me know as soon as you get tired. We don't want to overdo it."

She yanked her arm out of his. "Will you stop? I'm fine."

He held his hands in surrender. "I know. I just don't want to have to carry you home. You're a little heavier than my books." His mouth twitched.

She didn't see what was funny. Well, maybe a little. Okay, a lot. Laughter bubbled from her chest. He joined her, his laugh deeper, his warm body touching hers. For once, they were united.

Straightening, she glanced at him. "I'm sorry I've been such a bear."

"You're entitled."

"You're awfully reasonable...about everything. Why?" They started walking again. He put his arm around her shoulders. The weight felt good, steady.

"Why not?"

"That's not much of an answer," she said.

He exhaled. She thought he might finally yell at her. But he didn't. "Look, you were injured. Now you're recovering. Part of your recovery includes emotions you'll just have to get out of your system. Plus, I'm honestly too tired to jump at every cross word or inflection you might make."

Stabs of guilt pierced her. "I'm sorry."

"What for?"

She shrugged. "For not calling you, for not being grateful, for keeping you away from your studies, preventing you from sleeping..."

He pulled her against him, rested his chin on her head and rubbed her back. "You need to get something straight. I care about you." He pulled her away from him to stare into her face. "That means, I care about all of you, even the parts that might infuriate me, or frustrate me, or tire me out. It also means you're worth losing a little sleep, or not being able to study quite as much as I might otherwise. Got it?"

She nodded in wonder. It was as if the world paused for a moment, or her heart stopped beating, or the heavy silence after a loud concert. His words were foreign to her. This man whom she'd known for a little more than a month was making sacrifices, ignoring his own needs as if it was the most natural thing in the world. She'd always been the one to sacrifice herself for others. No one had ever done so for her. What in the world did this mean?

"It means he loves you," Hannah said the next day. They sat at Aviva's desk drinking tea Hannah had brought.

"He can't love me, Han. We haven't dated long enough."

"That means nothing. Do you love him?"

"How should I know? It's only been about a month." But she turned her mug around, rather than meet Hannah's knowing gaze.

Her stomach fluttered each time she thought about him. She'd never felt more cherished than when she was with him. He put her needs first. It used to be Hannah whom she'd call when something happened. Now she wanted to call or text Jacob first.

Did she love him?

"You know, don't you?" Hannah sipped her tea, hiding her grin behind the rim of the mug.

Aviva opened her mouth to protest. What was the point? "I don't know if I love him or if I'm falling for him. Or maybe I just realized I could fall in love with him. Crap."

"Why crap? Falling in love with someone, whether you already have or are going to soon, is a good thing. Isn't it?"

"Of course it is. I just don't want to lose myself."

"Why would you?"

Aviva fiddled with her mug. She tried to get her parents' relationship out of her head.

"You're not like your parents, Avs. Jacob isn't like your dad."

"Wow, was I that obvious?"

Hannah raised an eyebrow.

Aviva sighed. "I know Jacob and my dad are nothing alike. No matter how out of it I might have been over the past few days, even I saw the difference between the two." She raised her hand to stave off any comments. "I don't want to make judgments on my dad here. He is who he is. I love him anyway. But it doesn't mean I want that kind of person for my husband." At Hannah's look of shock, she continued. "Eventually. But I also don't want to just fall for the first person who isn't like my dad."

Hannah reached across the desk. She put her hand on top of Aviva's. "I really don't think you'd do that."

Aviva sighed. "I hope not." She looked at Hannah's wrist and gasped. "I hate to kick you out, but I've got to get to work. I didn't realize how late it was."

Hannah walked down the hall. When she turned the corner, Aviva returned to her desk. For the rest of the day, she waded through the work she'd missed, met with Meryl about the gala and didn't come up for air until Meryl stuck her head in the door at the end of the day. But it didn't stop the seeds of a plan from germinating in her brain. A plan to thank Jacob for his care of her. To celebrate the end of finals.

As she got ready to leave that evening, she nodded to herself. She knew what to do.

"So, you're not going to tell me what we're doing?" Jacob waited for Aviva to finish getting ready.

It took a little longer than usual since she could only use one arm. A week after her accident and she felt better. Not perfect, but better. By the time she fully recovered, Jacob would be in the midst of studying for the bar exam. If she was to execute her plan, it needed to be now.

"Nope. It's a surprise." She finished applying makeup, grabbed her keys and purse, and ushered him out the door. Downstairs, she directed him to the PATH trains. They took one to 34th Street. Once out of the station, she called a rideshare.

She gripped the door handle as the driver pulled away from the curb.

"You okay?"

She looked at Jacob. Concern etched his face. "Yeah, it's just this is the first time I've been in a car since coming home from the hospital."

"Come here." He drew her into him, his arm around her shoulders. Resting his cheek on the top of her head, he cocooned himself around her. She felt safe. Expelling a breath, she settled in for the ride.

Jacob looked out the window. "Central Park?"

"You're right," she teased.

He shook his head as they exited the car.

They entered the park, crowded with tourists and natives alike. Kids shrieked and ran around, parents yelled words of caution, tourists spoke in a variety of tongues, and lovers walked arm in arm on the walkways. Deeper in the park, the traffic noises receded, replaced by tweeting birds and buzzing insects. Crossing the lawn, the grass was soft beneath their feet.

"You don't have a picnic blanket, so I guess we're not laying out here," Jacob said. He pointed to some of the other couples who picnicked and relaxed on the grass.

"Nope."

"I never knew you were secretive."

She winked. "I have my moments. Come on, we're here." She brought him to the Boathouse. They approached the ticket booth. "Two tickets for the gondola, please."

He turned in a circle. His mouth dropped. "How did you know I love boat rides?"

She kissed his lips briefly. "I didn't know for sure, but since you like pirates, it wasn't too big of a stretch. I would have done the ones we paddle, but with my arm, we'd end up in circles and dizzy. My luck, someone would fall overboard."

He looked her up and down. Although she wore jeans shorts and a white T-shirt, she suddenly felt exposed. Her heart pounded.

"I wouldn't mind seeing you in the water."

She covered her chest with her one hand, though she was bone dry, and he couldn't see anything.

He stepped forward, took her hand. It was hard to breathe, but in a good way. His eyes darkened. He smelled good. She wanted to kiss him. Rising on tiptoe, she leaned against him. He bent his head, touched his lips to hers. This was where she belonged. She opened her mouth, but he pulled away.

"I don't want to hurt you," he whispered as he rested his forehead on hers.

"You won't."

"Excuse me."

She turned toward the awkward sounding voice in the ticket booth. "Your gondolier is ready."

She wanted to hide behind Jacob and let him deal with everything. But this was her treat, so she took Jacob by the hand and led him toward the water.

The gondolier and Jacob helped her settle into the gondola. The day was warm. A light breeze caressed their faces as they glided on the lake. From the shore, people waved. Jacob waved back. Aviva's attention was focused on him.

They floated along the lake, and the stress practically melted away. Jacob's eyes, which had developed a squinty focus, widened. The crease between his eyebrows flattened. His shoulders lowered. His mouth softened. If she'd wondered about her choice of excursions, she wondered no more.

She rested against his shoulder.

His arm tightened around her. "I'm not hurting you, am I?" he asked.

"No."

"Good." He stroked her hair. "I love this surprise."

"You deserve a break from all your stress. It's peaceful out here. Almost as if we're somewhere other than Manhattan."

"It's a great reprieve, although I love the hustle of the city. There's a vibrancy you just don't find anywhere else."

The gondolier's rhythmic strokes were hypnotizing. "True, but it's busy and hectic. There's noise everywhere."

"That just adds to the excitement. What about you?"

"I like coming in when there's something I want to do. But given a chance, I wouldn't be averse to somewhere else."

"But you're in PR. Can you do that outside of a city?"

"Yes," she said. "And I could also open my own business, which can be done anywhere."

"Is that what you want to do? Have your own firm?"

"I like the idea of it. I'd have to see how I feel in a few years. But the idea appeals to me."

"I think you'd be great," he said. "You should pursue it if it's something you want."

She smiled, once again warmed by his complete faith in her.

When their half hour ride was over, they disembarked and strolled through Central Park. Two guys playing Frisbee missed. Jacob leaped to catch it. He threw it to them, waved off their thanks and continued walking.

"Want to climb Belvedere Castle?" Jacob asked.

"Pirates and castles?"

Jacob shrugged. At the top, they admired the view of the Great Lawn, the Ramble, and Turtle Pond.

"Are you ready for the next part of our adventure?" Aviva asked.

"Will you tell me what it is?"

"Where's the fun in that?"

They got into another rideshare and held hands during the drive. Actually, he hadn't let go of her hand except for the few times that were absolutely necessary. She liked it. It was a physical expression of their connectedness; one she began to appreciate. She didn't want anything to separate them. Jacob stared out the window, but Aviva paid attention to his hand. His thumb, to be precise. It caressed the back of her hand, ran over her knuckles, absentmindedly, as if it was the most natural thing to do. The nail was square and neat, the skin was olive, the pads were smooth. She watched it, mesmerized.

The stillness, after their stop-and-go ride, distracted her from Jacob's thumb.

"South Street!" Jacob smiled. "I haven't been here in a while."

"It's on every pirate's to-do list." They strolled down the cobblestone street toward the pier. At this time of day, the place teemed with tourists. Street performers juggled and performed acrobatics to music and cheers. Gulls cried overhead. The briny smell wafted across the wharf.

Aviva led Jacob to the tall ships. "Want to go on board?"

He nodded. They purchased tickets for the ships. After walking around the lobby area of the museum and viewing the interpretive displays, they exited the building and boarded the Peking. For forty-five minutes, Aviva listened as Jacob extolled the virtues, history, and usage of the one-hundred-and-four-year-old ship. His enthusiasm was contagious. Though her interests lay elsewhere, Aviva was fascinated.

"I never knew it was possible to get excited about a ship that carried bird dung," she teased as they disembarked.

He spun her around. "I hope I didn't bore you."

"Not at all. Honestly, I liked touring the ship with someone who knew what they were talking about. You brought it to life."

"These ships fascinate me."

"I can see that."

Arm in arm, they strolled along Water Street.

"Do you mind if we go into Browne & Co.? I love their printmaking."

"Sure." Jacob held the door. They explored the shop and letterpresses and stopped to chat a few moments with the master printer before they returned outside.

"Hungry?"

"Starved," Jacob said.

They walked into the Trading Post and sat at a table overlooking the East River. After ordering yellowfin tuna tacos, as well as a Blue Moon and a Bronx Pale Ale, they admired the view.

"So, tell me what all this was about," Jacob said after a few moments passed.

She looked at him, relaxing in his chair. "I wanted to treat you to a day out, doing things you liked, without worrying about studying, or me, or anything else. Think of it as my graduation present to you."

They sipped their drinks.

"Well, it was great," Jacob said. "I enjoyed it. You're right. I am totally relaxed. Thank you."

"You're welcome."

"I'll think back to this every time I'm sick of studying for the bar exam."

Aviva shook her head. "When do you start?"

"I started in January, actually, but my study course starts right after graduation. The test is in July. That's why today was perfect."

"I'm glad."

Their food arrived. They stopped talking while they tasted it. In the middle of the afternoon, the restaurant was busy, but not packed. A low hum filled the silence as couples and groups at other tables talked in the background.

"What are you thinking?" Jacob asked.

"Nothing, why?"

"So, there's not even a tiny part of your brain wondering how much time I'll be able to make for you while I study for the bar exam?"

Aviva covered her mouth as she stifled a laugh. He knew her well. "I'm doing my best to learn from the past. You've made time for me before. You came through when I was hurt. I'm sure everything will be okay."

"Wow, I'm impressed."

"Well, that and you'll be finished by the end of July. I can handle being ignored for a couple months."

He threw his napkin at her.

She laughed. "Got ya!"

"Just when I started to think you might believe me." He forked a bite of food into his mouth.

She covered his hand with hers. "I do believe you. Truly. I care about you deeply. But I also know the bar exam is a short period of time. Worst-case scenario, if

I can't see you as often as I'd like, I'll manage. You're worth waiting for. Okay?"

He flipped his hand over to grasp hers. "Okay."

When they finished eating and Aviva had paid for the meal, they headed outside.

"Oh, I almost forgot," she said. "I have something for you." Reaching into her purse, she handed him an envelope.

"What's this?"

"Won't know until you open it."

He rolled his eyes, ran his finger through the envelope flap and pulled out the insert. "An invitation to your gala?"

"Yeah, I thought you'd like to go as my date."

His cheeks spread into a wide grin. "I'd love to." He leaned down, took her in his arms and kissed her.

She melted into him, savored his warmth.

"Thanks for inviting me." He pulled away. "Thank you for today. It was great."

"I'm glad you enjoyed it. Thank you for everything you did for me when I was hurt."

He chucked her under her chin. "You don't have to thank me. I'm your boyfriend. That's what we do."

CHAPTER EIGHTEEN

Aviva sat in the Prudential Center with Jacob's mother and the families of the other law school graduates as the names were called. After quizzing Aviva on her recovery from the accident, her ability to take time off for Jacob's graduation, and complimenting her on her dress, his mother *kvelled* next to her about Jacob. Aviva couldn't blame her. There was something awe-inspiring about watching these students reach their goal. Knowing how much effort Jacob put into this moment made it more amazing.

Especially when you considered she'd almost messed everything up for him. She shook her head to rid herself of the thought, wiping a tear from her eye.

Karen leaned over. "My son the lawyer." She beamed with pride. "You know what makes me even prouder of him?"

Aviva shook her head.

"Because for all the nagging I do about making time to see me and prioritizing things in life, he manages to balance everything and still do well."

Aviva tried not to show her reaction to Karen's words. Was this woman psychic? If she was, there could be definite problems down the road—a psychic mother-in-law? Holy cow.

"Don't look surprised, sweetheart." Karen patted her leg. "You think I don't worry about his finding time for life in his life? I do. All the time. But look at how well he did after your accident."

Aviva shook her head. "I could have messed everything up for him." Other audience members turned to look at her. She lowered her voice. "I feel guilty," she whispered.

"Nonsense. You didn't mess anything up. If you think he hasn't spent forever studying, you're crazy. He spends so much time doing it, if he misses a day or two, he'd still be fine. He was. Because he's there."

She pointed toward the sea of black mortarboards. He was toward the front, but she couldn't tell exactly where.

"Oh," she said, turning to Karen, "they just called his name." They pulled out their cameras and pointed them toward the podium as he exited his row, followed the line of other graduates toward the stage, and made his way across toward the podium. He shook hands with the dean, received his diploma, and turned toward the audience. Aviva would swear she saw him wink at her, but he couldn't have. He didn't know where they were seated, did he?

After he made his way to his seat, Karen leaned toward her once again. "Don't doubt for a moment he can't handle you and his studies. He doesn't talk a lot about his feelings, but he is excellent at managing expectations."

Aviva, lulled by the drone of names called from the stage, thought about Karen's words. She let go of the guilt. She had to believe, or at least try to believe, Jacob. There was simply no other option.

When the last graduate was called and the last speech was made, Jacob made his way to them. Karen grabbed him and held him in a hug. Arms wrapped around his mother, he made eye contact with Aviva. She smiled, warmed by his attention. Once Karen let go, he leaned toward her. She kissed him chastely—his mother was here, after all.

"I'm proud of you." She fingered the tassel that hung from his mortarboard.

He grabbed her in a hug, put his lips against her ear. "Would it be wrong of me to say I'm proud of you for dealing with my mother for the last hour and a half?"

She smacked his arm with her good hand.

"Okay, you two. Before we do anything else, has my son invited you to Shabbat dinner yet?"

"Ma!"

Aviva swiveled between Jacob and his mother. "No, but between my accident and his studying and graduation, there hasn't been time."

"That's sweet of you to defend him, but an invitation takes two seconds to give. He's very good at wiggling out of them. We'll take care of this right now. How is this Friday?"

When Jacob started to object, Aviva placed a hand on his arm. "I think it's okay. What time would you like us, and what can I bring?"

"Oh, that's not necessary, sweetheart. Just bring my son and come about six. Jacob, make sure to look nice when you come. I don't want her to think I raised a slob. Now, how about we go out for something to eat?"

"Ready?" Jacob asked Aviva.

She stood in the silver-carpeted hallway of his mother's condo, but his question had been a rhetorical question. She couldn't possibly be ready to deal with his mother for an entire dinner, even if she had managed to handle her during graduation. An hour and a half in an auditorium filled with people wasn't the same as a Shabbat dinner with just the three of them and no set end-time.

"Ready," she said.

Ah, the confidence of the inexperienced. He shook his head. He was leading a lamb to slaughter. She was used to bowing to her dad, there was no way she'd be able to stand up to someone like his mother. His mother met lots of girlfriends over the years. She was very vocal about her opinions, and she always had an opinion. The women were too familiar, too uptight, too boring, too loud, or not intelligent enough. She commented on their clothes, their hair, their makeup, and their manners. Except for the times she didn't. Those times, she was uncomfortably silent. Even with prompting, she said nothing.

Aviva would need a lot of help.

She took his hand and squeezed it. Maybe she was nervous. He wanted his mother to like Aviva, because he was starting to think he and Aviva might have a future together. As he put his hand on the doorknob, he realized how much he wanted a future with Aviva. He turned the handle and ushered her inside.

"Ma?"

Heels clattered on the tiled floor. His mother appeared in the darkened hallway. Her smile practically lit up the enclosed space. "Jacob! Aviva! How nice to see you!" She pulled Jacob's head down for a kiss, turned toward Aviva, and grasped her hand. "I'm glad you're here." She pulled her down the hallway, leaving Jacob to follow.

This was new.

"How do you feel?" His mother asked Aviva.

"Pretty good, Mrs. Black. I can't wait to get this cast off."

"Call me Karen, please. Now, I hope you like brisket. You're not a vegetarian, are you? Jacob didn't say anything about that..."

"Oh, I love brisket," she said. "Please don't worry about me. I'm sure whatever you serve will be delicious."

Jacob shook his head and followed the two women into the living room. They chatted as if he didn't exist. Chatted pleasantly.

For now, at least.

"Jacob, why don't you get everyone a drink," his mother said.

He walked to the sideboard and poured himself a scotch. "Aviva, what would you like? Mom?"

"I'll have a gin and tonic, Jacob, thank you," his mother said.

"Good idea, I'll have one too," Aviva said.

As he mixed, he looked out the window onto the deck. The deep gold velvet drapes had been pulled back. Although the sun had begun to set, it was still high enough on the horizon to provide a view of the tennis courts surrounded by trees. In this golden hour, everything glowed. Turning, he handed his mother and girlfriend their drinks, took his own, and leaned against the sideboard. He could get a good overview here and hopefully prevent anything bad from happening. You know, swoop in like a superhero. *Yeah right.* He rubbed the back of his neck and tried to mask the wry laughter bubbling inside as he imagined his mother's and girl-friend's looks if he showed up in cape and tights.

"Jacob don't stand there like a Ficus tree," his mother said. "Come sit down."

He sat on the pale gold upholstered chair, gripped his drink, and made circles in the gold and green Oriental carpet with his heel.

"Aviva, you were able to get off work in time to come here today?"

"During the summer, my office closes at four on Fridays. It's a nice chance to start the weekend early."

"That's wonderful," she said. "I guess you work longer hours during the rest of the week?"

"Usually until about seven, depending on the work that needs to get done. You have a lovely home, Karen."

"I moved here after Jacob graduated college. Our old home was wonderful, but I didn't want to be bothered with the upkeep."

A beep sounded in the kitchen. His mother rose. "Please excuse me. Help yourselves to hors d'oeuvres."

Jacob called out to her. "Do you need any help?"

She beamed. "No, I'm fine. But thank you for asking."

"I don't know why you were worried," Aviva whispered. "Your mother is so nice."

"Just wait." He leaned over and dipped a pita chip into hummus. Offering one to Aviva, he took another for himself.

"Should I offer to help?" Aviva asked.

"No, she said she's fine. Don't worry."

He tried to see the living room from Aviva's perspective. It was his mother's home, but he'd never felt relaxed here, especially in this room. The furniture wasn't comfortable, he was always worried he'd spill on it, and it wasn't the kind of "sprawl on your back and hang" kind of room he liked. But did Aviva like it? She sat in the corner of the sofa, legs crossed, her non-sling arm resting on the armrest. She didn't seem tense. In fact, she seemed more at ease than he was. Maybe the warm-up meeting during graduation was a good thing. He took a breath.

His mother returned. "Dinner's just about ready. Jacob, would you pour the wine, please? Aviva, come with me."

His mother led her into the dining room. When Jacob was finished, they lit the candles, said the prayer, and sat.

"Jacob, will you say the *bracha* for the wine, please?"

He did, and they each took a sip. He swished a little in his mouth before swallowing. It was a Yarden 2008 Merlot. His mother recited the *bracha* over the challah and passed around the food. Jacob served the brisket to his mother and Aviva.

"Avs, do you want noodles? Green beans?" He held her plate and waited for an answer.

"Of course. Thanks. Mrs. Black, oh, sorry. Karen, do you want some water?"

Distracted for a moment by the pretty blush that stained Aviva's cheeks at her slip, he held the serving spoon suspended midair. She was beautiful. Her graceful neck and delicate collarbone accentuated her high cheekbones.

"Yes, Aviva, thank you. Jacob! You're going to stain the tablecloth."

With a start, he moved the spoon back over the tureen. This time, he concentrated on serving people. Aviva wasn't prepared for his mother, who could squash her with one or two pointed comments. It wouldn't do to get distracted. He wouldn't be able to rescue Aviva if she needed it.

His mother turned to Aviva. "Is Avs a nickname?"

Jacob held his breath. See, they'd walked into an invisible minefield. His mother didn't like nicknames. He remembered how often she made comments to him about his friends and their nicknames. "Why ruin a perfectly good name your parents spent time picking out with something like that?" was a favorite refrain as he grew up. He should have remembered, made sure to use her full name in front of his mother.

Aviva grinned. "Yes. Mostly it's used by my friends."

"I love it. It's perfect for you. Although I think I'll stick with your full name, if you don't mind. It's pretty and unique."

He exhaled with a whoosh, trying to cover it with his napkin. That went surprisingly well. Maybe she was softening in her old age.

"I don't mind. And you're right. Growing up I was always disappointed to never be able to find anything personalized with my name on it. But now I like it."

They ate for a moment in silence. Jacob admired Aviva's ease at dealing with his mother.

"Everything tastes wonderful, Karen."

"Yeah, Ma, the brisket is terrific."

"Thank you both. Brisket has always been Jacob's favorite."

"I'd love the recipe if you don't mind sharing it."

Once again, Jacob held his breath. His mother was always reluctant to share recipes, especially with people she'd just met. There was no way she'd give it to her this soon in their relationship. He wracked his brain to try to come up with something to distract his mother.

"Hey, Ma—"

"Jacob don't interrupt. I taught you better manners than that. Aviva, I'd be happy to give you the recipe, honey. Remind me before you leave tonight. I love women who aren't afraid to eat and cook."

Whoa. Apparently, his fears were misplaced. All of them. Either that or an alien had abducted his mother and replaced her with this easygoing, pleasant woman. Because she proved he didn't need to be nervous.

Aviva laughed. "I do like to eat. Cooking, well, I'm not terrific at it. I don't have a tremendous amount of time, but I've always heard brisket isn't too complicated—not that I mean any offense!"

"Not at all. Brisket is pretty easy. It's a great meal to practice on. It's almost impossible to mess up."

"Good, you understand. I wouldn't want to offend you. Anyway, yours tastes so good. Hopefully I'll be able to maybe come close to this."

He silently applauded her as she extricated herself from a potentially difficult situation. This woman he'd fallen for was good. Aviva was a lot stronger than he'd thought.

"You know, if you want, you're welcome to come over sometime and I can make it with you. That way you can see how I do it. Sometimes it's easier to learn by example rather than a recipe."

Jacob's throat closed. He tried not to choke on his mouthful of food. Did his mother offer to teach his girlfriend to cook?

"That would be terrific! Maybe one weekend while Jacob studies."

"Are you free Sunday? It freezes well, so you'd be able to have it for later. It's always better reheated anyway."

"I am. I can't wait."

His girlfriend...his mother...

"Jacob, close your mouth and eat. Aviva and I are getting along just fine."

...liked each other. His mother was right. He focused on his plate and ate in silence.

Aviva was a genius. She deserved a lot more faith than he'd given her. Not only could she hold her own with his mother, but she'd also charmed her. Actually, charmed her. A foot beneath the table stroked his leg. Aviva smiled at him. He hoped she could read all the silent promises and apologies he was making.

In the meantime, he would step back and let his mother and girlfriend handle themselves without his help. Because a smart man knew when he was out of his element.

CHAPTER NINETEEN

"How was dinner with Jacob's mother?" Aviva's mom asked as soon as she picked up the phone the next day.

"Hello to you too, Mom."

"I'm sorry, sweetheart, but you know you called to tell me."

"You're right." Aviva sank onto her bed and kicked off her shoes. "Dinner was fun. We got along great."

"Really? Tell me."

She recounted their arrival, dinner, and conversations. "Her home was one of the most gorgeous I've seen. She's teaching me to make brisket on Sunday."

"Alone?"

"Well, Jacob's in his hole studying for the bar exam, so yeah, alone."

"And it doesn't worry you?"

Aviva paused to think. "Not at all. She was nice. Her brisket is Jacob's favorite, so I want to learn to make it."

"Aw, my baby's in love!"

Aviva sank against her pillows glad her mom couldn't see her face. "Stop. You make me feel like I'm four."

"Sorry. I'm happy for you, though, *bubbelah*. You deserve someone like Jacob. The fact you like his mother is even better. Have you told Jacob how you feel about him?"

Aviva squeezed the phone in her hand. Her heart pounded. "No. I...I kind of just figured it out myself and I don't want to pressure him."

"And you're not good at pushing him."

"I don't want to push him into confessing something he might not feel yet."

"You know, you don't just put yourself last by not talking to him. You put him last too."

"What do you mean?"

"Did you ever think maybe he wants to tell you how he feels but doesn't know how?"

Aviva frowned. "He knows he can talk to me."

"Yes, but you've said yourself he's bad at talking about his feelings. Maybe he really needs you to make the first move."

"You're the one who suggested I prioritize with him, Mom."

"Oh baby, I didn't mean important things like how you feel about each other."

Aviva wrapped her arm around her waist. "I may have taken your suggestion a little too far."

"I don't want to upset you, honest, but I want to make sure you don't brush aside your feelings because you could hurt more than just yourself."

"I appreciate it, Mom, I really do. I'll talk to Jacob and tell him how I feel. I promise."

"Good. In the meantime, have fun cooking and let me know what happens."

"I will."

As Aviva hung up, she promised herself she'd call Jacob tomorrow and talk things out. It was time he knew how she felt about him, regardless of what else was going on in his life. Her mom might be right.

Jacob's phone rang the next morning as he packed his books to head to the library. "Hey, Aviva."

"Do you have time to get together today?"

"Ugh, I'm totally swamped. Any chance we can talk now, instead?"

Her sigh echoed through the phone. "I guess." He put his books and keys on the table then dropped onto the wooden chair. "Is everything okay?"

"I just, I kind of wanted to talk to you in person. This isn't really something I want to say over the phone..."

He froze. There was only one thing he could think of that could only be done in person. "Avs, can you give me a second? I need to call you right back. Don't go anywhere, okay? I need two minutes."

"Okay."

He ended the call and sat at the table staring at his books. The refrigerator buzzed in the background, creating a white noise that was somehow comforting. The thing about the law that had always appealed to him was its logic. And right now, there was no logic to anything. Something was wrong with Aviva, something she wanted to talk to him about in person. The only thing that popped into his head was her wanting to break up with him. That was the last thing he wanted. His heart pounded in his chest.

He needed to keep calm so he could convince her they belonged together. They'd just had dinner with his mother. The two women had miraculously gotten along. Or he thought they had. Did something happen during dinner to make her want to break up with him? He wracked his brain trying to replay that evening, but nothing jumped out at him. What could he say to convince her to give him another chance?

Tell her you love her.

He straightened, thinking for a moment it was Adam who'd said that. But Adam wasn't home.

Did he love her? He thought he did. He thought about her constantly. When he was supposed to be studying, his mind wandered, and he'd daydream about her. He loved being with her, talking to her, touching her. When he listened to music, every love song sounded like it was meant for the two of them. He wrote notes about her in the margins of his books. For the first time in his life, he could imagine a future with someone, and it didn't feel impossible. His stomach fluttered every time he was around her, even now, while talking to her on the phone. Yeah, he thought it was love. So, he had to be willing to confess his innermost feelings to her, now, when she was asking. Even if those innermost feelings involved groundless fears that Aviva couldn't handle his mother.

He played with the spine of his book. He had to call her back. He had to tell her everything. He had to trust that confessing his feelings would change her mind. Picking up his phone once more, stomach clenched, he dialed her number. "Aviva? I'm back. And I'm sorry."

"For what?"

"For everything. For not being truthful about how I felt and even for now, interrupting you, hanging up to gather my thoughts and not being honest about that either. I know we've talked about your needing me to be honest. I didn't do a very good job about it. But I'm trying. I'll tell you everything."

"I don't understand."

He exhaled. "Please give me a chance to explain. Before you say anything else to me, please let me tell you how I feel." He waited, pain pulsing behind his eyes. What if she gave up and said no?

"Okay."

The silence on the phone weighed him down like a physical being. He swallowed, his tongue thick. "Aviva, I love you." He plowed right through the gasp on the other end of the phone, afraid he wouldn't get the words out if he waited a second longer. "I think I've loved you from the moment you beat me at bowling. I was just too afraid to tell you. I spend my life trying to avoid conflict, which is why I lied to my mother about you, and why I was afraid to admit, even to myself, that I was falling in love with you. Because if I admitted that, I'd have to figure out how to fit you into the rest of my life."

He gulped. "But the thing is, you already fit. You've fit in from the second we met. It was easy. And I can't picture my life without you. I don't want to picture it without you. I'm crazy about everything about you. Please don't break up with me. I don't know what happened at dinner with my mother, but I promise you, I'll fix it. I'll..."

"Jacob."

There was a slight pause. Aviva spoke, her voice filled with wonder. "I love you too."

His chest swelled. "Wait...what?"

"I love you."

"You do?"

"I do," she said. "In fact, that's what I called to tell you. Only it's not the type of thing I wanted to say over the phone."

"I thought you were going to break up with me."

"Why would I do that?" she asked.

"I don't know. I couldn't figure out what had to be said in person and I thought maybe something happened at dinner that I wasn't aware of."

"Dinner was great. I thought you knew that."

"I did. But my mom can be difficult. I've learned to deal with her, but I didn't think you'd be able to handle her, especially after the mess I made at the High Line. I was afraid of what would happen if she didn't like you. I need the two of you to get along."

"Jacob, you don't have anything to worry about."

"I know. It was a knee-jerk reaction, though. I've never seen her as taken with anyone. I kept waiting for another shoe to drop. Only, it never did. And now I feel ridiculous."

"Jacob, I've known you for almost two months now. Never once have you sounded ridiculous. You've been kind and thoughtful and always concerned about my feelings and everyone else's. You don't ever have to worry about that, okay?"

He expelled a breath he'd tried to talk around. "How the hell did I luck out with you?" He closed his eyes. He hadn't meant to say that out loud.

A soft chuckle came over the line. "I believe it involved sneaking out of a speed dating event. Apparently, we're both rebels."

"You were really calling to tell me you love me?"

"I was. I just wasn't sure if you were ready to hear it and I didn't want to distract you from your studying or scare you away."

"You'll never scare me away, Aviva. And you're worth so much more than any distraction. Please don't be afraid to talk to me."

"I'm trying. And I want you to talk to me too."

"I'm working on it. I love you, Aviva. I truly love you."

"I love you too. Still. Again."

"I hate to just stop talking, especially because I just got finished telling you you're not a distraction, but I have to study. Can we talk later?"

"Absolutely."

This time, when he ended their call, there was no sense of impending doom. For the first time in a long time, he was at peace.

He loved her. He'd actually told her. For a man who wasn't comfortable talking about his feelings, he'd certainly had no trouble expressing them. She couldn't stop thinking about it—or him—all day. The way his voice sounded when he said those words. It was like a caress, soft and intimate, meant only for her. She liked it better that way. She remembered a character in a movie who professed his love for the heroine by shouting it from an actual rooftop, with a bullhorn. It was a grand gesture. Aviva's roommates had swooned. But to her it seemed like it was a gesture made to demonstrate how awesome he was rather than how special the relationship was to him. Aviva's stomach had turned.

Jacob always made her feel special, made it seem their relationship mattered, that she mattered. He didn't play games. He didn't show off. He didn't care about that stuff. That was why she liked him. Actually, that was why she loved him.

She'd never felt like this about a guy before. Never felt the soul-baring comfort, the need to make the other person feel as good as he made her feel. She was used to putting others first, but it always felt like a sacrifice. With Jacob, it never did.

"Aviva, did you hear me?"

She started. Her face heated as she looked at Karen. "Um, I'm sorry, I missed that."

Karen shook her head. "You know, I said the recipe was easy, but it doesn't mean you're going to get it by osmosis. Where were you?"

Aviva leaned against the counter. "I was thinking about something."

"Something or someone?"

She looked at Karen, not sure how to answer.

"Ah, that's how it is. I hope this involves my son?"

Aviva nodded.

"And it's a good thing, right? I mean, you're not bursting into tears, and you came today, so..."

Aviva nodded again.

Karen put the recipe on the counter. She sat at the table, motioning for Aviva to join her. "Okay, I'm good, but I'm not a mind reader. There's only so much information I can pull out of you, so if you stay distracted, you'll have to talk to me. Otherwise, we can go back to cooking." She tented her fingers together and raised an eyebrow. The look was so similar to Jacob's, Aviva gasped.

"Problem?"

"No, but when you sit like you are and raise your eyebrow, you look just like your son. Or, rather, he looks just like you."

Karen smiled. "In all seriousness, you don't have to tell me if you don't want to."

"I don't mind. I love him."

Karen dropped her hands onto the table. "Really?"

"Really. I know it's only been a short time, but I do."

"Have you told him?"

"Yes." She smiled and bit her lip.

"How about him. Do you know he loves you?"

Her smile widened. "Yes."

A big grin crossed Karen's face. She wrapped her arms around Aviva. "Oh, I'm glad! He told you?"

Aviva nodded, unable to suppress the giggle that burst from her lips.

"Well, my son doesn't tell that to just anyone, so if he said it, you should believe him. I knew I liked you from the moment we met. Even during graduation, I had an inkling. Your liking my brisket was just a bonus."

Aviva ran her hand over the tablecloth. "I didn't doubt him." Not about that. Never about that.

"I know, you're just in that glorious haze of new love. Maybe we should postpone the cooking lesson?"

"No, no, I really want to learn. I promise. I'll focus now."

Karen patted her arm as they moved to the counter. "I'm usually pretty insistent my cooking protégés pay attention. However, in this case, I can probably make an exception. Now, like I said before, peel and slice the carrots."

CHAPTER TWENTY

A week later, Aviva sat at her desk trying to avoid looking at her calendar. Her to-do list was on it, though, so it might be necessary. But for now, her calendar reminded her of how long it had been since she'd seen Jacob. An entire week of quick phone calls and occasional texts, but no actual in-person dates. It might not sound like a long time, but she missed him. She sighed.

"Aviva, where are we on the RSVP list and menu?" Meryl asked.

With a start, she pulled them up on her computer. "We've heard from about three quarters of our guests. The caterer just sent the final menu for confirmation. Do you want me to print it out for you?"

"Please. We meet with Russell later today. I want to review everything beforehand. When will you follow up with the guests we haven't heard from?"

"This week. Our final count is due in two weeks. I want to stay on top of it."

"Good, perfect. Okay, I'll be in my office if you need me."

With reluctance, Aviva pushed thoughts of Jacob aside and made the calls. She continued calling most of the day with a short break for lunch. By the time of the client meeting, she'd whittled the list of people they hadn't yet heard from and printed the latest numbers.

As they sat with Russell and finalized the menu, Meryl turned to her. "You're coming to the gala, right? And you're bringing your boyfriend?"

Aviva's face heated. Meryl and Russell looked at her, waiting for her answer. It wasn't her attendance, but Jacob's, she was nervous about. "Yes, we'll be there."

"Good," Russell said. "I'm looking forward to meeting him. You said he's a law student?"

"He's studying for the bar exam right now. I can't wait for it to be over so we can actually see each other. Texting and calling gets old."

Russell laughed. "My son is a lawyer. I know the feeling. Luckily, he works for a small law firm, so we get to see him. His hours are long but manageable. Those big law firms? Whew, they're at their desks until two or three in the morning, then again at ten. Not a lifestyle I can understand."

A sour taste filled her mouth.

An hour later, they'd finished their meeting. Aviva took a short break to text Jacob.

so, ur coming to the gala
with me, right?

of course. can't wait!

really?

yeah, never made out in a science
center before. haven't been since
I was 8.

funny guy. luv u.

luv u too.

She put her phone away and smiled out the window. Come to think of it, she'd never made out there, either.

Jacob stared at the computer screen. He was supposed to study, but the words smudged into each other and created a pale color wash across the screen. Instead, his brain churned trying to decide what to do about Croft. He'd received a follow-up email from Stuart yesterday.

The email was friendly, as was the guy. He wanted to know how his finals went, how studying was going, and lastly, if he'd given any more thought to their proposal.

Most days, his brain barely had room for breathing and Aviva, but somehow, way in the back, he'd kept them there, thinking about the proposal in out-of-the-way places and during odd quiet times, like in the shower or on his way to the library. So yes, he'd given more thought to their proposal. The problem was, he didn't have an answer.

Stuart showed him something he hadn't considered before. The boutique agency tickled his fancy in unexpected ways. He'd be able to learn a lot, be involved in everything, and immerse himself in substantial projects. It appealed to him. But his dream had always been to be a high-powered lawyer. He loved the excitement and the power. He wasn't power hungry, at least not exclusively. But there was something appealing in it. He'd never been able to lose that desire.

With a sigh, he grabbed his phone and stalked out of the library. Outside, the muggy air did little to refresh him, but he inhaled anyway in an attempt to clear the cobwebs. Jabbing the buttons on his phone screen, he waited for Stuart to pick up. It went straight to voice mail.

"Hi Stuart, it's Jacob Black. Got your email. Listen, I'm sorry I haven't answered. Studying has been crazy. Give me a call when you have some time. Thanks."

They needed to talk. He didn't want to leave it to voicemail. Feeling a little more grounded about his decision, he returned to the library and settled in for another long day of studying.

When his phone rang, he was taking a lunch break. He answered and walked outside.

"Jacob, Stuart Rose here. Am I getting you at a bad time?"

"Not at all. Thanks for calling back."

"It's good to hear from you. Congratulations on graduating. I imagine studying keeps you pretty busy."

Jacob laughed. "You could say that."

"Just remember, it'll be over soon."

"That's what I tell myself every day."

"Good. So, have you come to a decision?"

Jacob took a deep breath. "I think I have."

"And?"

"And I appreciate the offer, but I have to pass. Smith Kane has been my dream since I first decided to go to law school and—"

"—you shouldn't have to lose out on your dream, Jacob. I get it. Can't say I'm not disappointed, but I'd hate for you to work for us and always wonder what might have been."

"Thank you. You don't know how much your understanding means to me."

"Well, I wish you the best of luck. Keep in touch."

"Will do. Thank you. And thank your associates as well."

"Take care."

As Jacob hung up, a little frisson of doubt traveled up his spine. He'd stuck to his plan and was following his dream. It couldn't be a mistake.

When the buzzing intercom announced Jacob's arrival, Aviva practically skipped to the doorway in anticipation. The elevator binged, the doors swooshed, and his lean form appeared silhouetted in the shadows.

"Hey there." He leaned down and kissed her.

She melted into him. His hands grasped her waist and caressed her back. He tasted good—his lips a little salty. She opened her mouth to encourage him. He spread his legs and pulled her tight to him as his tongue plundered her mouth. Every muscle and bone pressed against her. She moaned. She wanted—needed—to get closer. She sucked on him, raised her hands to run them through his hair. Closing her eyes, she inhaled his scent—spicy, male and all him. Too soon, he grabbed her waist and moved her away from him.

Her vision took a moment to focus. Her breathing was heavy as she came around. "What?"

"Not here," he panted.

Her gaze zeroed in on his mouth. She reached for his hand. Pulling him into her apartment, she shut the door with her foot and turned into his arms. He kissed her again and dragged his mouth away from her.

"Roommates?"

"Gone."

He lifted her up and hauled her along his body. The friction was pure torture. She wrapped her legs around his waist, her arms around his neck and opened her mouth to him once more. Supporting her bottom with his hands, he carried her to her bedroom, dropping her on the bed. She pulled her shirt off. His pupils dilated as he reached for his. With a wicked grin, she yanked the ends of the shirt out of his hands and pulled it over his head. His torso—hard pecs, flat stomach—was warm to the touch. His breath stuttered as she ran her hands over him. He pulled her into a kneeling position on the bed. Their bodies met, skin against skin. His hands reached around to unhook her bra. He paused, an unspoken question hanging between them. Nodding, she let him undress her.

Her body heated under the intensity of his gaze, but she remained where she was on the bed. He backed up a step. She could practically feel his gaze rove over every inch of her.

"You're beautiful," he whispered. He drew her close.

She sighed and buried her face into his neck. His fingers trailed down her back, around her hips and beneath the waistband of her shorts. She shivered. He repeated the action until she shifted. Her restless movements made him harden. She pressed her pelvis into him. His breath hitched. Trailing her fingers to his waistband, she joined him in their frenzy to remove the rest of their clothing. They squirmed out of their pants. He fumbled in his pocket before letting his shorts drop to the floor. The crinkling of foil pulled her up short as he held a condom in his hands.

"I hope you don't mind—"

"You brought—"

They spoke at the same time and halted together, a sheepish smile on his face.

"No, I don't mind," she said. "I'm glad."

She shimmied out of her panties. The condom dropped onto the bed, forgotten as he stared at her naked body. She picked it up, unwrapped it and sheathed him. His breathing became choppy. He leaned in to kiss her lips. She pulled away, teasing him. Biting her lip, his eyes widened as he followed her every move. She slipped off the bed and pushed him onto it, while she straddled his hips. He bucked, trying to join her, but she smoothed her hands over his pelvic bones and pressed him onto the bed. This was her time.

Leaning over, she trailed kisses from his forehead, down the bridge of his nose, over his chin, and across his throat. His adam's apple bobbed as her lips left a wet trail on his skin.

"Aviva," he whispered, but she covered his lips with her finger. He sucked it into his mouth and drew it in and out, mimicking what their bodies would soon do together.

A heaviness pooled in the pit of her stomach. She let him draw her finger deeper into his mouth. After a moment, she raked her fingers across his chest to his stomach. He bucked. This time, Aviva followed him with her body, rubbing against him.

Growling, he grabbed her waist. "I have to have you, now!"

He flipped them over, so he was on top. His eyes were almost black with desire. Now it was she who strained trying to reach him. A wicked grin crossed his face. He touched her, teased her, using his fingers to make her need build.

When she could stand it no more, she whispered, "Please."

Lowering himself, he penetrated her slowly, letting her body adjust to him. His weight was a relief. As they moved together, their bodies became one. They rocked, tension building in her as they reached higher and higher for climax. Pressure built. Her breathing increased in time with his. He plunged deeper and faster. She closed her eyes and arched her back. Wave after wave of climax rolled through her. Light burst behind her eyelids and pulsating sounds filled her ears. Moments later, Jacob roared her name as he joined her over the edge.

She floated down and lay spent, him draped on top of her, their breathing slowing together. His fingers fiddled with her hair. She stroked his back as she became more aware of her surroundings. Together, they drifted off to sleep.

When she opened her eyes, he lay next to her, watching her, a small smile on his face.

"I love you," he said.

"I love you, too."

"I've wanted to do this for a long time." He brushed her hair out of her face, traced her jawline with his finger. "You're beautiful."

Her face heated and Jacob laughed at her. She stuck out her tongue at him and joined in. Cuddling against him, she rested, listening to the beat of his heart.

"I spoke to Stuart today."

She smiled when she realized whom he was talking about. "Did you accept the job?" A position there would be perfect. He'd work hard and probably have long hours, but there would still be time for the two of them. They could find a way to balance things. She felt him sigh before he spoke.

"No, I thanked him for the offer, but I want to try Smith Kane. I've always wanted to do this. I need to see what happens."

How would they survive? They barely saw each other now. The only way she handled it was because it was short-term. Long term? She closed her eyes as her heartbeat raced.

She loved Jacob. He was different from her dad. She had to trust him.

She tried to stifle her disappointment. This had always been a possibility. Smith Kane was his dream. Who was she to get in the way of it?

"You should follow your dream." *Even though it's my nightmare.*

"You're not mad?"

Terribly disappointed. "No, I'm not mad. It's your decision to make."

He gazed into her eyes. "I will make time for us. I promise." He kissed the tip of her nose, and she tried to stifle the doubt that struggled to reach the surface.

CHAPTER TWENTY-ONE

The blare of an alarm penetrated Jacob's dreams. He reached his arm across his bedside table, shut it off, grabbed his phone, and held it to his bleary eyes. Some of his fatigue lessened when he saw the text from Aviva.

good luck today!

With a smile, he rubbed the sleep from his eyes. At seven in the morning, traffic rolled beneath his window. Horns honked and trucks rumbled. For most people, it was a regular day. For him, it was the start of his professional life. It would determine his future. He tried to shake off the nerves that twisted around him, clenched his stomach, and squeezed his head. Nerves were useless. They wouldn't help him ace the exam; they would only make him doubt himself.

He showered, ate breakfast, and headed to the Jacob Javits Convention Center where the exam was located. After registering, he waited until it was time to begin, his nerves buzzing like an electric wire.

Three hours and fifteen minutes later, the doors opened. He followed the other test takers out of the exam room for a lunch break. He was exhausted. His mind hummed with all the possible answers flitting through his brain. He continued to analyze the questions, turned over his responses, and wondered if there was anything he could have done differently. A bump on the shoulder brought him out of his reverie.

"Sorry," said another student, who continued down the hall.

With a shake of his head, Jacob made his way to the cafeteria, bought his lunch, and found an empty table. He pulled out his phone. "Hey, Avs, it's me."

"Hey, how's the exam?"

"Ugh, about like I expected, but exhausting. I still have the afternoon session to sit through, and again tomorrow."

"And then you're finished. You can do this. I know you can." Her voice was firm, filled with a belief he needed right now.

"Thanks. I needed to hear you, to know you were in my corner."

"Always," she said. "Are you at lunch?"

"Yeah."

"Well, eat. I can talk while you chew."

He laughed. Some of his tension escaped. He listened to her chatter about the last-minute preparations for the gala, a funny story about Hannah, a complaint about Meryl. By the time he'd finished his sandwich, he was much calmer. "Thanks for talking me through."

"Feel better now?"

"Much."

"Good, now go ace your test."

He cleaned his spot and returned to the test room. Three hours later, he finished with day one. He texted Aviva.

day 1 done. barely see straight.
going home. luv u.

so proud of you. 1 day left.
sleep. luv u too.

The next day was a repeat of the one before. By the end of the day, Jacob was wiped. He staggered out of the exam and almost missed Aviva, who stood by the side of the building waiting.

"Hey." She took him in her arms.

He leaned into her, soaking in the feel of her. Burying his face in her hair, he inhaled her floral scent. He tried to let the stress of the day evaporate.

After a moment, he pulled away. "What are you doing here?"

"I thought I'd meet you when you were finished." His exhaustion must have shown on his face because she cupped his chin and stroked his cheek. "Don't worry. I know you're beat. I'll just see you home and leave you to relax."

He took her hand as they turned toward the corner. "You're amazing, you know."

She swung their arms in time to their steps. "Do you want to walk or ride?"

"I need to stretch, so let's walk."

They walked without saying much. Her grip in his was firm, her skin soft. New York City at the end of July was like walking into a wet sponge—high humidity, high heat, little air movement. The Jacob Javits Convention Center was out of the way of most commuters and tourists, so the sidewalks were filled with other law students. Jacob was reassured to see everyone looked as exhausted as he felt. By the time they made it to Penn Station, he was done.

"Do you mind if we get a rideshare?"

"Of course not. Would you rather take the PATH?"

"Not in this heat." After waiting in the rideshare section for their car to arrive, he held the door for her. When he climbed in, he gave the driver his address. "I'll have him drop you off as well."

She rested a hand on his arm. "Wait. Let me see you settled first, then I'll go to my apartment."

He shook his head. "That's not necessary."

"You're barely functional. Let me make sure you get home okay. I promise I won't stay long."

As he leaned against the headrest, he muttered, "I don't want you to think I'm trying to get rid of you."

"Don't worry. I know. Now rest."

He closed his eyes. He should make sure she was okay in a cab. She was still recovering... What seemed like a moment later, she shook him. "Wake up," she whispered. "We're here."

He stumbled out of the car. "Do you want to get dinner?"

She laughed as she reached for his arm. "You're swaying on your feet. Come on. You need to go to bed."

As they made their way to his apartment, he tried to string words together to make a sentence. "Was the ride okay for you? I'm sorry I fell asleep."

She took his keys out of his hand and opened the door. "It was fine. You want to lie on the sofa or your bed?"

"Are you offering?" He wiggled his eyebrows.

She laughed. "I prefer sex when my boyfriend remembers who he's having it with, thanks. Or is even aware he's having it."

"Ouch." He collapsed on the bed. "At least come lie with me. I'll be fine in a minute."

"Mm hmm. Sure." But she lay next to him. Jacob let out a deep breath.

Her hands stroked his forehead. He closed his eyes. He couldn't have kept them open with toothpicks. His body felt weighted, his limbs heavy. He wanted to thank her, to tell her he would be fine, to say he loved her. He opened his mouth, but his tongue wouldn't form the words. He'd take a little nap after which he'd talk to her, reassure her, tell her he...

Aviva watched him sleep. She should leave, let him rest undisturbed. She'd told him she would. Of course, he hadn't expected to fall asleep. He probably didn't hear half of what she'd said.

He'd fallen asleep a half hour ago. She'd like to think it was because her hands stroked his face, but the truth was he'd probably have fallen asleep standing up. It was a little scary how tired he was. The Jacob she knew was always on, always prepared. He always looked out for her. This Jacob was an anathema.

She'd gone to the Javits Center because she couldn't wait to find out how the test went. She wasn't prepared for utter exhaustion on two legs to stumble out of the building. He didn't appear much different than anyone else who'd taken the exam. Adam had stumbled in a little while ago. By the crash that accompanied his movements, she was confident he was in the same shape as Jacob. Whoever created zombie movies was obviously a former law student.

Seeing him like this concerned her. She wanted to see him home safe into bed. Well, he was home safe and in bed. Snoring, actually. Why was she still here?

She ran her hands through his hair, which had grown a little long on top. She kind of liked the tousled look. It was silky against her skin. He'd probably cut it all off before he started his new job...she shook her head. Denial. That was the way to go. She wouldn't think about his job. Not now.

He'd been good to her when she was hurt. Better than she could have possibly imagined.

I mean, seriously, who else has a boyfriend in the middle of finals who camps out on her floor?

Now it was her turn to repay the favor. This didn't come close to what he'd done for her, but it was a start. Leaning over, she placed a whisper-soft kiss on his lips and left the room. In the living room, she found paper and a pen and wrote him a note:

> *Get some rest and call me when you wake up. I love you.*
>
> *Aviva*

Outside, she debated whether to call a rideshare or take the PATH train. Cars still made her nervous, but the PATH would be scorching at this time of year and day. So, she requested a rideshare on her phone, and five minutes later it drew up in front of Jacob's building. As she climbed in, she took a last look at his window.

He was one step closer to his dream. Now if only his dream and hers could mesh.

Aviva's hands shook as she fastened the clasp of her formal cocktail dress. A pale sage with sequins and beads, it oozed class and sophistication, in spite of not being black. Strapping on three-inch silver sandals, she grabbed her silver clutch and a gossamer shawl, and scrutinized herself.

Her hair was slicked back with a small rhinestone barrette. Her makeup was subtle. She gazed up and down at her reflection and let out a breath. Pretty good. Now she hoped Jacob wasn't late.

She checked her watch and turned out the bedroom light.

Erica was in the living room. "Girl, you look fab!"

"Thank you."

"Turn around."

Aviva spun in a slow circle. Erica let out a low whistle. "Jacob will be all over you."

She shook her head. "He can't. I'm working the gala."

"You've been working the gala all day. It's time you had a chance to enjoy it."

Aviva massaged her lower back. She sat on the edge of the sofa trying to not wrinkle the fabric. Erica was right. Today had been brutal. She'd been at her office this morning at seven, putting the finishing touches on the last-minute details. As soon as they were allowed into the science center to set up, she followed the caterer and Lacey around, making sure their set-up matched her plans. The lighting had been triple checked, as had the music. She'd returned to her apartment with enough time to shower and change. There was nothing left to be done. The gala would either be a failure or a success. Tonight, if she could put her nerves aside, she might actually be able to enjoy the evening.

"I hope so."

The doorbell rang. Erica motioned for her to stay where she was. "I want to see his reaction." She winked.

Jacob entered the living room. He stopped short. His eyes widened. He opened his mouth. His lips moved, but no sound came out. Clearing his throat, he tried again. "You look...stunning." He took her hand, helping her rise from the sofa, and spun her around.

Apparently both he and Erica wanted to turn her into a spinning top. Or maybe the twirling ballerina inside the music box, except no music played. Aviva shook her head. She was obviously exhausted if she had random conversations inside her head.

"Thank you." He filled out his tuxedo well. She resisted the urge to pull every shred of clothing off him. There was something about a man in a tux that made her mouth water. Jacob in a tux, well, she would have to walk with a feed bucket hanging around her neck to catch the drool. His broad shoulders looked broader. His flat stomach looked flatter. His debonair look made her want to swoon.

"You look amazing."

He ushered her toward the door. "Are you ready?"

"I hope so."

"Relax, it will be wonderful." He squeezed her shoulders then opened the door.

Downstairs, they took a cab to the Liberty Science Center. The line of cars to drop off guests at the museum was long. It took approximately ten minutes for them to be able to exit the cab. With a last adjustment of her skirt, she took Jacob's elbow.

Inside the main entrance, she paused. The entryway was light and airy, with mobiles hanging from the ceiling. Signs and displays directed patrons to various scientific galleries. With large windows and high ceilings, voices echoed throughout the hall, making it seem more crowded than it actually was at this time of night.

"Ready?" Jacob took her hand.

With a nod, she gripped his hand, her stomach trembling. They proceeded to the Governors Hall. She stopped at the entrance.

It was perfect. Colored lights bathed the room in muted reds and gold. Spotlights highlighted the statues of Apollo and Hippocrates. Tables were arranged with tablecloths, flowers, and tea lights. Soft music played from the quartet hidden to the side. In the darkness, the windows acted like mirrors, reflecting images from inside the vast room.

Guests milled about. Aviva spotted many she recognized. Meryl and Russell stood on the other side of the room. She turned to Jacob. "Come on, let me introduce you to my boss and our client."

They maneuvered through people and wait staff, grabbed a glass of white wine and a Pilsner glass of beer. Finally, they reached Meryl and Russell.

"Aviva, we were just talking about you." Meryl smiled. She looked with interest at Jacob as Aviva stepped forward.

"Hello, Meryl, Russell. May I introduce my boyfriend, Jacob Black? Jacob, this is Meryl Kreptke and Russell Newton."

Everyone shook hands, and she tried to breathe. It wasn't quite as nerve wracking as introducing a boyfriend to one's parents for the first time, but it was close. Added to the stress of the situation—a client event where Meryl had to make sure everything succeeded—Aviva didn't think anyone would show to their best advantage. But Meryl's smile was genuine. Russell wore a warm look on his face. Aviva exhaled.

"Ah, the famous Jacob," Meryl gushed. "I wondered when I'd get to meet you!"

"Nice to meet you, Meryl. I've heard a lot about you."

"Oh my, I hope it was good."

Jacob nodded, with a laugh. He pulled Aviva closer.

"Jacob, a pleasure," said Russell. "It's been wonderful working with Aviva." He looked around the room. "She and Meryl pulled off quite an event."

"I know they worked very hard on it," Jacob said.

Aviva was struck by his graciousness in including Meryl in his statement.

"They did. I've enjoyed getting to know her better," he said. "Have you two tried the hors d'oeuvres?"

"No, we just arrived," Aviva said.

"Well, go on, taste what you chose," Russell said.

Aviva turned to Meryl. "Is there anything you need me to do first?"

Meryl shook her head. "No, the cocktail hour runs itself. Russell will handle dinner and the presentations." She turned to Russell. "Is there anything you need from us?"

He shook his head. "No, as long as you're here to deal with any emergencies that might come up, you're free to enjoy yourselves."

"You heard him," Meryl said. "Go enjoy yourselves."

Jacob turned to her. "Shall we?"

"Alright, we'll see you both later." Aviva took his arm. They walked to one end of the room where they had a view of the entire venue.

As they helped themselves to hors d'oeuvres offered by passing wait staff, Jacob turned to her. "You're the loveliest woman in this room."

Aviva hastened to swallow her stuffed mushroom before she choked on it. Washing it down with a swallow of wine, she turned to Jacob. "Thank you."

"Is it wrong I want to kiss you?"

She looked at her feet to hide the blush she knew spread across her face. "No, but we're a little exposed."

"I can fix that." He pulled her into a corner adjacent to the main entrance of the room. With an overhanging soffit and shadows cast from the lighting, the area was less exposed than their previous location. He pulled her to him, but she pushed against his chest. "You can't kiss me here either," she said.

"Why not?"

"Because someone will see!"

"See you kissing your boyfriend? I can see how it would be a problem." He placed gentle kisses across her forehead.

Aviva blinked. Her body leaned toward him, as if it staged a silent mutiny.

"But this is a work event. I need to be professional." Despite her vocal protests, she tilted her head allowing him better access to her neck.

"You can do both," he murmured as he trailed kisses to her collarbone.

With a whimper, she gave in, wrapped her arms around his neck and pressed her body against his. He felt good, so solid and safe. Their lips met. All sound gave way to a rushing noise in her ears and the pounding of her heart. His hands skimmed her ribcage, lowered to her waist and cupped her buttocks. She wanted him.

Clasping her against him, he maneuvered so they were deeper into the shadows, with her hidden from view. She shifted against him. He groaned. Smiling into his lips, she slipped her hands beneath his jacket and stroked his back. His heart pounded as if in her chest. He hardened against her. She slid her hands lower.

He jerked. "Okay, we need to stop now." He tore his mouth away and took deep breaths.

She started to pull away, but he held her in front of him. "If you don't mind, I need a moment."

Aviva snickered. "Must be pretty embarrassing to be a man."

"You have no idea."

She let her gaze travel up and down his body as she licked her lips.

"You're not helping," he growled.

With her hand on his chest, she widened her eyes. "Oh, was I supposed to help?"

"Witch."

She laughed, rested her forehead on his shoulder. A few minutes later, she felt him take a deep breath. "Better now?"

"Yes, thanks."

"You know, if I'd known we were going to hide out and kiss, I'd have taken you to all my favorite spots," she said.

"You have favorite kissing spots? Here? How many times have you been here? I'm not sure I like that."

"Quite a few actually, both as a visitor and for my job. I also have a favorite kissing partner."

He folded his arms across his chest. His forehead creased into a frown. He was cute when he tried to look foreboding. "Oh?"

"Mm hmm."

"And who would that be?" He raised one eyebrow, reminding Aviva of a pirate.

She squashed the laugh as it bubbled up. "Oh dear, I really need to mingle with the guests."

He grabbed her elbow before she could get away. "Oh no you don't. Meryl and Russell both said you were free until the meal." He lightened his grip but continued to maintain pressure.

She stared at his hand on her skin. "I know, but I see people walking in whom I really do have to greet. You'll be okay on your own, won't you?"

She moved toward the group who'd entered.

"We're not done, you know."

Turning to look at him over her shoulder, she grinned. "Oh, I know." With a wink, she continued on her way. Catching up with the couple that had just entered the Governors Hall, she chatted with them about her client's medical research.

"This is beautiful," the woman said. "Superb job."

Her husband nodded. A flush of pleasure warmed Aviva's cheeks. After a sufficient amount of time, she moved on to a group of five people, colleagues of Russell.

"You must be the woman responsible for all of this," one of the men said.

"Meryl and I are, yes. We worked with some amazing people on this."

"Modesty, a trait I most admire," another man said.

"I admire this room," a third said. "If the fundraising is even half as impressive as the venue, you'll have my admiration for life."

Aviva thanked them before making her exit. Twenty minutes later, after mingling with more than half of the guests, she found Jacob near the bar, and made her way toward him, shaking hands, accepting a glass of wine, and smiling at everyone. It was another five minutes before she finally reached him. She still glowed from all the praise she'd received. She couldn't wait to share it with Jacob.

He spoke with a tall, older gentleman with grey hair. Jacob placed an arm around her shoulders as she approached. "Avs, let me introduce you to John Smith, founder and hiring partner of Smith Kane. John, this is my girlfriend, Aviva Shulman. She's the one responsible for tonight's event."

Aviva held out her hand. John's hand was strong and hard. She felt each bone and ligament working to grasp hers. She looked into warm brown eyes overshadowed by bushy white eyebrows.

"It's a pleasure to meet you, Aviva. You've pulled off a remarkable event. I look forward to experiencing the rest of it."

"Thank you. I hope you enjoy yourself."

"I am. I just talked to Jacob about ways to deal with the adjustment to a large law firm such as ours."

"Really?" She tipped her head, wondering what advice he'd given.

"Well, especially during those first five years, the hours are taxing. He'll need to adapt to little sleep and lots of pressure. Of course, it helps to have a girlfriend as successful as you." He spread his arms around to encompass the room. "You'll understand the pressures he faces, as I'm sure you faced similar ones in order to pull off such a successful event."

Aviva felt a chill. She wondered if the air-conditioning suddenly kicked down a few degrees more. She nodded and rubbed her arms. They were cold to the touch.

"Of course, you'll have to get used to not seeing each other often, although I know many of the first years arrange to meet their girlfriends and boyfriends for lunch or dinner at their desks."

Jacob's arm tightened around her, but she felt no warmth.

"Despite those negatives, your learning experience can't be beat. You'll get to work on some of the most nationally recognized cases, meet some of the world's most prominent attorneys and judges, and mingle with some of the most successful businessmen and women, as well as society's elite."

"It sounds impressive," Jacob said.

"What would you think of working on cases for the New York Supreme Court, Appellate Division?"

Aviva felt Jacob's intake of breath. His ribs contracted against her side. His hand gripped her shoulder. "That would be amazing."

John's eyes gleamed. They reminded her of a hawk eyeing his prey. "We've got one case there now with two more headed there soon. The attorneys on those cases are some of the most renowned in the country. You'll get a chance to work with them. If you play your cards right, you'll also go to the courtroom."

"I would love that."

John placed his hands on both of their shoulders. "Stick with us, Jacob. The possibilities are endless."

Aviva blinked. She forced her mouth into a smile. "I think they're just about to make an announcement for us to sit down."

As if on cue, the lights blinked.

Russell took to the microphone. "Ladies and Gentlemen, please take your seats. Dinner is about to begin."

Jacob shook John's hand. "It was great to meet you, John."

"You too, Jacob. I look forward to working with you."

Aviva led the way to their table near the front of the room.

"I can't believe I ran into him here." He held out her chair and sat next to her.

"Did he recognize you or you him?"

"I recognized him. He had no idea who I was until I introduced myself. But I thought he was very nice."

"Yeah, he seemed it."

Jacob turned toward her. "What's wrong?"

She spread her napkin on her lap, smoothing it over her dress. "Hmm? Nothing."

He stared at her for a minute as if trying to figure her out, but this was a business event. She'd never be anything but polished and professional. She couldn't crack here. Her gaze swept the room. It was filled with the sort of people John talked about to Jacob. The crème of society. At $10,000 a table, they had to be.

Jacob was in his element. He'd schmoozed with John. Now he talked to the person on his left, someone from Russell's firm. Aviva didn't remember his name, but as course after course was served, Jacob kept the table entertained with stories. Aviva joined in where appropriate. She talked to the woman on her right, but in the back of her mind, she thought of Jacob's future.

She bit into her salmon with lemon-herbed butter.

"My lobster is delicious," the woman on her right remarked.

Aviva nodded. "As is my salmon." She didn't taste any of it. She continued to eat, trying not to gag. A few moments later, the room darkened. Aviva let out a sigh of relief as she lowered her fork. The fund-raising portion of the evening started, alleviating the need for conversation.

Of course, it provided time to think.

Russell ascended the podium. She listened with half an ear to his welcome speech and introduction of the CEO, all the while thinking about what John had said. Jacob rested his hand on her thigh. Its warmth seeped into her leg, but she was still cold. Freezing. As she would be every night she spent alone. The CEO joined Russell and thanked him, made a joke, and waited for the laughter to subside.

Aviva joined in along with the rest of the room, but it was hollow, even to her ears. There was a camaraderie here she couldn't adjust to, but Jacob was in his element. When the CEO called Meryl to help display the items for auction, Aviva tried to get more comfortable in her seat. But the seat was hard. No amount of padding or shifting changed her discomfort. Just like no amount of reassurance from Jacob could ease her worries about his new job. Jacob put his arm around her and pulled her against him. His arm was muscular, the tuxedo jacket soft to the touch, yet still she fidgeted. With a shake of her head, she pulled away. She sat straighter in her chair.

Meryl held the first item: a certificate entitling the bearer to a three-day weekend in the Hamptons, including guest lodging at a private estate on the ocean, golf and tennis privileges at one of its premier country clubs, a private winery tour for two, and dinners at two of the area's most famous restaurants. Bidding started at $5,000. The winner paid $25,000.

The next item was a private dinner for four cooked by a celebrity chef at the winner's home, with a wine steward and world-renowned French pastry chef. The opening bid was $10,000. It sold for $50,000.

Despite her mood, Aviva was astounded at how easily items sold. She craned her neck to see who bid. She found many hands raised for each item up for auction. Throughout the event, as coveted spots in private schools, weeklong vacations, luxury cars and boats, theater experiences, and more were auctioned off, Aviva could almost feel her jaw drop.

Yet Jacob remained unfazed. It was if he belonged in this world of the über rich, as if the lifestyle John enticed him with sank into his pores. He could be a part of this life. From his reaction, or lack of one, maybe he already was.

By the time the auction ended, and dessert was served, Aviva's stomach was heavy, as if she'd already eaten more than she could fit into her body. She picked at her Schaum torte without actually tasting it.

"Are you alright?" Jacob whispered in her ear.

She gave a half smile. "Yes, I'm just full. Do you want this?"

With a nod, they switched plates. He dug into her untouched dessert with gusto.

Russell came over and leaned toward her ear. "Come with me, I'd like to introduce you to our CEO."

She followed.

"Marcus, this is Aviva Shulman, the woman I told you about. She and Meryl are responsible for this evening."

Marcus shook her hand, his grasp firm. "Aviva, it's good to meet you. Thanks to your amazing event, we've raised more than two hundred fifty thousand dollars for medical research. We couldn't have done it without you."

She nodded wondering when he'd release her hand. "It was my pleasure. I enjoyed working with Russell and Meryl on this. I'm happy it was a success."

Marcus handed her a business card. "I'd like to talk to you about some upcoming events we have planned."

Aviva took his card. "Meryl and I would be happy to help you."

"Good. I think you and I should get together to go over the preliminary details first. I'll have my secretary call you."

He walked away, leaving Aviva staring after him.

Russell laughed. "Don't worry, he's always like that."

"Okay, but he really should talk with Meryl too."

"You'll remind him of it when he calls. I'm glad he was taken with you. I think we can continue to do some great work together. Now, if you'll excuse me, I have to say good-bye to some people. Thanks again for an amazing night."

Russell was right—it was an amazing night. She couldn't guarantee tomorrow, though.

CHAPTER TWENTY-TWO

Jacob stood outside Aviva's apartment, filled with despair. He stared at the closed door wondering what happened. He was on the wrong side of it. Instead of standing in the hallway alone, he should be inside with Aviva.

One look at her in her spectacular dress, and he'd envisioned an after-gala scenario far different than this. It included removing her dress inch by inch, kissing her bare skin and making love to her all evening, with a walk of shame sometime around sunrise. Standing in the hallway, wearing his suddenly annoying tuxedo, and feeling frustrated wasn't in his event plan. Except she'd pleaded exhaustion and shut him out. Literally. With a sigh, he jammed his hands in his trouser pockets and strode to the elevator. He punched the button and traveled to the lobby, staring at his glossy shoes the entire way.

By the time he made it home, he was frustrated, tired, angry, and confused as well. Why did she shut him out? What was wrong? Why wouldn't she tell him?

He reflected on the evening. She'd seemed nervous, but fine when he arrived to pick her up. Once at the gala, she built a wall of professionalism he'd never witnessed before, but it filled him with pride. He'd put a chink in the wall when he dragged her into the shadows to kiss her. Those kisses softened her for a few moments, whet his appetite for later. Her comments about kissing places and partners turned him on, even as he'd pretended jealousy. But she'd left and everything had changed. What had happened?

When she'd joined him and John, talking about his future law position, she'd been quiet. Could it have been the focus on his hours that bothered her? He tried to remember exactly what was said and how she'd reacted.

At the table, he'd put his hand on her leg, hoping to reignite the spark from the shadows, but he wasn't sure if she'd realized it was there. Sure, she was there in body, but her mind and spirit were far away. When they had left? She'd barely spoken a word to him.

Of course she was tired. It had been an exhausting event. Hell, it had been an exhausting week for her. But fatigue wasn't stopping her from letting him in. Something else was. He was determined to find out.

He dialed her number, but it went straight to voicemail.

"It's Aviva. Sorry I missed your call. Please leave a message."

"Aviva, it's Jacob. Are you okay? Call me."

Placing his phone on the dresser, he undressed and got ready for bed. As he climbed into bed, he checked the phone for the last time, but there was nothing. He texted her.

hey, what's up?

He stared at the screen for five minutes, but she didn't respond. With a sigh, he put the phone on the nightstand and turned out the light. He'd give her tonight, but tomorrow he would get some answers.

Aviva awoke to her buzzing phone. Before she reached for it, she knew it would be Jacob. It was. Multiple texts, starting last night:

hey, what's up?

r u okay?

please answer me.

i need to see u.

i'm coming over.

She sat in bed and typed her response:

meet @ coffee shop.

10 minutes?

40

k

She scrubbed her face free of leftover makeup. She splashed it with cold water to try to get the swelling down, but a night full of tears had done damage. There was no way he'd miss it. He was too observant. Throwing on jeans shorts and a T-shirt, she stuffed her feet into flip-flops—those heels last night had hurt—grabbed her purse and left the apartment.

Jacob stood outside the coffee shop, the one they thought of as theirs. His forehead was wrinkled. He scanned the sidewalk looking for her. His face cleared as soon as he spotted her, but at her approach, his frown returned.

She took deep breath. "Hi."

"Hi." He leaned forward to give her a kiss, and she turned and gave him her cheek. "I was worried about you," he said. "Is everything okay?"

The hostess waved them to an empty table. The waitress appeared with a coffee carafe. Both nodded, and she poured and left them alone.

"Not really."

He took both her hands in his. "Tell me what's wrong. I thought the gala was fantastic."

"It was. It's not that."

He swore under his breath. "Did John freak you out? I knew he did. Listen, Aviva, it's not going to be…"

"Jacob, stop. It's not John. I mean, it is, but it's not. There's always going to be a John, whether it's him or someone else. I can't compete with that."

"Compete? What do you mean? There's no competition."

She chewed her bottom lip. "I can't compete with your dream, Jacob."

"What are you talking about? The hours? Sure, they'll be long in the beginning…"

"You don't understand me, Jacob. Your dream is to be a big, high-powered attorney. You'll be amazing at it. I watched you when you talked to John. There was a light about you I can't even explain. Sure, the hours will be long, but your attention will always be on your work, as it should be. I can't live that life."

"Is this about your dad? I've told you over and over I'm not like him. I showed you how different I am from him."

She placed a hand over his. "You're a completely different person than he is. I'm not comparing you to him, but you'll always be drawn to that high-powered life. I can't, and I won't, stop you from trying a case in front of the Supreme Court! I don't want to be that kind of girlfriend, but I don't want that kind of boyfriend, either."

He reared back in his chair. "Are you serious?"

She nodded as numbness spread throughout her body. She felt like she was getting a buzz, but the only thing in her coffee was milk.

Jacob's chair screeched as he pushed away from the table. He stalked out.

Aviva closed her eyes. She wanted to call him back. She wanted to run after him. But she couldn't. He needed to make a choice. This time, it couldn't be her.

Jacob's breathing was labored. His chest was on fire. At the corner of James Street and University Avenue, he bent over, hands braced on his knees. He tried to catch his breath as he and Adam waited for the light to change. Adam had decided they needed to get into shape—too many days and nights studying and eating crappy food had taken their toll—and he'd chosen running, dragging Jacob along with him. It had been three days since his breakup with Aviva. Jacob tried to protest, but Adam hadn't listened. He simply pushed him into the hallway and only allowed him to turn around to don shorts and running shoes before pushing and prodding him along on the sidewalk. Too depressed to care, it was easier to go along with Adam's wishes. However, an inability to draw in enough oxygen and Jacob started to think staying holed up in his dark room, surrounded by stale pizza would be an improve-ment over this.

"I'm done," he gasped, right before the light changed.

"No, you're not." Adam pulled him off the curb. It was either cooperate and move his feet, or land on his face in the middle of the intersection. He didn't think "roadkill" was high on the "Jewish Mother's List of Their *Kindelah's* Achievements," so he forced one foot in front of the other. He plotted ways to kill Adam in his sleep.

After what seemed like ages, they stopped. Jacob sank onto the nearest bench. He forced his head be-tween his knees.

"That was pretty good for your first time, Jake. You'll feel much better after we do this for a few weeks."

It took Jacob a few seconds to register Adam had spoken. It took several more until he could control his breathing long enough to speak. "You're out of your effing mind."

Adam laughed. Jacob would have gotten angry his friend was laughing at his obvious misfortune except he was amazed he had enough breath to laugh.

"Come on. This run was good for you."

"Are you insane?"

Adam stretched. He fixed Jacob with a knowing stare. "Tell me what you thought about on the run."

"All the different ways to kill you."

"Exactly."

Too tired to parse out what Adam was talking about, he stared at him.

"You spent all your time thinking of ways to kill me, rather than moping about Aviva."

Hearing her name was like getting hit in the chest with a fastball. Once again, Jacob struggled to breathe. He tried to hide it by drinking from the bottle of water Adam tossed him. He had difficulty swallowing. Yeah, he'd been distracted. But if jogging was what it took to get Aviva off his mind, he really might die.

"You don't have to kill me."

"No, but if that's what it takes to get you out of your room, maybe I do."

Should he talk to Adam? Aviva was the only person he'd ever confided in before, but she wasn't an option any longer. Maybe Adam could help him. "I'm pissed at her. She has no faith in me, no matter how many times I showed her I was different from her father. I showed her. Her father's an ass. I'm not like that. I can't believe she compares me to him."

Adam clapped him on the shoulder. "I'm sorry, Jake, that's a tough one. But think of it this way. You'll meet lots of women when you start your job next week, ones you'll have more in common with. So maybe this was a good thing."

As he hauled himself off the bench, he followed Adam on rubbery legs to their apartment. He thought about what Adam said. He couldn't possibly meet anyone better than Aviva.

CHAPTER TWENTY-THREE

Jacob stared bleary-eyed at the computer screen. The lines blurred and swirled before him. All the As swirled like Aviva's. He blinked. His fourth night in a row working until two in the morning. Technically, it was his twentieth, as he hadn't gotten home before four since he started here a month ago. Reaching blindly for his sixth—was it his sixth? Maybe it was his seventh?—ultra-large sized cup of iced coffee, he chugged it and wiped his mouth. Around him, muted conversations buzzed, punctuated by the occasional thump as another exhausted first year associate's head hit the desk. Usually, the person would wake up, mutter or groan and get to work. Occasionally, they'd be so tired they'd sleep right through, sometimes until morning. There had been more than one occasion when Jacob passed an associate leaving, yesterday's clothes rumpled, his or her face stained with drool, as

Jacob was coming in for the day. They'd nod, not even embarrassed anymore. Embarrassment took too much effort. All of the first years' efforts were focused on survival.

Survival. That was something you did on a deserted island, or after an accident or trauma. It wasn't something you should have to associate with your job, especially when you were twenty-five. Visions of Aviva's face filled with recrimination, flitted through his brain. He was losing it.

"Hey, wake up! We're going out. You're coming with."

Jacob jumped at the sound of Chuck's voice. Chuck was also a first-year associate, a stereotypical frat boy. He had appointed himself the cruise director on this "ship from hell," as he called it. He always came up with ways to entertain everyone. Jacob spent half the time wondering how the heck he didn't get fired. But he'd read some of his briefs. They were brilliant, so maybe they saved his ass.

He shook his head. "Going out? Where the hell are you going at two in the morning?"

"Last call is in an hour. There's a bar across the street a little way. If we hurry, we can make it."

"Sorry, I can't. Too much work."

Chuck closed Jacob's books. "There will always be too much work. It'll still be here later. Let's go."

Too tired to argue and somehow finding logic in his argument, he followed Chuck out of the office.

There were four other associates in the bar, as tired as he was. They all gave halfhearted waves.

Nursing their drinks, they made some small talk and discussed their cases. Like Jacob, they had put in inhuman hours for the past month. Like Jacob, they were all single.

"Do you ever wonder if it's worth it?" Jacob asked, when there was a lull in the conversation.

"Doesn't matter if it's worth it," said Katie, the blonde on the end. "I have college and law school loans to pay."

The others nodded.

"But there has to be more to law than this."

"There is," said Phil, Jacob's office mate. "It's called *making partner at thirty.*"

Thirty. Five years from now. Five years of working his ass off like this, alone, with countless days of falling into bed at four in the morning and returning at ten. Great if you were a robot, less if you were human.

"Come on," said Chuck. "It's only the first month. We'll get used to it."

Conversation moved on to the partners they worked for. All agreed Jacob's boss was by far the best.

"You lucked out." Matt was in the firm's malpractice division. "Cole is a hard ass. I can't stand him."

Jacob thought about Robin. She was brilliant and passionate about environmental law, but tough. Not unfair, though, if you discounted her motto "work was life." She had no family. She spent as much time in the office as he did. This was what they thought was lucky?

"Yeah, but where's her life? She's a partner but still at the firm the same number of hours as I am."

"That's much better," said Katie. "At least she shares the time with you. Mike puts in some time and goes to the golf course. He expects me to have everything ready for him when he gets back. I can't wait until I have associates under me."

The others agreed, but Jacob stayed silent. He didn't want to make others miserable. Abject misery wasn't what he'd bargained for. He grabbed his phone to check the time. He started when he saw a voice mail notification. Aviva? As his eyes focused, he identified the sender as his mother. His stomach dropped. He'd barely talked to her since he started working. He hadn't told her about the breakup.

When are you and Aviva coming to Shabbat services with me?

He swallowed. Luckily it was too late to respond. Looked like they'd have an interesting conversation. If he ever had time to talk to her.

Aviva's voicemail message notification was highlighted. She frowned. Other than Hannah or her mother, she hadn't spoken to too many people recently. Tapping her phone, she listened to the message.

"Hi, Aviva, this is Karen."

Aviva's stomach dropped.

"I hope you don't mind my calling, but it's impossible to get hold of Jacob these days, as I'm sure you know, so I thought I'd call you to find out how things are. Please call me when you have a chance. I'm worried."

Mind her calling? Guess it depended on how much she liked breathing, eating, and functioning. Because Karen's voice made her stomach hurt. Her throat squeezed shut. Any thoughts about her current work project flew straight out the window. She looked toward the sun filtering into her office, without noticing the beauty. Should she call her back?

With a sigh, she closed the door and dialed Karen.

"Hi, Aviva. How are you?"

Did she really ask her that question? "I'm okay, Mrs. Black, and you?"

"Aviva, I've told you...what's wrong? You don't sound like yourself."

She sighed. "I'm doing the best I can."

"Oh, honey, are Jacob's hours getting to you?"

"Um..." Wait, it wasn't possible, was it?

"You know it won't be for forever, right? He'll be able to have more flexibility as he works longer. Although, I have to admit I don't like them either."

She didn't know. "Mrs. Black?"

"Karen, Aviva."

"Karen?"

"Yes, dear?"

"We broke up."

The silence on the other end lengthened. For a moment, Aviva thought the phone had been disconnected.

"You what?" The question was whispered. From her interactions with Karen, Aviva knew she never whispered, unless she spoke about a friend getting some disease. Or plastic surgery.

"We broke up. I'm sorry, I thought you knew."

"No, I didn't. When was this?"

"The beginning of August. I'm really sorry. I didn't mean to be the one to break it to you. Certainly not like this." More than a month ago, and Jacob hadn't said anything to her.

"No, sweetheart, don't apologize. What happened? Was it his hours?"

She didn't like having to talk about it, but since Jacob hadn't said anything, she probably should answer. "It was my fault. I couldn't continue to see him knowing I'd prevent him from pursuing his dream." Aviva took a deep breath. "I know what it's like to love someone who is so dedicated to their job. I don't want to stop Jacob from doing what he loves."

"No, honey, of course not. It was very noble of you. I'm sure it was very difficult."

"Yeah," she whispered.

"I've just made it worse, I'm sure. Listen, Aviva, I'm going to let you go. But I'd like us to catch up one of these days. I'll call you, okay?"

"Um, okay." *Please don't.*

Jacob knocked on his mother's door. He listened for her footsteps trying to block out the last time he'd been here for dinner—three months ago—with Aviva. He wasn't sure which was worse, the length of time or the memory of Aviva. Liar. He knew. He just couldn't face it.

Somehow, he'd gotten the dinner break he'd asked for. He'd probably pay for it by working later than usual, but he needed to talk to his mother in person. This wasn't the kind of conversation they could have on the phone.

She opened the door. Her face lit up briefly with joy and longing, soon replaced by anger, which she tried unsuccessfully to mask.

He sighed. "Hi, Ma. Can I come in?"

She stood back. He walked into the apartment. After weeks holed up in his office, only departing at night, it was disorienting to be out in the daylight. He walked around the living room, touching the backs of chairs and sofas, feeling the soft carpet under his feet as if for the first time.

"Did you get Marcy's wedding invitation?"

He blinked. This was the first topic she wanted to discuss? The invitation had been addressed to him and a guest. At one time, that guest would have been Aviva. Not now. "Yeah, I looked at it briefly. I can't go."

"She's your cousin, Jacob."

"I know, but I have to work."

"On a Saturday night?"

"Every night, Ma."

She nodded. "Probably better that way. It would have been awkward for you to have to explain why you weren't bringing a plus one."

He froze. When he met her gaze, he saw recrimination reflected at him. She knew.

"How do you know?"

"Aviva told me."

Her name sliced through him, leaving a wake of pain. He staggered. What the hell?

"Bet you didn't expect that answer, Jacob, did you?"

"No, I didn't. When did you talk to her?" What did she sound like? How was she? Does she miss me? None of which, he could ask.

"Do you have any idea how awful it is to hear news like that from someone other than my son?"

"Ma, I haven't—"

"Why wouldn't you tell me you and Aviva broke up? Don't tell me you haven't had time."

"I haven't."

She fisted her hands on her hips and glared at him.

"Okay, I'm sorry. I haven't had a lot of time," he held his hands up to prevent her interruption," but I should have made time to tell you about it. I'm sorry."

"That's better. Now, talk to me. What happened?"

"What did she tell you?"

"That it's her fault."

He frowned. He hadn't expected that.

"Is it not true?"

"I don't know," he said. "She doesn't believe I'll make time for her, though I've shown her countless times I want to."

"Why doesn't she believe you?"

He ran his hand through his hair. He blew out a sigh. "I have no idea. I've never once not made time for her, ever."

"Yet you work where you do."

He squinted at her, trying to understand her goal. "Yes. But she knew that when we started the relationship."

"Just as you knew when you started the relationship, she wasn't interested in high-powered guys who are overly devoted to their jobs."

"I'm not overly devoted. I'm paying my dues."

"You're not the only one."

He jumped off the sofa and spun on her. "What does that mean? Are you trying to sneak in some dig? Because I don't need that right now."

"Relax, Jacob. It was meant exactly as it sounds. You're not the only one paying these dues. There's no dig."

She paused.

He returned to his seat, still confused.

"I pay the dues every time I want to see my son but can't because he's working. She paid the dues every time she couldn't talk to you or see you or spend time with you because you were studying. Every time she adjusted her schedule to fit yours. Every time she planned out her conversations with you in the moments you had to spare. I'm not judging you; I'm just stating the facts."

"But this is temporary. She knows I'm happy to make time for her."

"Is it? Does she?"

"Of course. We discussed it lots of times."

"What happens when you have the chance to be promoted, to have an important job or work on an important case? Is it 'paying your dues' or is it your lifestyle she has to adjust to? How is she a part of your life if she only fits into the leftover holes?"

"Are you on her side? Do you suggest I quit?"

"I'm always on your side, Jacob, no matter what. But I'm trying to make you see her side of things. That's all."

He dropped his head into his hands. He stared at the carpet between his feet. The Oriental pattern made him dizzy. He closed his eyes. "What the heck do I do?"

"You decide what your dream is. You pursue it. But you understand not everyone can follow your dream. Sometimes dreams cost you. So, you need to make sure your dream is worth it. If it is, you go full steam ahead. But if it isn't, change your course before it's too late."

She rubbed his back like she'd done when he'd been a child. For a moment, Jacob yearned to return to the easier, earlier time when the worst thing he faced was a monster under the bed. When a kiss could make everything bad go away. But he was an adult now. It was his job to fight the monsters and carve out his future.

He spent a half hour with his mother, catching up on all he'd missed in the past month, and eating the dinner she'd made him. He tasted nothing, heard little, but tried to give her the attention she'd lacked. Inside, though, he was lost.

After shoveling in his food, he headed back to work. He was late, but he didn't care. He took a few extra minutes to look at the people around him on the sidewalks. Most wore business attire and headed home. He, on the other hand, didn't. Like a salmon swimming against the current, he bobbed and weaved around the harried commuters, taking twice as many steps as he would if he were walking the same direction as the rest of them.

When he finally reached his office, swarms of people piled out the doors. He waited for a break in the pedestrian traffic to enter the revolving door. The elevators were another wait, as most stopped on each floor on their way down to the lobby. Finally, he stepped into one and made it to his office.

"Jacob, good, you're back. We're defending a motion tomorrow. I need you to finish this brief."

Jacob suppressed a laugh as one of the senior associates handed him a stack of papers. 'Brief' was a relative term. He took them and headed toward his desk, stopping when the senior associate continued speaking.

"Oh, and you'll come with us to court tomorrow. Wear a good suit."

Heart quickening, he sat at his desk and went to work, fisting his hand as it automatically reached for his phone to call Aviva. He no longer shared things with her. As much as his heart hurt, this was what he'd waited for. This was why his dream was worth it.

CHAPTER TWENTY-FOUR

The next day, after only three hours' sleep, Jacob met the senior associate and several other lawyers from his firm at the courthouse. He was prepared. His new suit fit perfectly. His shirt and tie coordinated. His shoes shone. Would Aviva have liked it? He shook his head to clear the thought. He knew the brief backward and forward, had rehearsed answers to questions, could provide information on any topic related to the brief, could cite multiple precedents. He was ready. He had no time for stray thoughts of her.

The senior associate looked him up and down. "Nice suit. Great tie. Wait here." He pointed to a bench outside the judge's chambers.

"I thought you said I'd go with you."

Mark pulled him aside. "I know. I'm sorry. But there are already four of us. If we bring anyone else inside, it will look like we're grandstanding. Wait here.

I'll fill you in when we're done. Good job on the brief, by the way."

Shock and disappointment flooded through him as he watched the doors close, leaving him out in the hallway. The last time he'd been on the wrong side of a door he'd lost his girlfriend. He loosened his tie and sat. And fumed. He'd done all the work. Put in all the hours. Rehearsed. For what? A chance to sit on a bench outside chambers? What kind of a learning experience was this, unless he was ever called upon and asked the number of floor tiles in the hallway? How many more times would he have to kill himself without the benefit of reaping the rewards? Probably too many to count.

"Jacob?"

Stuart Rose from The Croft Firm walked toward him.

He rose. "Stuart, how are you?"

"I'm well. Are you here to see Judge Abrams?"

"The senior associate is. And some others from my firm."

Stuart nodded knowingly. "You write the brief?"

Jacob nodded. His face burned.

"Good luck. I'll see you around."

Jacob clenched his jaw. His days on the wrong side of the door were over.

He was done.

Two and a half weeks later, Jacob took a deep breath and dialed Aviva's work number. The phone imprinted on his hand as he gripped it. She answered on the third ring.

"Aviva Shulman."

"Avs? It's Jacob."

The silence on the other end stretched for a long moment. He wondered if he should have given his last name. She wouldn't have forgotten him already, would she? Jacob was a pretty common name, but she'd recognize his voice, right?

Then he wondered if she'd hang up on him. He strained to listen for her breathing, for any sign she still was on the other end of the phone.

"Hi."

He melted into the chair as sweat popped on the back of his neck. It was only one word, but it was a start. "Hi. I was hoping you'd meet me for lunch."

"No."

His throat clogged. "Please?" Another silence. Jacob closed his eyes.

"It's not a good idea."

Okay, not the answer he'd hoped for, but she hadn't hung up. "Maybe, maybe not, but I want to discuss something with you. Please?"

"We're already talking. Can't you just tell me now?"

"No, it has to be in person."

She sighed. Within that breath of air, Jacob heard pain and frustration and something he couldn't identify. He willed her to agree. "I'm not trying to make things harder for you, Aviva. But it's important and I need you to meet with me."

"Alright."

"Thank you. I promise you won't regret it. Four thirty-one Greene Street, Jersey City. I'll meet you out front. Twelve, okay?"

"Yeah."

"I'll see you then. And Aviva? Thank you."

The clock on his computer read ten o'clock. Two hours to get ready.

She was an idiot. A glutton for punishment. *meshugener.* It had been eight weeks since she'd broken up with Jacob. She finally slept again, was finally able to go a few hours without thinking of him. Now she was meeting him. Why did she do this to herself?

Because he asked.

Aviva shook her head and looked out the car window. Just because he asked to meet her didn't mean she had to say yes. She wasn't his girlfriend. She was no longer at his beck and call. In fact, she had work to do.

But I'm curious.

He hadn't called her since she'd broken it off. When they'd dated, he'd contacted her at odd hours when trying to stay awake, or when he'd had a free moment late at night. She missed that, and the lift from hearing his voice. And the first time he did call, she agreed to make the biggest mistake of her life.

She was stuck in traffic at the light right before the address she'd given the driver. Through the window, she saw Jacob outside a building entrance. Her heartbeat increased. Her throat went dry. He looked better than she remembered. Sun glinted off the crown of his head, casting mahogany highlights in his hair. He leaned against the wall, one knee bent, hands in his pockets. Tears pricked her eyes. She wanted him. She leaned forward to tell the driver not to stop, but he pulled over before she found her voice.

Hands shaking, she fumbled and opened the door.

"Hi." Jacob held out his hand.

His body occupied all the space. He seemed to suck all the oxygen as well. She tried to take a deep breath but couldn't.

Lifting her head, she took his outstretched hand and climbed out of the car. "Hi."

His gaze devoured her. She willed herself to stop trembling. Movement from the corner of her eye distracted her. She looked around. "Where are we?"

He smiled at her. "Not yet. Come with me."

"Where are we going?"

"It's a surprise."

She balked and resentment returned. All her frustration from the past few months came to a head. "No, you don't get to surprise me. I'm not your girlfriend anymore. I've done everything you asked. I came here, even though I didn't want to. Now you have to tell me."

He looked at her, surprise on his face.

It mirrored her own.

He nodded. "You're right. I want to give you a tour of my office."

She frowned. "Your office? But I thought you worked—"

He held up his hand. She stopped mid-sentence.

"I know. Come see?"

Opening the door, he ushered her into the brownstone. She admired the architecture while at the same time feeling confused. What was this place? Her gaze stopped on a sign: The Croft Firm.

"Wait, what? I thought you worked for Smith Kane?"

"I quit. I started here three days ago."

She shook her head. Before she could speak, someone walked over.

"Aviva, this is Ann. Ann, this is Aviva Shulman."

Pasting a bland smile on her face, Aviva shook the woman's hand. Jacob crossed the foyer. She rushed to catch up with him. He pointed out the conference room, the kitchen, and the library as they passed. Walking upstairs, he led her down a hallway and finally into an office. There were two desks, but neither was occupied. He shut the door.

"This is my office. My officemate, Charlotte, is out." He perched on the desk. She burst into tears. "Wait, what's wrong?" He leaned toward her, but she shook her head. She stood by the window, as far from him as possible.

She'd leave, except she didn't know how to get out of the building without being seen. "Aviva, please tell me what's wrong. I thought you'd be happy."

"Happy? Why would I be happy?"

"Because I don't work for Smith Kane anymore, which means I don't work the crazy hours anymore. They're still long, but nothing like before. I thought if my hours were better, maybe we could get back together."

White hot anger flashed before her, drying her tears faster than anything else. She spun around. "You thought we broke up because of your *hours*? You think fixing your hours will suddenly make things okay?"

He started to walk toward her but stopped. He held up his hands in surrender. "Yes, no, wait, let me explain. I'm sorry, I planned everything out and then you started crying and I couldn't think of anything but stopping your tears. I messed it all up. Can I start over, please?"

She wiped her cheeks and nodded.

"Okay. Originally, when you broke up with me, I was angry. I thought you doubted my desire to put you first, and you'd given up on me. That anger burned in the back of my mind as I went to work for Smith Kane. But the work and the hours and the complete exhaustion made my anger disappear. It made everything disappear, actually. I was numb and miserable, but I didn't know why. I didn't want to think about it or admit I'd made a mistake. I worked and tried to forget about you. Unsuccessfully, by the way."

He smiled but she couldn't return it. She couldn't remember the last time she'd smiled.

His faltered. "Anyway, then my mother interfered."

"I had nothing to do with that." Karen hadn't called her again.

"I know. For once, I'm glad she did. Because she was able to get me to understand your side."

"My side?"

His adam's apple bobbed as he swallowed. "The lifestyle I choose by working for Smith Kane is not what you want to be a part of. No matter how hard I try to make sure you're not left out, it will never be enough because it's more than just me working a lot. Am I right?"

Her throat closed. She could only nod.

"But I still didn't listen. I went back to work. I created this fantastic brief for a client. The senior associate told me to be prepared to go to court. I assumed I'd play a key role. I was psyched. This was my dream, and I got to live it. Except, I didn't. Because I went to court, the building, but I didn't get to do anything except wait on a bench out in the hallway while everyone else defended my brief."

Her mouth dropped open. Despite everything, she hurt for him.

He shook his head when she started to speak.

"While I waited outside for them to do their thing, I ran into Stuart Rose, the lead partner here. He asked what I was doing. I told him. He didn't say anything, but I knew, I just knew, if I'd taken the job he'd offered, I wouldn't be seated outside in the hallway. I'd be defending my brief."

Embarrassment for him made her cheeks burn. "What did you do?"

"I quit. I called Stuart to see if the job was still available. Here I am." He pulled papers off his desk and walked toward her. "Listen, I had a dream. It didn't work out. I saw what it was going to cost me. It turned into a nightmare, and I lost you to boot. No dream is worth losing you. I've changed my dream, not because of you, but because of me. I'm happy now. I'll be happier with you as a part of it, though." He handed her the papers.

Her pulse pounded in her ears. He was choosing her. Her hands shook as she took the papers from him. "What is this?"

"This is a printout of what this firm sends to the families of the people whom they hire. It's a kind of contract they make with the families. Don't tell them I printed it, because we're supposed to be green, but I wanted to give this to you. Read it."

She skimmed the papers. Her eyes widened. "Are they serious?"

"Yes."

"They really believe family comes first?"

"They do."

She read the information more carefully—how they didn't believe in working all night and all weekend, how personal days and vacations were mandatory, how families were encouraged to stop by to visit and to attend outings planned by the firm. When she was finished, she looked at him. Her throat was thick, and her lips quivered.

"It's not perfect," he said. "I don't think anywhere is. But it's a whole lot better than where I was. I'd like you to be a part of this. Part of me. Part of us. Because I'm choosing you, Aviva, if you'll let me."

Joy flickered. "What about paying back your law school loans and taking care of your mom?"

He shrugged. "It'll get done, just a little slower than I originally planned."

She blinked. "I don't want you to resent me if this choice doesn't make you happy. It has to be your decision, not mine."

"I could never resent you, Aviva. You let me choose my own course."

Her heart pounded. "But the lifestyle..."

He took a step forward and grasped her upper arms.

Her skin burned beneath his touch. She'd missed him so much. His touch almost made her cry with need.

"No lifestyle is important to me if it doesn't include you."

Finally. She dropped the papers on the floor, stepped forward and melted into him. He'd made his choice. He'd chosen a new dream. This dream included her. For the first time in her life, someone was choosing her.

CHAPTER TWENTY-FIVE

Aviva and Jacob held hands as they entered Karen's synagogue on Shabbat. Aviva looked around at the stately building. An impressive foyer with wine-colored carpeting, pale beige walls filled with photos and event flyers, and signs directing people to the various places within the building, it spoke of an active Jewish community, similar to the one in which Aviva had grown up.

Jacob greeted the people he knew, introduced Aviva, and led her into the sanctuary. His hand was clasped around hers and added to her sense of belonging. The setting sun filtered in through the stained-glass windows in the sanctuary, lending a soft colorful glow to the holy room. All around them, well-dressed people filed in and greeted friends and family.

His mother stood near the front of the sanctuary in the third row and gave them a big smile as they approached.

"Hello, *bubbelah*, hello, Aviva. I'm happy to see the two of you together. Aviva, your dress is beautiful. Doesn't she look gorgeous, Jacob?"

"Thank you, Karen," Aviva said.

"Yes, Ma, she does, as always."

Aviva smiled and squeezed his hand. He kissed his mother on the cheek and rubbed Aviva's back.

"Oh, look, there's Amanda and Joseph," his mother said. "Jacob and Amanda were in religious school together. They just got engaged. Don't they look adorable?" Karen waved. The two walked over, big smiles on their faces.

They greeted each other; Karen asked to see Amanda's ring, and the five of them made small talk. Aviva asked all about the engagement, admiring Amanda's ring. As other people walked by, Karen introduced Aviva and Jacob to her friends, and soon, everyone was asking Aviva and Jacob how they met.

"Speed dating," Jacob said.

"Well, *technically*, it was escaping the speed dating," Aviva corrected.

"The best escape ever," Jacob agreed.

"You two are so cute," Amanda said, before she and Joseph excused themselves to sit. Karen's friends all nodded in agreement, and Karen turned to her son.

"My son, the escape artist."

Jacob shrugged. "I believe the idea was Aviva's, originally."

Karen raised her eyebrows. "Really? I never would have suspected you to suggest something so rebellious."

"What can I say," Aviva replied. "Sometimes you have to bend the rules a little in order to find your perfect match."

Jacob whispered in her ear. "Am I your perfect match?"

"Always."

As they sat in the seats Karen had reserved, Aviva fingered her chai necklace. Chai, the Jewish symbol for life. A long life with Jacob. It was exactly what she wanted.

The End

Acknowledgements

There are so many people who have been instrumental in helping me publish this book. All of my writer friends who also self-publish have been after me for years to do it. I can't possibly name them all, but I thank every single one of them for their persistence.

Nancy Light, my developmental editor—thank you so much for helping to make my characters shine!

Paula Gardner, copy editor—thank you for catching all the grammar errors that remain no matter how hard I try. Any errors I missed are entirely my fault!

Lisa Verge Higgins, formatting—in addition to being a fabulous critique partner, you're a fantastic friend to volunteer to help me format the book. I really appreciate your time.

Donna Stevens Simonetta—thank you for your recommendation for a cover editor.

And, I can't believe I actually have to say this, but this book was written by me, not some AI bot or whatever. A reader's time is too precious to waste.

About Jennifer Wilck

Jennifer Wilck is an award-winning contemporary romance author for readers who are passionate about love, laughter, and happily ever after. Known for writing both Jewish and non-Jewish romances, her books feature damaged heroes, sassy and independent heroines, witty banter and hot chemistry. Jennifer's ability to transport the reader into the scene, create characters the reader will fall in love with, and evoke a roller coaster of emotions, will hook you from the first page.

You can find her books at all major online retailers in a variety of formats.

Jennifer started telling herself stories as a little girl when she couldn't fall asleep at night. Pretty soon, her head was filled with these stories and the characters that populated them. Even as an adult, she thinks about the characters and stories at night before she falls asleep or walking the dog. Eventually, she started writing them down. Her favorite stories to write are those with smart, sassy, independent heroines; handsome, strong and slightly vulnerable heroes; and her stories always end with happily ever after.

In the real world, she's the mother of two amazing daughters and wife of one of the smartest men she knows. She believes humor is the only way to get through the day and does not believe in sharing her chocolate.

To learn more, go to http://www.jennifer-wilck.com